HEKATE JONES

NIMHUE WYNN

TYRON GREY

CHIEF INSPECTOR SIBYLL

PRAISE FOR
PEREGRINE QUINN
AND THE COSMIC REALM

'An electrifying read – full of fast-paced action,
endless fun and fearless imagination.'
A. F. Steadman, author of the Skandar series

'Mythology with a modern makeover – Peregrine Quinn's
battle to save the Cosmic Realm is an epic adventure!'
Maz Evans, author of *Who Let the Gods Out?*

'A thrilling, rip-roaring adventure through portals and the
legends you thought you knew in this fresh and exciting start to
an action series with a fantastic and lovable cast of characters.'
Lizzie Huxley-Jones, author of the Vivi Conway series

'This debut just sings with excitement – a boldly imagined
world bursting with myth and magic.'
Jasbinder Bilan, author of *Asha and the Spirit Bird*

'Ash Bond's deep learning meets irrepressible wit in a
whirlwind of waistcoats, lasers and magic! I couldn't stop
smiling as I chomped through her debut: *Peregrine Quinn
and the Cosmic Realm*. I want to chase after adventure with
Bond's characters – no matter how sweaty – and I want
to *be* Rowan Strong of the Seven Strong Sisters! Would
GlamPasses work for a Terran like me?'
Amy Jeffs, author of *Storyland*

PEREGRINE QUINN

AND THE
COSMIC REALM

PEREGRINE QUINN
AND THE
COSMIC REALM

ASH BOND

Piccadilly
PRESS

First published in Great Britain in 2024 by
PICCADILLY PRESS
4th Floor, Victoria House, Bloomsbury Square, London WC1B 4DA
Owned by Bonnier Books, Sveavägen 56, Stockholm, Sweden
bonnierbooks.co.uk/PiccadillyPress

This is a work of fiction. Names, places, events and incidents are
either the products of the author's imagination or used fictitiously. Any
resemblance to actual persons, living or dead, is purely coincidental.

A CIP catalogue record for this book is available from the British Library.
HB ISBN: 978-1-80078-680-6
TPB ISBN: 978-1-80078-796-4
Exclusive edition ISBN: 978-1-80078-987-6
Also available as an ebook and in audio

1

Typeset by Envy Design Ltd
Printed and bound in Great Britain by Clays Ltd, Elcograf S.p.A.

Piccadilly Press is an imprint of Bonnier Books UK
bonnierbooks.co.uk

For John, who was always too crafty to have had just one life.

And for Jacquie, who has always shown me
the magic in this one.

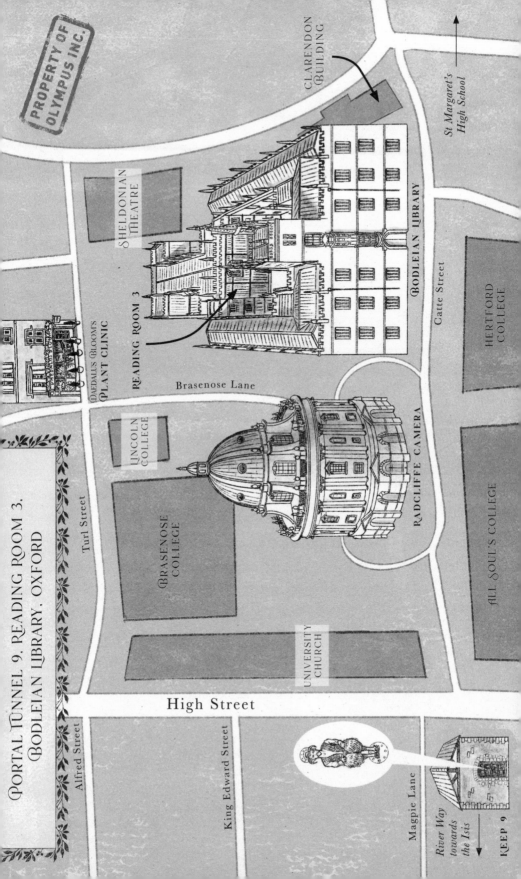

PORTAL TUNNEL 9, READING ROOM 3.
BODLEIAN LIBRARY, OXFORD

CLARENDON BUILDING

St Margaret's High School

SHELDONIAN THEATRE

BODLEIAN LIBRARY

Catte Street

HERTFORD COLLEGE

DAEDALUS BLOOM'S PLANT CLINIC

READING ROOM 3

Brasenose Lane

LINCOLN COLLEGE

Turl Street

BRASENOSE COLLEGE

RADCLIFFE CAMERA

ALL SOUL'S COLLEGE

UNIVERSITY CHURCH

High Street

Alfred Street

King Edward Street

Magpie Lane

River Way towards the Isis

KEEP 9

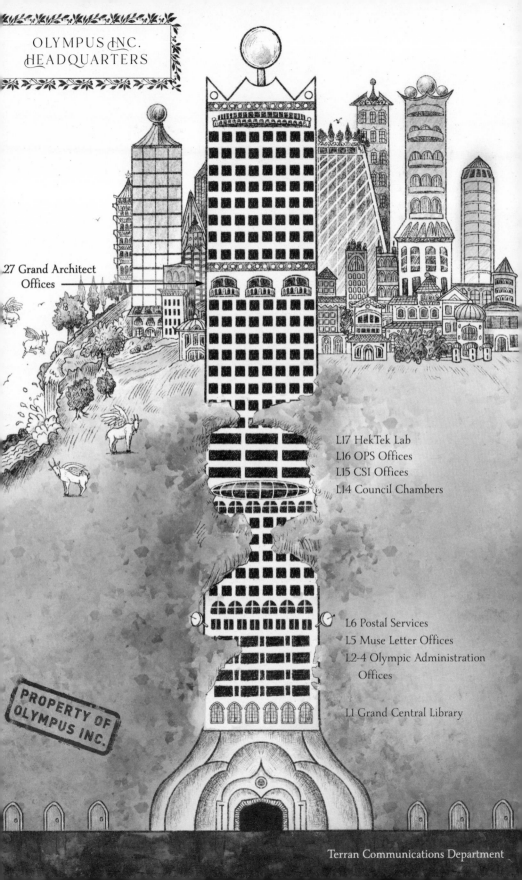

OLYMPUS INC.
HEADQUARTERS

27 Grand Architect
Offices

L17 HekTek Lab
L16 OPS Offices
L15 CSI Offices
L14 Council Chambers

L6 Postal Services
L5 Muse Letter Offices
L2-4 Olympic Administration
Offices

L1 Grand Central Library

PROPERTY OF
OLYMPUS INC.

Terran Communications Department

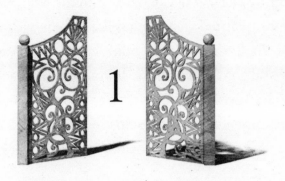

1

PEREGRINE

Location: Portal Tunnel 9, 52nd Bookcase, Reading Room 3, the Bodleian Library, Oxford, England

'Are you *sure* she's just sleeping?' Peregrine whispered. 'Not, you know . . .'

She was peering at the Librarian, whose forehead rested on the desk in front of her. The girl's bowler hat had rolled off, and a pair of pointy green-tipped ears were poking out from underneath her shower of black curls.

'What? *Dead?*' Peregrine's godfather, Daedalus Bloom, picked up the Librarian's limp wrist and checked her pulse against his pocket watch. 'Quite, quite sure. Indeed, apart from being unconscious, this young lady is in tippity-tip-top health.' He tutted at the open bag of jelly beans on the desk. 'But sugar is *terribly* bad for a dryad's digestion. She really should know better.' He sighed, then winked at Peregrine.

It had in fact been Daedalus himself who had planted the jelly beans: planted them *and* spiked them with enough herbal sedative to knock out a small kangaroo. Peregrine leaned forward and gently placed the Librarian's hat back on her head; it felt a very personal thing to see those vibrant, delicate ears. 'A dryad.' She let out a low whistle. '*Wow*.'

'Wow indeed,' Daedalus said, glancing back down at his pocket watch.

Peregrine could not stop staring. She fancied herself quite the expert on mythological beings, but despite all her reading, she'd never actually *met* a real immortal. Apart from Daedalus, and he just looked like your average seventy-something-year-old human, albeit one who ate lots of organic broccoli and went to Pilates twice a week.

But a dryad – a tree nymph – well, that was *really* something.

As Peregrine readjusted the Librarian's hat, she noticed a golden pin in the shape of an apple attached to the dryad's collar. It glittered like a shiny penny in the low lamplight of the library, and she found herself reaching towards it.

'What is *that*?' She whipped her hand back immediately and squeezed her palms tight under her armpits. This was *not* the behaviour of a Library Break-in Assistant. Rather, this was the behaviour of a magpie. A very grabby magpie. She flushed with embarrassment.

Daedalus didn't seem to mind, though. 'That apple, my dear, is the insignia of Olympus.' He set the dryad's wrist down gently. 'Well, the new one. There was some rebranding when Zeus retired a couple of millennia ago. It used to be a lightning bolt – very flash, very *macho*.' He shuddered.

'Oh.' Peregrine scanned the other items on the Librarian's desk. A pot of pencils, a few books, and a framed faded photograph of seven laughing girls in what looked like graduation gowns.

Removing her hands from her armpits, Peregrine picked up the frame and studied it. The girls in the photograph were almost identical: they had the same hair, the same smiles, but with slight differences – a mole here, a bit of extra height there. 'Septuplets,' she whispered. She looked closer. There was another girl, shorter and younger than the others – one she hadn't noticed at first – standing a little apart, her hands shoved firmly into her pockets. Peregrine liked her immediately.

Daedalus cleared his throat, and Peregrine quickly returned the frame to its proper place. 'Sorry,' she mumbled.

'Now that we're sure our Librarian friend is . . . sleeping –' his gaze darted to the jelly beans – 'let's get this show on the road, shall we?' He rubbed his hands, then spun balletically on his heels.

Peregrine shook her head. She was always amazed at how spry her godfather was for somebody who remembered carving the blueprints for Stonehenge.

'Voila!' Daedalus pulled back the midnight-blue curtain behind the desk with a dramatic swoosh. 'Or as we say in the Cosmic Realm . . . voila!'

'Whoa.' Peregrine felt the magic before she saw it: her arms began to prickle, as if a thousand spiders were tap-dancing across her skin. She shivered, and her smile grew wider. So *this* is what magic felt like. It was a sensation she'd only felt snatches of before. She bit her lip, pushing down the urge to whoop with un-Assistant-like glee.

With the curtain drawn back, Peregrine could see an intricately patterned metal gate, the kind you might find over the door of a lift in a fancy hotel, like the one she and her mum had stayed at once in Athens. A melancholic chord in Peregrine's heart twanged, and she shook her head in annoyance. She did *not* want to think about her mum right now.

The gate was made of shining silver and gold interlocking circles, complex spirals and lines that zigzagged their way across, backward and forward, up and down. Peregrine's eyes followed the lines like the loops of a rollercoaster, swirling round and round. Then, remembering she was supposed to be on lookout, she glanced over her shoulder at the entrance. Not that anyone would be able to see much of them in the dim pre-dawn light.

She and Daedalus had decided on a dress code the previous evening and, as discussed, Peregrine was dressed in a manner befitting a stealthy Top-Secret Library Break-In. Her gangly frame was clothed in black: black T-shirt, black jeans, black socks, even especially-soft-soled non-squeaky black shoes. Her hair – which was the approximate colour and texture of a golden retriever – was tied as usual in messy plaits and tucked into a tight black beanie. Daedalus, on the other hand, had interpreted 'stealthy' slightly differently. He was wearing a dapper navy-blue suit with seventies-style flared trousers and a bright turquoise waistcoat embroidered with a scattering of silver stars.

When she had questioned him about his outfit, Daedalus had responded simply. 'If I am going to be caught on closed-circuit television, my dear,' he said, adjusting his fuchsia handkerchief square, 'I may as well look fabulous.'

'Hold these please, Peregrine.' Daedalus passed her a book on ferns of the British Isles, then a couple on woodland fungi and finally a particularly dusty tome on the life cycle of polar bears. He paused, his hand hovering over the last book. 'Maybe we don't need the bears,' he muttered. Turning back to the gate, he traced his finger along the innermost circle until he found a keyhole in the shape of a star, no bigger than the nail of a pinkie toe.

'Aha!' He tapped tentatively around the lock, then leaned forward to peer through. 'Hmm. Just as I thought. OPS have upped the security a little in the last century or so.' He stood back up and cracked his knuckles. 'Best to stand over there, in the corner.'

'B-but . . .' Peregrine spluttered. She'd spent the last *three* years listening to stories about the Cosmic Realm, and now Daedalus wouldn't even let her see the portal? It was always like this – magic was *right* there, just an arm's length away, but she was never allowed to get close enough to touch it. Her face flamed and she jutted her chin over the teetering pile of books. 'Couldn't I just . . . look?' The books wobbled and she veered to the side.

Daedalus raised an eyebrow. 'I appreciate your enthusiasm, but this is just the *door*. If you got any closer to the portal itself, well, you might be lucky . . .' He plucked his spectacles out of his waistcoat pocket and put them on.

'Lucky how?' she asked, her eyes narrowed.

'Tentacles will only sprout from your –' he edged his glasses down and stared at her – 'nose!'

Peregrine snorted, so a little bit of snot splattered onto the cover of *Indigenous Forest Fungi*.

Daedalus chuckled. 'I'm deadly serious! You Terrans lost your tolerance for the mystical centuries ago. Why, I remember the first time young Arthur tried to pull that sword out of that stubborn stone . . .'

Peregrine sniffed. She didn't have any hands free to wipe her nose. 'What happened?'

'Mucus.' Daedalus sighed. 'EVERYWHERE.'

Peregrine snorted again, and this time *The History of Carnivorous Fungi* slipped from her arms and fell to the ground with such a loud *th-dunk* that they both looked towards the dryad to check she was still sleeping. They needn't have worried; she'd obviously eaten quite a few of the jelly beans.

'Ugh!' Peregrine picked up the fallen book. She wasn't squeamish exactly, but she was rather fond of her nose. It was small, slightly upturned and covered in freckles. It was, in fact, almost identical to the nose of her mother. Anyway, when there's a choice of whether to get tentacles or not, she would choose *not*.

'Fine!' she said, before shuffling backwards.

'Thank you. Now if you wouldn't mind –' Daedalus rolled up his jacket sleeves and bent down to click open his leather doctor's bag – 'please take a further three steps back.' Without looking up from his bag, he held up three fingers.

Peregrine glared at him. Maybe her fragile mortal self

would fizz into nothing if she saw too much magic, or maybe it wouldn't. But clearly Daedalus didn't think she was ready, and *that* stung.

Daedalus waited to lower his fingers until Peregrine – who really *did* mind actually – had stepped further away from the spiral gate. Then, from the depths of his holdall, he took out what looked like a shining golden stethoscope. Peregrine had seen lots of Daedalus's odd magical contraptions over the years. This was, in fact, how she had discovered that Daedalus was not your average godfather. When she was nine, she had arrived at the house unannounced, to find the lawn being mown by a clockwork lawnmower while a mechanical crow read Daedalus the morning papers. Still, she had *never* seen an instrument like this.

As soon as Daedalus placed the stethoscope earbuds into his ears, its golden tubes began moving towards the gate. Peregrine blinked in surprise as the tubes sprouted tendrils that grew smaller and smaller until finally they travelled straight through the tiny keyhole.

In an instant, golden sparks began swirling around the bookcase. Peregrine sucked in a mouthful of air, a gleeful whoop once more bubbling in her throat. She was seeing it – this was *real* magic. She peered closer, watching the sparks fizz and pop like tiny fireworks. 'What are you doing?'

Daedalus put a finger to his lips. A faint hum emanated from the portal, sounding like the rotors of a low-flying helicopter. 'Hmm. Hmm. HMMM.' He nodded. 'Interesting.' He tapped his bottom lip in contemplation.

'What? WHAT is interesting?' Peregrine leaned forward

on her tiptoes, *The Life Cycle of Polar Bears* sliding slowly out of her arms.

Without glancing up, Daedalus caught the book inches from the ground and placed it carefully back on top of the tottering pile. '*Very* interesting . . .' After an agonising minute, he finally took the earbuds out and put the stethoscope back into his bag. '*Tempus fugit,*' he muttered. His usually cheerful tone was etched with worry.

Peregrine frowned. Daedalus *never* sounded worried, not about anything. Ever.

'But we still have time . . .' He paused, as if considering whether to say anything else. He shook his head and placed a hand tenderly on the bookcase; a few stray sparks licked his fingers. 'I will bid you farewell for now, old friend.' He took hold of the midnight curtain and gently pulled it closed. 'We should go.' He turned to Peregrine. 'I can't be keeping you up all night with criminal activity.' He picked up his bag. 'Not on a school night, anyway.'

'But what about *her?*' Peregrine indicated the dryad, who was starting to drool.

'Oh, she'll be all right.' Daedalus stood up and looked at his pocket watch again. 'She won't notice a thing.'

ROWAN

Location: Portal Tunnel 9, 52nd Bookcase, Reading Room 3, the Bodleian Library, Oxford, England

Precisely twenty-three minutes later, Rowan Strong snorted awake – and noticed something. In fact, she noticed a number of things. First, drool was dribbling down her chin; second, her hat was on at a jaunty angle that was completely against Olympus Inc.'s agent-attire regulations; third, she had fallen asleep.

ASLEEP!

She shot to her feet, slammed her palms down on the desk and pushed her chair back so it squealed like sharp nails on a blackboard.

She, Rowan Strong of the Seven Strong Sisters, had fallen asleep on the job; she had snoozed on her sacred duty; she had *dozed* by the door to the Cosmic Realm! Shame washed over her like a bucket of icy Styx water.

'The three golden rules of being a Portal Librarian.' Her Academy professor's voice boomed in her head. 'Vigilance, vigilance and vigilance!'

'*Flooharght!*' she swore.

As the youngest of her sisters, she always got the worst shifts, the hand-me-down jumpsuits and the battered, moth-eaten manuals. Now she would be the first Librarian *ever* to have been fired from the sacred guardianship of a portal, and on her very first day on the job! Her sisters would disown her; she would be sent back to Olympus in disgrace.

She gulped. She could see her future now: wearing the ill-fitting lilac uniform of a Mountain Mall security guard or carding teenage nymphs at neon-lit Enchanted Forest raves.

No, she was getting ahead of herself. Rowan spun around and pulled back the portal curtain in panic. The gate looked exactly as it always did: shiny. She snatched up her CosPad, fingers swiping clumsily as she scanned for any incoming transports that she might have missed. Nothing. Any messages? None. All portal readings were coming back within acceptable limits. She scrambled for her spectrometer, checking for any other life forms – perhaps a night porter had wandered into the Reading Room by accident? She exhaled.

Everything looked absolutely, well, fine.

Rowan slumped back into her chair and adjusted her bowler hat. She had made a mistake. OK, a *big* mistake, but there was no harm done. She had gotten away with it. *This time*, her old professor snarled in her head. Rowan winced.

Her night shift would be over in a couple of hours; maybe she could wash away some of her guilt by doing some cleaning. The area around the CosPort desk could definitely do with a tidy. Sweet wrappers and old portal arrival tickets were scattered across the floor, and there was a blob of something suspicious stuck to the drawer handle. She sighed. As much as she loved her big sister, Hazel was kind of a slob.

She took out her key chain and flicked through the keys that the shift manager had given her that morning: desk drawer, portal gate . . . Ah, there we go. Cleaning cupboard. As Olympus's front-line operatives on Earth, only Librarians had access to these keys, and they were DNA-melded too. It had been a rush to imprint them, as Rowan wasn't even supposed to be here – not really, not *officially*. She'd interned with Hazel once or twice, but she was still in her last year at the Academy; she hadn't even taken her oath yet. Then Hazel had gotten a nasty case of bark-flu, and Rowan was the only replacement available. Of *course* she'd said yes – it had felt like such a huge opportunity.

'Yeah, a huge opportunity to mess up,' Rowan muttered as she opened the cupboard. The Oxford Desk in Reading Room 3 might not be the most prestigious of CosPort assignments – it *was* only Portal Tunnel 9, after all – but it was Rowan's first gig. It was important to *her*. As she took out the mop, something caught her eye beyond the Reading Room door caught her eye. There was something on the second step. Something she hadn't noticed before.

She shuffled as close to the edge as she dared. The something was rectangular and laminated, like an ID card. 'A GlamPass?' Rowan whispered, squinting at it suspiciously. 'What in Hera's highlights is *that* doing there?'

GlamPasses were tech-enhanced glamours that made the wearer look like whoever was on the ID badge. These were given out to immortals who needed to hide their true form – extra legs, antlers, that kind of thing – when visiting the Terran Realm. They were also Class Delta CosTech. If any Terrans found a GlamPass – well, it would be disastrous! Worse than that, she corrected herself, it would mean *disciplinary action.*

Rowan tutted. She would have to ask Hazel to check the logbooks to see who could have dropped it. That would be fourteen points off someone's portal licence for sure.

Rowan bit her lip and glanced behind her. *The Librarian's Handbook* was very clear: never, under *any* circumstances, leave your CosPort while on duty. Never. NEVER. But . . . it would only be for a moment, and surely it would be worse to leave a piece of CosTech just lying around until the morning when a caretaker – or, worse – a *student* might see it. Wouldn't it?

Rowan leaned the mop against the nearest bookcase and slowly unclipped the red velvet rope at the top of the stairs to Reading Room 3. Holding her breath, she edged the toe of her boot over the step. Then Rowan Strong, who never EVER broke any rules, broke her second one in as many hours.

One step. Two steps.

She leaned down to pick up the GlamPass and turned it over in her hand. It was a pass to transform the wearer into a Terran office worker. 'Sharon Batterson,' Rowan read out loud. 'Recharge every twelve to fourteen hours.' She tucked it carefully into her jumpsuit pocket. Today was turning out to be a very strange day indeed.

'WARNING! WARNING!' The CosPad on her belt buzzed

like a swarm of angry bees. Rowan scrambled to grab the flashing screen. '"Portal malfunction"?' Her whole face reflected the red, then blue, then red again. 'WHAT?!'

There wasn't a minute to lose. Rowan spun around to sprint up the steps, but . . . the door was gone. Not shut, or closed, but *gone* – as in, vanished. Poof! Even the red velvet rope had disappeared. In its place was a solid metal wall.

Rowan pounded her fists against it. 'This.' Smack. 'Can.' Smack. 'NOT be happening!'

The metal clanged in disagreement.

'No, no, NO!' She punched the wall one more time, then stepped back and tried to steady her breath. She had been trained for this. Well, not exactly *this*; no Academy simulation had ever been this dramatic. But she *had* been trained for high-level crisis situations. She was Rowan Strong of the Seven Strong Sisters.

Her knees wobbled.

'First, assess the situation,' she reminded herself. She pressed another button on her CosPad and shimmering holographic displays popped up in front of her – status reports of all known global portals: Baghdad, Bologna, Istanbul, Nairobi.

Rowan blinked. The always-green dots were now red, red, red, RED.

'INCOMING CALL,' the CosPad shrilled.

In an instant, the broad leathery features of Chief Inspector Sibyll materialised on her screen. Sibyll was a very big deal, and not just because she was a giantess. War hero, decorated strategist *and* head of the Cosmic Sprite Investigation Unit of Olympus HQ. Sibyll was, in short, a legend – and you didn't use that language lightly in the Cosmic Realm.

'Agent Rowan, we have a problem.' Sibyll's voice boomed through the CosPad and echoed off the library walls. She appeared to be moving at a galumphing speed through Cosmic Headquarters: Rowan could see the familiar marble pillars, each hung with an 'Olympic employee of the month' photograph, shake as she stormed past.

'Our readings show a mass collapse of the Portal Tunnel Network. Do you concur?'

Rowan nodded. 'Yes, Chief, I see it, but you should know –'

A high-pitched squeak interrupted her confession.

'Do keep *up*, Simon.' Sibyll rolled her eyes.

The turquoise face and translucent wings of a struggling weather sprite appeared then disappeared from view. He was holding a clipboard.

'Our readings *also* show that you are not in your CosPort. Is this correct?' Sibyll leaned in towards the screen so Rowan could see the blue veins on her temples pulsing.

Rowan chewed the inside of her cheek. This was it. She was *definitely* getting fired, and before she'd even officially got the job. 'Yes, I –'

Sibyll held up a hand. 'All of the other Portal Librarians who *stayed* at their posts –'

Rowan's heart flopped down to somewhere near her Olympus-issue boots.

'– appear to be trapped within their CosPorts.'

'Trapped?' Rowan glanced at the thick metal wall that had appeared from nowhere.

'Yes. We've got visuals, but there seems to be some kind of

CosTech interference, no communications in or out.' Sibyll sighed. 'The thing is –' she leaned even further into the screen, so only her eyes were visible – 'it turns out our engineers are quite useless.'

There was an indignant snorting sound from off-screen.

Sibyll turned to the troupe in her wake. 'My apologies, gentlemen.' She turned back to the screen. '*Absolutely* useless,' she repeated. 'And you know what this means?'

It means they needed a professional Portal Librarian, one who didn't abandon their post, one who didn't SLEEP on duty, one who would know exactly what to do in this situation . . .

'It *means* we need Daedalus,' Sibyll announced. 'Grand Architect Hekate *insists* that she has it in hand, but there's no point tiptoeing around it –'

Rowan could not imagine the giantess tiptoeing around anything.

'Daedalus designed the Portal Tunnel Network, and *Daedalus* is the only one who can fix it.' Sibyll shook her head, so that her impressive neck wobbled back and forth. 'Essentially, without Daedalus Bloom, we are *all* in a big pile of . . .'

'*Flooharght?*' Rowan offered.

'Exactly.' Sibyll nodded sagely. 'He's on your side of the portal. *We* will find out how this malfunction happened, but I need *you* to find Daedalus. We can give you remote help, but otherwise you're on your own.'

On my own? On. My. OWN?

'I . . . I . . .' The portals between the Cosmic and Terran realms had broken. That meant there was no way through, and – more importantly for her – no way back. Rowan suddenly felt very small, very alone, and very much like the youngest of the Strong Sisters. She breathed in too fast and coughed. 'I can do this,' she choked, her eyes watering.

Sibyll nodded. 'Your mission, which you have now officially accepted –'

Rowan gulped.

'– is to locate Daedalus and figure out what in Tartarus is going on.' Sibyll's pace quickened. 'I'm putting you in touch with Callimachus Thorn. I'm reliably informed he's our expert on Daedalus, though he's only been in the job for –' Sibyll paused as the weather sprite flew up to whisper something in her ear – 'two hundred years?' She snorted.

Rowan scrunched up her nose. Great, *another* amateur.

'Details are coming through to your computer now.'

Rowan scanned her own holo-displays again. 'But –'

'I know this is not what you expected from your first day as a Librarian.' The giantess's finger hovered over the screen. 'And, Rowan?'

'Yes?'

'Whatever you do, don't mess this up.' The giantess gave one final, decisive nod, then the screen went blank.

Rowan blinked. Well, at least her first day couldn't get any worse.

3

PEREGRINE

Location: Daedalus Bloom's Plant Clinic, 4 Brasenose Lane, Oxford, England

Books, socks and underpants whizzed through the air and into the battered old suitcase that lay open in the middle of the room. Peregrine yawned as she watched her godfather throw a travel pillow with the precise aim and determination of a professional basketball player.

She pulled off her black beanie and tossed it angrily onto the sofa. Daedalus had been a whirlwind of activity since they'd returned from the library, just a couple of hours ago. She *could* have had a nap, but she was too twitchy. She knew what a suitcase meant – it meant that Daedalus was leaving. And only one suitcase meant that Daedalus was leaving *without* Peregrine.

The apartment – in which the offending suitcase now sat – was situated above the florist's that Daedalus owned, and which he ran with no small amount of help from Peregrine, though the apartment's rooms were now so stuffed with plants that they looked much less like living quarters and more like terrariums with a few sofas in. There were peace lilies in the bath, orchids in the sink, cactuses in the airing cupboard, ferns in the hallway, banana plants on the balcony and spider plants on the stairs. From each stalk hung a label written in neat copperplate handwriting, stating who the plant belonged to and what the plant needed to bounce back to life. For example:

Mrs E. Russell, 511 Morrell Ave.

Three millilitres of valerian essence, a teaspoon of gin and a Shakespearean sonnet twice daily.

Originally the plants had been limited to the greenhouse, then the greenhouse *and* the shop, but word of Daedalus Bloom's Plant Clinic had spread so fast that the plants eventually *had* to be moved upstairs.

Peregrine's mum – whose apartment it *actually* was – had not been entirely happy about this, but Daedalus had reassured her that the plants would absolutely stay in his bedroom 'and maybe a few in the dining room – just to brighten up the place'. This had been the case. For three whole days.

At least Peregrine's bedroom had remained a relatively plant-free zone. It was nice – and necessary – to have somewhere she could go to read that wasn't covered in leaves, petals or potentially poisonous thorns.

The number of plant patients only increased as Daedalus's unique approach to botanical health made him famous on the British horticultural scene. He was a regular, if irreverent, guest on *Gardeners' Question Time*, and his latest discovery, that kitchen herbs preferred to grow to the sound of nineties hip-hop between four and seven in the morning, had caused quite the stir in *Floristry Weekly*.

'I am calling in reinforcements, Peregrine dear.' Daedalus threw a toothbrush over his shoulder. It landed neatly in the suitcase, beside a pair of daisy-printed socks that sported the slogan *Flowers make you look cool.*

Peregrine's freckly face paled. 'No, please. Not –'

'Ms Kidman.'

'But she hates me!' Peregrine dodged a pair of flying sunglasses. Ms Kidman was her ad hoc babysitter, whose idea of a Super Fun Afternoon was getting Peregrine to conjugate Latin verbs while she organised the cutlery drawer.

'She does not *hate* you, Peregrine. Watch out!'

A pair of Bermuda shorts flew past her ear. 'But she is so *boring*.'

'Hmm, yes, she is quite, quite boring. Anyway, I have spoken to your mother, and she agrees.'

Peregrine brightened. 'That Ms Kidman is boring?'

'Yes.' He nodded. '*And* that Ms Kidman will look after you while I'm away.'

'Ugh!' Peregrine let out a loud huff. Her mum, who was anything but boring, was away again on an archaeological dig in the Jordan Valley, filming series three of *Penelope Quinn's World of Wonders*, a smash hit with history buffs and armchair archaeologists alike. Smitten scientists, love-struck Librarians and besotted boffins from around the globe were always sending Peregrine's mother long, complicated love letters and boxes of expensive luxury chocolates. Peregrine used the letters as fuel for their wood burner and ate the chocolates (apart from the strawberry creams, which she left for Daedalus).

Her mum phoned every evening at six o'clock exactly, and asked about Peregrine's algebra, archery, Ancient Greek and aikido, and whether she was eating enough leafy green things. She was especially keen on the aikido, as it was Penelope who had taught her that – before *World of Wonders* had become such a huge hit and Daedalus had officially been named as Peregrine's designated guardian.

Peregrine felt a familiar knot twist in her stomach. This knot tightened with every week her mum was away, and was always there, coiled and heavy. She inhaled slowly, forcing the knot to unwind a fraction.

Out of the corner of her eye, Peregrine spotted another item Daedalus was about to launch into the suitcase. Something that looked very much like –

'Your *passport*?' She shot up a hand and caught it in midflight. 'Why are you taking your passport?' A passport meant that Daedalus was not only leaving the city, he was leaving the *country*, and that was far more distance than Peregrine was prepared to put up with. Daedalus had been Peregrine's primary guardian for the last three years, and since she had already lost a mother to travel's exotic temptations, she refused to lose a godfather too.

Then another, even scarier, thought struck her. What if he

was going somewhere Cosmic, somewhere that Peregrine, as a Terran mortal, couldn't follow? She clutched the passport tighter. What if he didn't come back?

'It's only for a few days.' Daedalus took off his hat and fiddled with the indigo feather he always kept there. Its reflection in his glasses made his eyes look as if they had purple stars swimming in them. 'That should give me enough time for the round trip.' He put his hat firmly back on, and held his hand out for the passport.

Peregrine hesitated. She went to hand the passport over, but then pulled it back at the last moment. 'Round trip to WHERE?'

'Sneaky!' He snatched the passport and tapped her nose with it affectionately. 'Well done.'

'But it's not even a real passport, is it?' She scratched her nose where he had tapped it. 'I mean, your name isn't *really* Daedalus Bloom.'

'It most certainly is!' He tucked the passport into his pocket. 'Well, sort of. And when you have lived as long as I have, you appreciate just how important names are. Remember that, Peregrine Quinn.'

Peregrine glared at him, hoping her gaze would be fierce enough and serious enough to make him stay.

It was not.

Daedalus took out his pocket watch. 'Now, Ms Kidman is due here at three o'clock exactly, so she will be here when you get home from school.' He bent down to try to zip up his suitcase, and failed miserably. 'Maybe I didn't need the toothbrush . . .' he muttered.

He sat down on the bag and began to bounce.

Peregrine stopped glaring; it was exhausting. 'But what about all the plants?' she tried desperately. 'And the customers!'

'Ah yes, let's go through the list, shall we?' He pulled out a crumpled sheet of paper from his jacket pocket. 'Mr Roberts will be phoning about his *scarletis iridiscia* bird of paradise flower tomorrow afternoon.' Bounce. 'Four tablespoons of hot chocolate and three hours of Bach played *fortissimo* every morning.' Bounce. 'Bernadette needs watering every forty-seven minutes during daylight hours.' Bounce. 'Sing them our lullaby at least twice daily.' Bounce. 'And most important. Absolutely.' Bounce. 'Under no circumstances.' Bounce. 'Let Bernadette anywhere near fire, flame or electrical sparks.' Bounce, bounce, bounce. 'Got it?'

'Got it.' Peregrine had heard that *particular* plant's instructions dozens of times. She bet Ms Kidman didn't get this much information on how to look after *her*.

'Good.' Daedalus sprang off his suitcase, spun on his heel and zipped up the case in one graceful movement. 'Time to go!' he sang.

A squeak made him turn. 'Ah, Bernadette, of *course* I wouldn't go without saying goodbye!' Daedalus picked up his favourite plant and hugged them to his chest. Bernadette's turquoise, star-splattered pot matched Daedalus's waistcoat almost exactly. This was not a coincidence. The small purple plant had always been Daedalus's special project; he had cooed and cajoled and sung to them as a delicate seedling, and when they had been just three inches tall, he had taken them for long walks around the university parks and introduced them to the ducks. He hardly ever even left the shop without the plant tucked safely into his bicycle basket. Peregrine wondered why he wasn't taking Bernadette with him. She supposed he might get some rather odd looks at customs, wherever it was he was going . . .

She looked up. Bernadette was tickling Daedalus's chin as he poured himself a final cup of coffee into a mug with a handle in the shape of a moon.

Hundreds of plants passed through the shop – thousands, probably – but Peregrine had never seen one quite like Bernadette. Uncurling from a sturdy copper-coloured stem, their leaves were spade-shaped, a vivid, almost-neon green on top and an iridescent petrol-spill purple underneath. Though she was still quite annoyed, Peregrine couldn't help smiling at the plant. With the morning light streaming through the window, it sort of looked as if they were glowing.

Clutching his mug's crescent-moon handle, Daedalus began to sing Bernadette's lullaby. Swirls of steam spiralled around his face, clouding his glasses, as he crooned:

> Light and bright and airy thing,
> Rarer than a fairy's wing,
> Bring your strength to grow your leaves,
> Through you nature's power weaves.
> From stem to tip you glow and shine,
> Your roots the unknown magicks mine.
> The first and last of your wondrous kind,
> In you a precious gift we find.

His song was interrupted by the clock. 'Chick-a-cheep, chick-a-CHEEP.'

The clock was another of Daedalus's inventions. Every hour a different bird would appear through the door at the top of the clock and chirrup the time. Seven o'clock in the morning was a wren. Peregrine yawned again. She *really* should have had a nap.

'Chick-a-cheep, chick-chick-a-cheep.' The little wooden bird flapped its wings. 'CHEEP!' She sounded quite insistent.

'Ah!' Daedalus thumped his mug on the table so abruptly that coffee sloshed onto the tablecloth. 'Oops, sorry about that.' He smiled sheepishly and thrust the plant into Peregrine's arms. 'You'll have to take Bernadette to school with you of course.'

Bernadette let out a faint squeak as Peregrine struggled to keep hold of them. It sounded like they weren't too happy with this arrangement either.

'WHAT?' Peregrine groaned. 'But they're a plant!'

Bernadette squeaked again, louder this time.

Daedalus looked at Peregrine blankly. 'And?'

Peregrine screwed up her face. 'And everyone at school already thinks I'm weird –'

'Weird?' Daedalus blew a raspberry. 'You mean *interesting*.'

'No, I mean WEIRD.' Peregrine's voice got louder. 'So, I can't turn up for registration with a *plant*.'

Bernadette's leaves wilted slightly and a sweet peppermint smell wafted up towards Peregrine. She lowered her face and breathed it in. 'Sorry, Bernie,' she whispered. It wasn't Bernadette's fault; they were a magical plant in a non-magical world. They didn't quite fit, and Peregrine knew exactly what that felt like. She hugged the pot tighter.

'Coswallop,' Daedalus muttered as he took Peregrine's raincoat off the peg and stuffed it in her rucksack. 'That Caspian chap – you said he brought in a, er, what's it called? You know, floppy ears, smells, terribly popular –'

'A puppy.'

'Yes, one of those.' Daedalus nodded. 'It's just like that.'

'It's *nothing* like that!' Peregrine couldn't quite imagine Candice and her gang cooing over Daedalus's pet plant like they had over Caspian's four-month-old cockapoo.

'Well, how else will you water Bernadette every forty-seven minutes?' He paused, then added a water bottle to the bag. 'Peregrine, please be reasonable.'

Peregrine stared down at the precious peppermint-smelling plant, who was now batting her braids with their leaves. This seemed like such a lot of responsibility, even for just a few days. 'I don't know if I can do this,' she said quietly. 'Maybe –' she coughed – 'I could just . . . go with you?'

'One day, I promise.' Daedalus squeezed her shoulder, then lifted up her chin. 'You were born for adventure, Peregrine Quinn.' His eyes twinkled to match his waistcoat. 'That is why your mother gave you a name with wings.'

4

CAL

Location: Terran Communications Department, the Basement, Olympus Inc., the Mountain
CosDate: 300.23.241

Callimachus Thorn spat out the segment of this week's *Muse Letter* that he'd been chewing, then read the CosMail again. *Sibyll wants to see you.*

He bleated once, then let out a little moan. You see, Cal was a hoofer. That is, half hoofed animal, half human. More specifically, he was a faun.

Cal put the half-chewed paper down and picked up his CosPad. He flicked back to the CosMail. Why was Sibyll contacting *him*? Chief Inspector Sibyll was head of the Cosmic Sprite Investigation Unit (CSI for short), which was the investigative branch of the Cosmic constabularies. That meant *she* was important, whereas Cal was . . . well, not very important at all.

Maybe it was a mistake? Yes, that must be it.

He bit another chunk out of the paper and looked around his office warily, as if Sibyll herself might jump out from behind a pile of paperwork. This was unlikely. For one, the chief inspector hardly ever made it down past Level Ten of the Mountain, and for another, the Terran Communications Department was barely big enough for Cal, his maps, his Terran artefacts and – most importantly – his coffee machine, let alone a giantess.

Cal's CosPad bleeped again. It was another message. *Sibyll wants to see you. NOW.*

Ah. Not a mistake then. Cal's human half was now sweating quite considerably, damp patches forming on the cardigan that Nanny Goat had so lovingly knitted him. It got chilly up here on the Mountain.

Cal gulped and scooted his swivel chair over to his console. Sibyll's Vesuvian temper was almost as famous as the time she had solved the mystery of the uni-foal smuggling ring. What did she want with *him*? Before he could click on his CosMail, a *Muse Letter* article unrolled itself on the screen.

Live Update: Panic at Mass Portal Failure
Embarrassing Blunder or Enemy Attack?

A holo-pic of Thoth Thompson materialised under the article, his pixelated wings folded over his feathery chest.

Reports are streaming in from across the Realm of
multiple inter-realm portal transfers being cancelled

at the last solar-second. Immortals who have been waiting decades for portal visas have been turned away, with 'technical difficulties' cited as the reason for the disruption. In shocking news, dear readers, we at The Muse Letter have discovered that the portals have in fact <u>Shut Down.</u>

Is it a malfunction? This is possible. However, our reliable and – dare I say – dashingly handsome source from inside Olympus Inc. has told this reporter that Cosmic Sprite Investigation's highly trained Librarians have been locked – or trapped? – inside their very own CosPorts.

Designed by the great Grand Architect Daedalus himself, the portals have been part of our way of life for millennia. In fact, who could imagine Cosmic life without a connection to our cousins in the Terran Realm? Grand Architect Hekate and her team are, our insider confirms, working furiously to resolve this situation, but we at The Muse Letter must ask, as you no doubt are asking yourself: if the portals can fail, WHAT will be next?

Thoth Thompson dipped his beak, and the article rolled itself back up, disappearing from the screen with a blink.

Cal's ears flattened. He had never even heard of a glitch in the portal system, let alone it failing. 'It's not possible,' he whispered.

'And yet, here we are!' The booming voice filled the room, making even the maps tremble.

A heartbeat later, Sibyll marched in, her saucer-like eyes scanning the tiny space. 'Wait outside, Simon,' she barked as the door swung closed in the face of a bemused-looking weather sprite.

Cal scrambled out from under the desk, where he had launched himself. 'Hello Sibyll, what a surprise, and an honour, to –'

'I take it you received my CosMails?' Sibyll cut in, raising a bushy eyebrow the approximate size and shape of a lesser-spotted slugger-eel.

Cal looked sheepish, which in itself is quite an odd look for a faun.

At that moment, a CosMail flew out of the printer and slapped Cal in his blushing face. 'Yes, absolutely,' he mumbled, grabbing at the fluttering page. 'I was just about to –'

'You will have heard about the portals.' Sibyll's huge fists bunched, as if imagining punching *The Muse Letter*'s Thoth Thompson right in his feathery face.

'Yes, I –'

'That means I have a job for you.' Sibyll said this slowly, chewing the words as if they were a slightly awkward and unusually flavoured toffee.

A job? Cal puffed up his chest. He couldn't believe the tufts of his ears. He had dreamed of this moment – the moment when someone up there on the Mountain would notice his potential. Whatever the task was, he was ready to leap into action. The leap wouldn't be very fast, or even particularly high, but it would certainly be filled with a lot of enthusiasm.

'Not the most important job,' she added.

'Oh, no, of course not.' Cal's enthusiasm fled, like air from a punctured balloon.

Sibyll fixed him with her infamous analytic gaze that had made much braver immortals than Cal – and there were many – faint in terror. The loose skin around her eyes twitched. 'We have a trainee Librarian, Rowan Strong, who, by some Cosmic *miracle*, has not been trapped in their CosPort like the others.' She paused. 'I am assigning you both – her Terran-side, and you as her Cosmic liaison – to find Daedalus.'

'*Daedalus?*' Cal's ears twitched. 'The Grand Architect?' He had worked with Daedalus before, but he had also been the subject of his final-year dissertation at the Academy: *Daedalus Bloom: Crafty or Crackpot?* Cal had concluded, after some research, that he was likely both.

'*Former* Grand Architect,' Sibyll corrected. 'We have our best sprites on the portal problem, and Grand Architect Hekate insists she is making headway.' She coughed. 'The point is, we need to explore *all* possibilities. The portals can't be replaced for obvious reasons, so if there's even the smallest possibility that they *can* be fixed, if it is just a glitch, and not a . . .' Her voice trailed off.

An attack. Cal gulped. The idea that anyone would attack the Cosmic Realm was inconceivable. No, it was definitely just a glitch, something that Daedalus would be able to fix. He understood now: they just had to find him.

'The thing is, with the portals shut down, none of our TraxTech is working.' She sighed, pulling a huge hand down her face, lengthening her frown. 'Seeing as you are our resident Daedalus expert, Mr Thorn, and you have the necessary –' Sibyll gestured towards the atlas, and Cal's ceramic duck collection – 'tools, I am hereby enlisting you to help in this mission. I need you to make it TOP priority – do you understand?' Sibyll leaned over so she was looking him straight in his bespectacled eyes.

'I understand –'

Sibyll snorted so loudly that Cal jumped, and let out a little bleat.

'That is unlikely.' Sibyll straightened up. 'Nevertheless, my Investigation Unit is stretched lacewing-thin trying to figure out what exactly has caused this clattering Cosmic calamity. And let me tell you –' she lowered her voice – 'OPS are chomping at the bit to take over this investigation. They are *convinced* that this is an attack on the Cosmic Realm.' She glowered. 'Not that Admiral Prim needs an excuse to spend more of our budget on HekTek laser blasters.' She sighed.

Cal nodded. As the investigative branch of Olympus Inc., CSI snooped, hacked, prodded and probed to get answers. They were the quiet ones who worked in the shadows, and their dull grey uniforms reflected their shady role. In contrast, OPS – the Olympic Punitive Squad – were the cool guys. They were the military strong arm of Olympus Inc. and had a well-earned reputation for laser first, ask questions later. They also had the flash gold outfits, all the latest CosTech and frequently made the front page of *The Muse Letter* – usually when they had just blown something up. The organisations hardly ever worked together. If CSI *and* OPS were involved, then this really *was* top priority.

'We've got twenty-four hours to sort this mess out quietly,

Thorn. Admiral Prim has got that Captain Pine waiting in the wings to take over.' Sibyll snorted. 'But with that cowboy in charge, who knows what might happen?'

'Captain *Pine?*' Cal felt the hair on his haunches lift up. Hansel Pine had been in his year at the Academy and was the Olympic Punitive Squad's current golden boy. The nymph was faster, bigger and much, *much* more violent than Cal, and had taken every opportunity to remind Cal that his secret dream – of being a full CSI agent – would never, ever come true. You see, no faun had ever actually been a CSI agent; they were too scared, too small, too . . . sweaty.

As if hearing his thoughts, Sibyll tapped her fingers on her CosPad. 'It says here that you applied to be an active operative with CSI?' She flicked through the screens, her eyes narrowing. 'That is very unusual for a faun . . .'

Cal twiddled his thumbs, eyeing his hiding place under the desk. He didn't want this to get awkward. He, more than anyone, knew what an oddball he was. His parents reminded him frequently.

'You *did* fail the physical . . .' Her gaze drifted from his stubby horns all the way down to his goatish hooves. 'But, hmm, you also had the best scores in the written exam of any immortal in over a century.'

Cal squirmed as Sibyll's eyes flicked across her CosPad.

'Look, it's not *all* stick and no carrot. I'm not a *monster*.' The giantess paused to pick a spider out of her hair and pop it in her mouth. 'If you help Agent Strong retrieve Daedalus with *zero* drama –' she made a circle the size of Cal's head with her giant thumb and index finger – 'then I might – *might* –

consider letting you apply for my Investigation Unit.'

Cal squeaked. 'The Investigation Unit? Really?' He took out a moss-green hanky to wipe the sweat off his brow. 'This is most unexpected. I –'

'Don't count your cockatrices before they've hatched,' Sibyll snapped. 'You still have a job to do.' She indicated the maps.

Cal felt his face flush as he wheeled his swivel chair over to his console.

'And not that I'm complaining . . .'

Cal could feel Sibyll's glare burning a hole in his neck.

'. . . but Daedalus has been *uncharacteristically* quiet lately. The last time I checked on him was after the –' she lowered her voice – 'Florence Incident.' She glowered at the memory. Understandably, that particular Daedalus debacle had made the front page of *The Muse Letter* for a month. Not to mention the Terrans almost discovering air travel three centuries too early.

'So?' Sibyll growled. 'Where is he *now*?'

'Right, of course.' Cal stood on his chair to pull the weighty *Off-Realm Register* down from the shelf and traced his hairy finger down its index. 'Ah! Here we are.' He licked his fingers and prodded at the page.

'You're joking?' Sibyll looked over his shoulder. 'The Cosmic Realm's most famous inventor works in a . . . florist's?'

'A *boutique* florist's,' Cal corrected her. Then turned red at the very cheek of it. 'Does very well apparently,' he mumbled, checking his notes. 'A good amount of foot traffic. And we're lucky – it's just around the corner from the Bodleian Library.'

He scratched his beard. 'I think he wanted to stay close to the Oxford portal.' He pushed his glasses a little further up his nose and lowered his voice. 'I always suspected that he checked in on it.'

'*Highly* illegal of course.' Sibyll looked mildly impressed. 'Is there any more data you can give me?'

Cal's ears itched. He was on a roll now. 'He has two known Terran associates.' He clicked a button on the console and an image of a tall, grey-eyed woman in a suit jacket, horse-riding boots and a wide-brimmed fedora hat appeared on the console. 'Penelope Quinn and –'

'No!' Sibyll's eyes widened. '*The* Penelope Quinn?'

Cal nodded. 'Yes, though her location varies. She never seems to be in one place for very long. There is a daughter, though – Peregrine Quinn.' The image of the woman was replaced with a shorter, surlier version. The same shock of white-blonde hair, but rather than pulled into a neat ponytail, it was tugged into two messy pigtails that reached to just below the girl's shoulders. 'We have a school address for her. A *St Margaret's*.'

'Hmm.' Sibyll raised her eyebrows. 'Do you remember the protocol for Terran interaction and interview?'

Cal scrunched his face up and shut his eyes, trying to remember that particular Academy lesson. 'Yes. ARC – Approach with caution. Reveal absolutely nothing. Contact CSI immediately for memory-wipe.' He hesitated. 'But *I'm* not actually going to be –'

Sibyll took a deep breath. 'SIMON!'

Cal snapped his eyes open to see the weather sprite bustle

into the office holding a holo-transporter and a lavender-coloured pillow, both of which he placed on the floor.

Cal sprang up from his swivel chair so fast that the chair spun backwards, bounced off the wall and fell over. 'What are those for?' A rising sense of dread told him that he knew *exactly* what they were for. The chair wheels squeaked mournfully in the air.

'I'll send the florist coordinates to Agent Strong. I need *you* to locate that Peregrine girl, see if she has any leads on Daedalus's whereabouts.'

'But –' Cal began.

'Don't worry, it's perfectly safe.' Sibyll and Simon took two steps back. 'With the portals out, there's no telling how long we'll have holo-communications.' Sibyll nodded to Simon, who pressed a button, sending an arc of sparkling blue towards Cal's hooves. 'So it's now or –'

'Never?' Cal offered hopefully, as the blue holo-scan reached his belly, then his cardigan buttons, then the tufts of his beard. His heartbeat picked up pace.

'Calm *down*, Callimachus. You're not even really going to be there.' Sibyll gave him a terrifying stare.

Cal's heartbeat was at a gallop now. But what if he was transported to the wrong place? What if Simon had forgotten to scan his CLOTHES? He wobbled sideways.

'Don't worry, we haven't had a fatality in . . .' Sibyll leaned in towards Simon, who whispered something in her ear.

'Oh' was the last word Cal heard as he fell nose-down onto the waiting cushion, his consciousness evaporating into a glittering shower of blue sparks.

5

ROWAN

Location: The Steps Outside Reading Room 3, the Bodleian Library, Oxford, England

'A ... florist's?' Rowan blinked as a stream of information poured onto her screen. No, that couldn't be right. She pressed the refresh button, and the screen blinked off, then on again. 'A ... *boutique* florist's?' She shook her head. And she'd thought today couldn't get any weirder.

Her heartbeat throbbed in her ears as she input the coordinates into her CosPad. The florist's looked like it was close. *Maybe* this whole mission would be easier than she thought – she might even be home, safe with her parents in the Enchanted Forest, before nightfall.

A warm feeling spread across Rowan's chest, like acorn butter across a chrysanthemum crumpet. What were her parents doing right now? Would they be worried about her? Did they even know that the portals had shut down?

It was time to do her job. Rowan gave the wall separating her from her CosPort one more long, hard stare. Then, with one hand on her hat, she turned and sprinted down the steps, through Reading Room 2, past the reception desk and towards the main entrance. There she skidded to a stop and performed a quick uniform check. Underneath her cavernous overcoat was an olive-green jumpsuit akin to work overalls. Not quite as fancy as the full agent uniforms, which were skin-tight, grey and shot through with CosTech, Rowan's uniform was still that of a trainee: made from comfortable, hardwearing fabric with a lot of pockets to fit her gear in. She patted them down now: keys, check; spectrometer, check; ration pack, check; *The Librarian's Handbook* and moth repellent, check and check.

She balled her hands into fists, stepped out into the street and immediately wrinkled her nose. 'Eww!' A potent stench, disturbingly similar to that of blocked drains, wafted towards her. Where was it coming from? Holding her nose with one hand and her CosPad in the other, she set off at a jog towards the coordinates.

Her heart skittered in her chest. There it was! The crisp morning light glinted off golden copperplate signage:

She rushed to push the door, but before she could, the door flew open to reveal a lithe, bespectacled man holding an overly full polka-dot suitcase. 'Oh! Hello!' He lifted his glasses up and blinked at her.

Rowan looked the man up and down. His star-spangled waistcoat, his twinkling eyes, his *excellent* choice of footwear. This was Daedalus Bloom all right. Just like in the textbooks.

Pushing down a sudden urge to ask for an autograph, Rowan spoke quickly. 'My name is Rowan Strong, and I am here on behalf of –' she panted – 'of Olympus Inc.'

'I see.' The man seemed neither impressed nor particularly surprised. 'Well, I was actually just about to head out.' He tapped his suitcase. 'But do you fancy a spot of coffee before I go?'

'No time!' Rowan barged past him into the shop. 'This is a Cosmic crisis!'

Daedalus shrugged. 'All the more reason to be properly caffeinated, surely?'

Rowan spun around and glared at the old inventor. 'The portals – *your portals* – have shut down!' she yelled, then slapped her hand over her mouth, not because she was being rude, but because she was being loud.

Daedalus let the door swing shut behind him. It clicked, and the silence widened.

'Shut *down?*' he asked calmly.

Rowan nodded.

'Already?' He scratched his head. 'But I just checked them this morning.' He coughed. 'And by my calculations we had at *least* another –'

'This *morning?*' Rowan narrowed her eyes. Again the idea that her falling asleep was not a complete coincidence pulled at Rowan's attention.

'Oh dear.' Daedalus was still muttering to himself. 'This means they *are* using the window. We'll need to speed things up.

Hmm.' He tapped his chin. 'We'll need Bernadette, of course, and Peregrine if she'll come.'

'Peregrine?' Rowan knew that name. Oh yes, that was the Terran the faun was in charge of finding. 'The CHILD?'

'Yes, Peregrine is twelve, so I suppose technically she *is* a child,' Daedalus said matter-of-factly. 'And Bernadette – that's the plant that is in her possession.'

'But –'

Daedalus picked out a pocket watch. Rowan huffed. So *now* he was worried about the time.

'I will tell you what I know of the situation, but we'll have to move quickly before –'

He was interrupted by a low, harsh laugh from the street outside.

Daedalus moved quickly, his eyes darting around the shop. 'Rufus, my friend,' he whispered urgently in the direction of a giant flytrap in the corner, 'I need you.'

Rowan gasped as the flytrap's lime-green waxy sides cracked open to reveal a bright fuchsia mouth lined with yellow needle-like teeth.

'What the –' Rowan began.

'I do apologise for this.' Daedalus coughed again, then promptly pushed Rowan into the plant's jaws, which clamped down, knotting together almost completely. 'Remember, find Peregrine, and find Bernadette.'

Still dazed, Rowan peered out between the needle-teeth. Daedalus just had time to smooth down his waistcoat when the door burst open and a blast of purple light hit him right between the buttons.

6

PEREGRINE

Location: Class 7B, Bramwell House, St Margaret's High School, Nosebag Road, Oxford, England

'SPEED –' Mr Alkhaki's voice boomed over the class – 'equals DISTANCE travelled – ' he mimed marching on the spot, his thin toothbrush moustache twitching in time with his feet – 'divided by TIME.' He tapped the watch at his wrist. 'As so.' He indicated the board with his finger, then let his arms return to their usual position, swinging from his shoulders like a pair of socks hanging from a coat hanger. 'Any questions, 7B?'

In the inevitable silence that followed, Peregrine's eyes traced the thick lines that Mr Alkhaki had drawn. The vertical blue line was labelled 'time' and the long red line that stretched across the board, like a scar, was 'distance'.

Letting her imagination roam, Peregrine followed the red

line off the board, around the rows of Class 7B, out the gates of St Margaret's and through the University Parks towards town. She followed the swerving, wriggling line until it stopped, coiled like a snake, at the door of the Plant Clinic. Her fingers squeezed her pencil like a python as she imagined Daedalus heaving his battered old polka-dot suitcase out of the door. How *far* was he travelling exactly? The pencil dropped from Peregrine's hand as her eyes darted to the vertical blue line. And how *long* would he be away?

The pencil rolled and then, as if in slow motion, dropped off the desk. With a quick glance at Mr Alkhaki, Peregrine ducked down and unzipped her rucksack. 'Hi, Bernie,' she whispered. Bernadette's leaves rustled in greeting as Peregrine tipped some water into the soil.

Candice Welch sniggered in the front row. Peregrine exhaled slowly. In just a few short hours she'd be out of here and back at the Plant Clinic where she could be as weird – no, as *interesting* – as she liked.

She stroked the silky underside of Bernadette's leaves as she glanced up to the classroom window. Bernadette didn't fit in here either; *nothing* unusual did. At St Margaret's, even being academically clever, like Raj, was considered impertinent. Daedalus had said once that if St Margaret's were a flavour, it would be boring. 'Not *bad* like, I don't know, *cat hair*, but just a bit . . . meh.'

From underneath the desk, Peregrine had a clear view of the perfectly ordinary recycling bins, which were next to the perfectly boring tool shed, and next to the tool shed was . . . Peregrine blinked, then narrowed her eyes. *Something* was happening, and that something was *unusual*. She blinked again.

That same spidery feeling she'd had when she was near the portal skittered across her arms. Peregrine inhaled. This was magic – it had to be. Blue sparks fizzed at the base of the now-very-interesting shed, then faded to reveal a . . . faun.

'Aargh!' Peregrine yelled, banging her head on the underside of the desk.

A faun – an actual curly-haired, red-faced faun, just like she'd read about in her mythology books – was standing right by the now-very-*not*-boring recycling bins. There were a few differences: in her books, fauns were usually shown without any clothes and playing pan pipes, not – like this one – wearing a forest-green cardigan and holding what looked like some kind of iPad. Peregrine blinked again. Was this real? If so, this was the second immortal she'd seen that day. It couldn't be a coincidence. She felt around in her rucksack for her phone. She had to tell Daedalus immediately!

'Everything all right, Peregrine?' Mr Alkhaki called from the front of the class.

'Yes, sir.' Peregrine rubbed the back of her head and stared at the faun, who was scratching his beard and muttering to himself. 'Just dropped my pencil.' Her breath quickened. What would happen if someone *else* saw the faun?

'Freak,' Candice sniped, accentuating the end of the word so it sounded like it had two, very mean syllables. There was a ripple of giggles from the class. Peregrine scrambled back onto her seat, scowling.

Mr Alkhaki sighed and flicked to the next page of the textbook with a flourish. 'Now, DISTANCE –'

Raj put his hand up. Peregrine had always liked Raj. Sometimes when they did group projects together, they talked about his parents, who were vets, and his love of fossil-hunting, and how he had secretly always wanted a pet woolly mammoth. It was in those moments that Peregrine thought that if she was going to tell anyone about Daedalus being an immortal, it would be Raj. But of course she wasn't allowed to tell anyone, so she didn't.

Raj pointed towards the window. 'Sir, I think there's a dog outside.'

All the blood drained from Peregrine's limbs as one by one the class turned towards the window.

Mr Alkhaki shook the open textbook so the pages flapped like paper wings. 'Please concentrate, 7B! *Everyone* has seen a dog before.'

Not like this one, they haven't. Peregrine's heart was racing: she had to do something, she *had* to distract them. Taking a huge gulp of air, and with one last glance at Raj, she stood up. At the screech of Peregrine's chair legs on the floor, the class's collective attention swivelled back towards her. It had worked!

'I need to –' her brain swirled in panic – 'go.'

Mr Alkhaki stopped waving the textbook, mid-flap. 'You need the toilet?'

Peregrine could hear Candice whisper something which made Nadine snort into her blazer. She groaned. The toilet excuse would only last for so long. What if Mr Alkhaki sent someone after her? What if he sent *Candice*?

'Not the toilet, sir.' Peregrine picked up her rucksack,

Bernadette's leaves still poking out the top. 'I need to go . . . home.'

'Home?' Mr Alkhaki looked genuinely baffled. 'Are you ill?' He walked towards her, concerned, as behind him Candice mimed vomiting into a bucket.

Peregrine gritted her teeth. 'Not *ill*, sir.'

'I see.' Mr Alkhaki placed the maths textbook solemnly down on her desk. 'Are you saying that you have no reason for leaving my classroom?'

Yes, I have a reason. My reason is that there is a goat man with glasses leaning on the recycling bins.

Peregrine shook her head. 'No reason, sir.'

Mr Alkhaki's moustache twitched. 'Leaving class without permission . . . that could mean suspension.'

Suspension? It was as if someone had turned up the gravity in the room. Peregrine's fists tightened. This wasn't fair.

'Really, Peregrine, I advise you to sit . . . back . . . down.' Mr Alkhaki said the last sentence very slowly, as if offering Peregrine as much time as possible to make what he considered the *right* choice.

Peregrine squeezed her eyes shut. She liked Mr Alkhaki, she really did, but more and more she was realising that having a small amount of magic in your life – even if it wasn't really *yours* – made ordinary things, like being honest with your teachers, very, *very* difficult. This wasn't a choice she could make alone; she needed Daedalus. The knot in her stomach tightened, reminding her of who it was that she *really* needed. She needed her mum.

Peregrine opened her eyes and jutted her chin forward. 'I'm

sorry, sir.' Shrugging apologetically at Raj, whose thick eyebrows were knotted in understandable confusion, she gritted her teeth, turned and marched out of the door.

Whatever reason the faun had for being here, it had better be a good one.

Splinters of morning sunlight fell through the leaves and onto the concrete as Peregrine jogged across the playground, Bernadette squeaking in time with her steps. She could just about see the faun flickering in and out of view with a fuzzy blue light. 'Hello?'

The faun poked his head out from behind the bins, then shuffled towards her. 'Thank Hera!' He took off his spectacles, rubbed them on his cardigan, then put them back on his nose. 'Oh! How *fascinating*.' He leaned forward. '*Very* fascinating.'

Peregrine blinked. She definitely wasn't imagining it; the faun really *was* flickering.

He leaned in so that their foreheads were almost touching. 'The holo-pic really doesn't show . . .'

'What?' Peregrine inched back as the faun inched forward. 'What doesn't it show?'

'You look just like her, but –' he shrugged – 'I suppose you would, you being her daughter and all.'

'Daughter?' Peregrine's hand instinctively flew to her nose.

'Well, better get this over with.' He picked his iPad-style device out of his oversized pocket.

'Wait, do you mean –'

The blinding flash made her blink stars. 'Hey!' Peregrine

staggered backwards, her previous question forgotten. 'What is THAT?'

'It's a CosPad Pro, *latest* edition. Standard issue for all Olympus Inc. employees.' He put the device back in his pocket, then held out a hand. 'A pleasure to meet you, Pear-grinn. I am Callimachus Thorn from the Terran Communications Department. I've been sent here to ask you a few questions.'

Peregrine bristled. *She* had a few questions herself: like, how did the faun know her name, and how could she get one of those CosPad things? She looked at the outstretched hand in front of her, then back at the faun. He was about her height, maybe a bit shorter. He was also clearly nervous, with beads of sweat forming on his forehead. She went to shake his hand, but instead her fingers went straight through the flickering blue light.

'Oh, sorry about that.' The faun coughed. 'Just a holo-projection, I'm afraid.' He wiggled his fingers. 'Can't actually touch anything.'

Peregrine stared, trying to remember all her faun-related facts. Pan piping? Yes. Dancing in forest glades? Yes. Worshipping at the altar of the wine god Dionysus? Yes. Appearing at schools as holograms? No, no, her mythology books definitely had *not* mentioned that.

She lowered her hand. 'What did you say your name was?'

'Callimachus Thorn.'

Peregrine paused, trying to move the syllables around her mouth. She very much wanted to say his name properly: her mum always said names were important and you should try to say them correctly if you can. 'Cally—'

'Cal,' the faun cut her off, not unkindly. 'You can call me Cal.' His hoof made a clacking sound as he tapped it on the concrete.

'Cal,' she repeated slowly. 'You're from the –' she lowered her voice to a whisper – '*Cosmic Realm?*'

Cal nodded proudly. 'Yes, from Olympus Inc.' He pointed to his T-shirt, which had a golden apple printed on it. 'I work on the Mountain or, more specifically, in the Basement.'

Peregrine's head was spinning. There really was a faun in front of her. She needed to get him to the Plant Clinic, and quickly, if they were going to catch Daedalus before he left. 'It's not safe here.' She peered around the recycling bins. 'People might see you, I think we should go and talk to my godfather –'

BEEP. BEEP. BEEP.

An alarm filled the air around them, smashing any hope of a quiet escape into a thousand beeping pieces. Peregrine spun, trying to locate the source of the sound.

BEEP. BEEP. BEEP.

'What is that noise?' she wailed.

Cal was staring at his CosPad. It was flashing red, then blue, then red again. 'It's a distress signal.' The faun's brows knotted together. 'M-my colleague, she's with your godfather. Something has happened.'

7

PEREGRINE

Location: Daedalus Bloom's Plant Clinic, 4 Brasenose Lane, Oxford, England

Peregrine's heart beat like a bird throwing itself against her ribcage. It pushed her onward as she hurtled down the cobbled high street. What had happened to Daedalus? Was he hurt? Images, each one worse than the last, ticker-taped across Peregrine's mind as she swerved right towards the Radcliffe Camera. She didn't even care when a student dropped their coffee cup onto the library steps as they stared, slack-jawed, at Cal, who was flickering on and off as he jogged next to her.

Peregrine scooted right again into Brasenose Lane, and there it was – the shopfront, its familiar golden letters dazzling as they reflected the morning sun. Cold dread trickled over her palms as she moved towards the door.

'No, Pear-grinn! Wait!' Cal's fuzzy blue light suddenly

appeared in front of her, blocking her route to the door.

'But Daedalus –'

'SHHH!' Cal put his fingers to his lips. He pointed to a row of large plant pots that Peregrine could hide behind and still see through the shop window.

Her breath caught in her throat, and she slapped her hand to her mouth to stop herself from crying out.

Two men in dark glasses were standing by the door. They were dressed in brown suits and ugly paisley ties, and one of them had a boxy metallic briefcase. They looked like regular office workers, except for their sinister expressions and the array of scary-looking knives glinting on their belts. But where was Daedalus? Peregrine scanned the shop for her godfather.

'No!' She gasped into her fingers. Daedalus was lying crumpled on the ground, his eyes closed and his face a pale papery grey. The trickle of dread grew, becoming a rush then a tidal wave that roared in her ears. The only thing that was keeping her from being washed away was Cal's flickering presence next to her. 'No,' she whispered, her voice barely audible. 'No, no, *no!*'

'I LOVE these new HekTek hand blasters!' The taller of the men stepped forward, waving what looked like a state-of-the-art laser weapon.

Peregrine went to move but Cal's image fuzzed. 'Lasers have stun settings,' he whispered quickly. 'Daedalus is probably just sleeping.'

Peregrine took her hand from her mouth. 'Sleeping?' she hissed, then added, '*Lasers?*' Not in all of her reading had she heard of any mythological creature having access to *lasers*.

'Yes, what *are* these Terrans doing with Olympus-issue HekTek blasters?' Cal mused next to her.

Peregrine stared at him.

The taller man sighed. 'What do I always tell you, Stan?'

The stockier of the two put his finger in his mouth to pick something out of his back teeth. 'Er, always floss in between your fangs?'

Fangs? Peregrine squinted. These men didn't have *fangs*.

'No. Well, yes, you *should* always do that. I meant the *other* thing I always tell you.'

'Um . . . shoot first, ask questions later?' The stockier one grinned and stalked over to Daedalus.

'Exactly!' The man had a slight build and an angular face with a delicate moustache. 'So, my question is, is he dead?' He shook the weapon and twitched his nose.

Peregrine held her breath. A grim scene flashed before her eyes: she was standing in front of a grave draped in a blanket of purple flowers, tears streaming down her cheeks, dripping from Bernadette's leaves and falling into the turquoise plant pot in fat, wet drops.

Stan leaned over Daedalus. 'Nah, not dead. Just knocked out.'

Peregrine exhaled sharply, and the grave vanished in a swirl of petals.

The taller one tucked his laser weapon inside his suit. 'Thought his old heart might have given out. Shame. Still, orders is orders.'

Stan pointed to Daedalus's hat. 'I like this . . .'

The taller man knelt down and opened his briefcase. 'This is no time for *hats*, Stan. We are on a very important *professional* mission. She wants us back in Alexandria.'

She? Peregrine strained to hear what they were saying through the window. And wasn't Alexandria in *Egypt*?

'I want a trophy!' Stan stuck his tongue in between his teeth and prised Daedalus's flat cap off his head. 'The *harpies* get to take trophies.'

'Well, you're not a harpy.' The man was taking some small silver discs out of the briefcase. He held one up to the light. 'Anyway, the harpies take thumbs, not *accessories*.'

'He's not wrong,' Cal muttered, shuddering. 'But how does a Terran know that?'

'Whatever,' Stan mumbled. He smoothed down his buzz cut and pushed Daedalus's cap down onto his own bulbous, balding head. 'I think it looks distinguished. Does it . . . does it suit me?'

'What do you care? This isn't even your real skin!' The man threw Stan the discs.

'Of course!' Cal slapped his forehead. 'They're using GlamPasses!'

'Glam . . . what?' Peregrine asked.

'A kind of disguise. I'll explain later.'

Stan was arranging the discs around Daedalus, and grunting. Peregrine saw he had temporarily shoved Daedalus's hat into his pocket, denting the feather. 'You never let me have any fun, Earl!'

'If blasting people with lasers isn't fun, Stan, then I don't know what is.' Earl stroked his moustache. 'Besides, it's better than Sewage Detail on the Mountain for another three centuries.'

Stan shrugged. 'Yeah, I s'pose.'

'*Sewage Detail.*' Cal's eyes narrowed. 'BogBrethren! I bet on Nanny Goat's knitting that's what they are.'

'BogBrethren?' Peregrine whispered.

'Lizard folk. Slimy skin and an even slimier nature. Also –' Cal wiggled his fingers – 'webbed feet.'

Stan prodded Daedalus with a finger. 'We sure it's him? Don't wanna take the wrong guy.'

Earl pulled a mobile-shaped device with two antennae from inside his jacket pocket. 'He's the Grand Architect all right. CosRays are off the charts.' He tucked the device back into his jacket. 'Hurry up and get the transporter ready.'

Stan shuffled around Daedalus, placing the metallic circles on the ground. 'You could help, you know.'

Earl adjusted his suit cuffs. 'I'm the supervisor, remember.'

'That was when we were on Sewage Detail. *She* never said you were the boss.'

'It was implied.' Earl straightened his tie. 'Is the transporter ready?'

'Yeah.' Stan huffed.

Earl took out a CosPad from his jacket and spoke into it. 'We're a go,' he growled. Immediately the room was filled with a strange thwumping sound. The discs crackled with purple electricity and thin tendrils of violet-coloured smoke slithered out of the metal circles and wrapped themselves around Daedalus, over and over again, like ropes.

Sparks fizzed over the discs as Daedalus was lifted off the floor, spinning like a sycamore seed. Then, just like that, the mist evaporated. Daedalus was gone.

8

ROWAN

Location: Daedalus Bloom's Plant Clinic, 4 Brasenose Lane, Oxford, England

In the cracks between the flytrap's fangs, Rowan could just make out Earl, the taller of the two thugs, looking down at his CosPad. 'They've got him,' he snarled. 'He's in Alexandria.'

Alexandria? Rowan's mind whirred. This was transport *within* realms – not even the latest CosTech could do that! She would have to report this immediately.

Plant goo bubbled at her feet. Well, maybe not *immediately*.

Brushing off his trousers, Stan loped towards the kitchen table. 'Canf we goff nowf?' He picked up Daedalus's toast and stuffed it into his face. 'Thisf glamour is itchy.'

Just then, Rowan's CosPad vibrated.

Buzzz.

Earl was at the table in a flash and thrust his hand towards

Stan's face. Rowan thought Earl was going to punch him, but instead he yanked the half-eaten toast out of Stan's mouth.

'Hey!' Stan went to grab it back. 'I was eating that!'

'Shh!' Earl threw the slice of toast across the room, where it splatted – butter-side – on the wall and slid down. 'I cannot HEAR when you are CHEWING –'

Buzz buzz buzzzzzz.

Rowan scrambled to turn off her CosPad. Earl *must* have heard that. What was she going to do now? The plant gurgled unhelpfully.

'But –' Stan began.

Earl held up a hand, took his sunglasses off and tucked them inside his jacket.

Rowan gasped. Behind the glasses swivelled bright yellow eyes with black slits for pupils, the only aspect of a person GlamPasses couldn't hide. BogBrethren. Slimy, sneaky, *stinky* BogBrethren.

Earl's beady gaze whipped towards where Rowan was hiding and trying not to breathe. A grin rippled across his face, making his moustache twitch. He reached back into his jacket.

If Earl got that blaster out, then she really was done for.

Rowan inhaled sharply. There was only one option. 'Let me OUT!' she yelled. The plant unhinged its jaws with a sticky SNAP!

Whatever Earl had been expecting, it probably wasn't a dryad rolling out of a flytrap's mouth like a gooey green bowling ball. He swore and swiped at the air, just missing Rowan's slimy curls. 'Stan! Catch her!'

Rowan half sprinted, half slid towards the door to the shop, but Stan was too quick. 'Not so fast, sprite!' He stepped in front of her and snapped his teeth.

Sprite? Who was he calling a *sprite*? 'I'm a *nymph*!' she spluttered, as she backed up. 'And a *Librarian*!' Her gaze zipped around the room, desperate for anything she could use to defend herself. Perhaps one of those umbrellas? A hanging basket? There was a bucket of trowels next to the sink – maybe if she got to them she could use them as throwing knives?

Rowan chewed on the inside of her cheek. Who was she kidding? She was *terrible* at throwing things. Also, she was surrounded. Earl was moving towards her now too, but slowly. His prey had frozen, and all he had to do was slide steadily forward and swallow her whole.

Stan wrenched the blaster out of his jacket and pointed it directly at her. 'Sprite, nymph, you fry all the same.'

Rowan gulped. She supposed that *was* technically true.

TAP. TAP. TAP.

Both Rowan and Earl spun. A short, blonde-haired mortal was beckoning to her through the window. Next to her was a holo-com of a faun – that must be Cal, and was he . . . waving?

'The window!' Earl yelled to Stan. 'And no stun this time! We don't want any witnesses!'

Rowan caught the mortal's eye and then, just in time, darted sideways as a purple flash of light zoomed past her ear and shattered the shopfront window.

9

PEREGRINE

Location: Daedalus Bloom's Plant Clinic, 4 Brasenose Lane, Oxford, England

'Look out!' Cal yelled.

Rather unusually, Peregrine did as she was told, and dived back behind the plant pots just as glass from the shop window showered over the cobbles. She looked up to see the bowler-hatted Librarian from the Bodleian leaping through the window frame.

'You're Callimachus Thorn?' the dryad panted, as she scrambled up. 'The liaison?'

'Cal is fine.' Cal nodded, his form flickering. 'And this is Peregrine – Peregrine *Quinn*.'

The dryad's eyes widened for a moment, then she held out a hand to Peregrine. 'Quinn?' she repeated. 'As in *Penelope* Quinn?'

Thinking she was going for a handshake, Peregrine reached

out her hand too. 'Yes, she's my mum –'

But instead of shaking her hand, the dryad used it to tug Peregrine forward into a sprint. 'Nice to meet you. Please start running.'

Anger flashed through Peregrine's limbs. Two yellow-eyed laser-wielding hitmen were shooting at them. She didn't need to be *told* to run, and she didn't need to be dragged either.

She wrenched her hand away but followed the Librarian as she dashed over the cobbles of the Radcliffe Square, then sped down the lane and onto Oxford High Street. She pulled her rucksack onto her front and felt for Bernadette. She sighed in relief. They were in one piece at least and – her hand went to her nose again – so was she. Her hand lingered on her nose a moment longer. How did *every* immortal she met seem to know her mum? Was *Penelope Quinn's World of Wonders* as big a hit in the Cosmic Realm as it was on Earth?

A blare of sirens echoed down the road, blasting through her thoughts, and were swiftly followed by two flashing police cars that swerved around the corner. Were they going to the Plant Clinic? A scream from the crowd made Peregrine look up. Stan was running along the rooftops towards them, his face set in a frightening rictus grin.

Peregrine forced her gaze forward as she raced after the dryad, zipping between open-mouthed tourists, all of whom were pointing upwards. Some even had their phones out.

'Can't we fight him?' Peregrine's words came out in breathy gasps. 'You know, with . . . *magic?*'

'You can't just go around zapping people with magic.' The dryad's gaze was darting side to side. 'It doesn't *work* like that.'

Peregrine huffed. She was currently sprinting through Oxford with a dryad and a faun while carrying a sentient plant. Using magic didn't seem like *such* an outrageous idea.

Cal flickered next to them. 'Well –'

'OK, it does *sometimes* work like that,' the dryad snapped.

Peregrine's gaze pinballed between them. 'What *can* we do then?' she hissed.

'We can run really fast.' The dryad indicated their fast-moving feet. 'And then we can hide *really* well.'

Before Peregrine could respond, a metallic groan split the air. Peregrine looked back to see Stan, his biceps as big as watermelons, leap from the roof onto a shiny SUV, which crumpled as easily as a tin can beneath his weight. Stan smirked as he jumped down from the now not-so-shiny car, glass crunching like diamonds under his patent leather shoes.

'This way!' The dryad veered down an even narrower alleyway. It was so narrow that even Peregrine had to step sideways to move at any kind of speed. Finally they stopped, panting, in front of an old wooden door with a brass knocker in the shape of a faun. The faun had his arms crossed, and his eyes were closed.

'What –' Peregrine began.

'Allow me.' Cal cleared his throat and addressed the faun. 'Brother, your Cosmic kin require sanctuary. We beseech you to grant us access –'

'NOW!' Rowan interrupted.

Peregrine heard a commotion down the lane. Was that Stan trying to get through the gap? She didn't know how he was going to manage it; the thug had the approximate dimensions of an armoured hippo.

The brass knocker opened its little mouth and yawned, making a sound like an unoiled bicycle wheel. Suddenly its eyes shot open and it turned its head so it was staring straight at Peregrine, who yelped, loudly. The faun smirked then began to sing in a thin, squeaky voice:

> *What is hidden from view*
> *When the grass hangs with dew,*
> *But will appear before us*
> *When the owl sings her chorus?*

'It's a riddle!' Peregrine gasped.

'It's not a very *good* riddle,' the dryad muttered. 'It doesn't even rhyme properly.'

'They must still be using the old software.' Cal sighed as he tapped his CosPad.

'We *really* don't have time for this.' The dryad stepped forward and addressed the knocker. 'Open up!' She tapped the apple on her collar, as if the pin itself was a door-opening button. 'This is an Olympic emergency!'

The tiny faun coughed twice, then began again. '*What is hidden from view –*'

The dryad groaned.

'Wait!' Cal stopped typing. 'I know this!' He clicked his fingers. 'It's –' He flickered once, and was gone.

'CAL!' Peregrine cried. She waved her hands about in the space where Cal had been. Cal was her guide, her *ally*. She needed him. 'Where did he go?' She turned to the dryad. 'Bring him back, please!'

'He must have lost signal.' The dryad slapped her forehead. 'This is NOT happening! Who uses riddles any more?'

'*But will appear before us –*' the brass knocker trilled.

The sound of footsteps echoed through the lane. They were slow but they were definitely getting closer.

'*When the owl sings her chorus?*'

What did her mum always say? *Think beyond the horizon.* Peregrine imagined her mum standing next to her as she stared up at the tower of University Church. She and Daedalus often sneaked up the tower on full moon, or when it was a particularly clear night so that Peregrine could practise her astronomy. Astronomy! That was it!

'Stars!' she yelled. 'The answer – it's stars!'

'Took you long enough!' squeaked the knocker, and the door creaked open. As soon as the gap was wide enough they fell in, and the dryad slammed the door shut behind them. Peregrine shivered as she pressed her back to the cool, hard metal.

Harsh fluorescent lights buzzed on to reveal a space that looked like an odd mix between a nuclear bunker and a log cabin. The walls were concrete grey and littered with notes, maps and Polaroids of the same seven nymphs she'd seen in the library, their arms around each other's shoulders. On one side of the cavernous space were cosy-looking bunk beds covered with neatly folded crocheted blankets; a small kitchen; an old sofa; and a coffee table stacked with unfamiliar board games. On the other side was a vast multi-screen console and a wardrobe of what looked like disguises (some, like the armour, were probably a little out of date). In the far corner, sitting at a slightly wonky angle on its ramp, was a vehicle that looked a bit like a rusted submarine crossed with a spaceship. It had *River Run 4000* engraved on its side.

BASH.

Peregrine leapt away from the door and spun around. 'This door . . . it will hold, right?' she asked.

'Of course!' The dryad chewed her lip. 'The door is reinforced with Mountain ore, it has a Boggart-built security system –'

BASH.

The dryad winced. 'It was built to withstand siege –'

BASH.

She raised her voice over the noise. 'But that *was* in the fourteenth century. Even *we* didn't have lasers then –'

Peregrine cut her off. 'Those – what did you call them? BogBrethren? They're going to find a way in.'

The dryad rubbed her temples and let out another little moan.

BASH. BASH.

Peregrine flicked her gaze to the screens. Stan, his hippo-sized body wedged in the alleyway, was thudding on the door while the taller one, Earl, looked on. Peregrine jogged over to the console and pressed a button with a mouth on it. A crackle of static flooded the room.

The dryad staggered up. 'Did you TOUCH something? That is highly complex CosTech –'

BASH. BASH. BASH. B—

The taller one, the one called Earl, held up his hand. 'Stop!' His voice echoed in the room. 'It's her. She wants a report.'

'*Her?*' Peregrine hissed.

'Shh!' The dryad paused, moving her face closer to the screen.

Stan's hand hovered off the door. He looked quite angry that his bashing had been interrupted. 'But I swear that knocker just mooned me –'

'Leave it,' Earl snarled. 'They can't go anywhere. They're trapped like marsh maggots in a sewer barrel.'

Stan screwed up his eyes, his face going red as if he was about to argue, but Earl had already turned and stalked back towards the high street.

A papercut smile sliced over Stan's face. 'Don't go anywhere,' he growled, looking straight into the camera. With one final punch of the door and a very rude hand gesture at the knocker, he followed Earl back down the alleyway.

Peregrine stared at the monitors. They were leaving – they were really leaving! Adrenaline still pumping through her veins, she exhaled and turned around. She was done with guessing; she needed information. And now. Peregrine set her glare to stun. 'Who. Were. *They*?!'

'I don't know.' The dryad was busying herself flicking stray plant goop off her coat. 'Those men – the BogBrethren . . .' She looked up, her face flushed green to match her ears. 'They came to the shop –'

Peregrine's eyes blazed, turning her glare up to kill. 'What were *you* doing in *our* shop?'

'I had to find Daedalus for –' the dryad paused, not meeting Peregrine's gaze – 'for something.' The useless word hung in the air.

Daedalus. Peregrine shook her head, but the image of Daedalus lying unconscious on the shop floor was impossible to shake out, like a bee tangled in her hair.

The dryad ran her fingers through her curls. 'I . . . I need to call this in.' She got out her CosPad and pressed the call button, then pressed it again. 'Why isn't it working? And where is Cal?' She slammed her CosPad down. 'Zeus's bolt! I am so tired of this stupid realm!'

Exhausted by the glaring, and the running, and whole crazy morning, Peregrine slumped to the ground and pulled her rucksack towards her. With just the smallest of shakes, she brought out Bernadette. Bernadette ruffled, lifting up their leaves and letting them sag. Peregrine stroked her finger down the leaves until she felt Bernadette calm and her own heartbeat slow.

'*Light and bright and airy thing, rarer than a fairy's wing . . .*' She needed to think. '*Bring your strength to grow your leaves, through you, nature's power weaves . . .*' She inhaled Bernadette's sweet peppermint smell. Maybe songs and riddles were a Cosmic thing? 'It appears,' she said quietly, 'that we have a common goal: we both need to find my godfather.'

She looked up. The dryad was staring at her. 'That plant . . .' The dryad stepped forward, reaching out for Bernadette. 'I've never seen anything like it – not even in the Cosmic Realm.'

Peregrine smiled smugly. 'Bernadette's very rare, according to Daedalus anyway.' She dripped water into the soil. 'Now, how about you tell me what you were doing snooping around our shop?' Her voice sounded so calm it was creepy, even to her.

The dryad chewed her lip. 'I have no idea how I'm going to justify this to the Investigation Unit.' She took her hat off and scratched the tip of her right ear.

'You'll tell me?' Peregrine hugged Bernadette to her chest. Finally, some answers.

The dryad nodded. 'I don't think we have much choice.' She inhaled. 'My name's Rowan. Rowan Strong of the Seven Strong Sisters.'

'What number are you?' Peregrine asked.

'What?' Rowan snapped.

'Of the Seven Strong Sisters? What number? Are you third, or sixth, or second, or –'

'Eighth.'

Peregrine stopped looking at Bernadette and raised her eyebrows. 'Eighth?'

'More *importantly*. . .' Rowan pulled her bowler hat down over her ears, 'I'm a Librarian. Well, a *trainee* Librarian. I haven't taken my oath yet. This is actually my first day,' she admitted, flushing a little. 'Librarians guard the portals to the Cosmic Realm – they are CSI's primary operatives on Earth.' Her flush deepened. 'We also make sure no one finds out about Olympus and its affiliate organisations.'

'I see.' Peregrine nodded. 'What's CSI?'

Rowan sighed. 'CSI is the Cosmic Sprite Investigation Unit of Olympus Inc.' She stood up straight, making her almost a foot and a half taller than Peregrine who, though very strong, was perhaps a tiny bit shorter than average.

'It's elite,' Rowan continued. 'Only the best of the Academy are invited to apply.'

Peregrine mouthed the unfamiliar names: the Academy, CSI, Olympus Inc. She tasted each word on her tongue before swallowing it hungrily. 'That is SO cool.'

Rowan smiled shyly. 'It *is* cool. Anyway –' the smile vanished – 'I've been told to find Daedalus. We, that is *Olympus Inc.*, need him to fix the portals between the realms.' She tapped the console. 'He designed them, and they've stopped working.'

Peregrine scrunched her brows together as she processed this information. *The portals have stopped working.*

'Don't worry.' Perhaps seeing Peregrine's expression, Rowan's tone turned haughty. 'It will be almost impossible for you to take much of this in. Mortals have such a *low* tolerance for the mystical.'

Peregrine gritted her teeth. This was reminding her a little too much of Daedalus's speech that morning in the library. If she wasn't allowed to talk to mortals about the Cosmic Realm, and *immortals* thought she wouldn't be able to handle any magical information, then how could she ever find out about *anything*?

'I've seen a portal.' She couldn't help it. 'Daedalus showed me.' Peregrine blushed. This was very *almost* true.

'He WHAT?' Rowan's eyes widened.

Bleep bleep.

'Aargh.' Rowan jumped. Then, recovering, took a mobile-phone-sized device with two antennae out from her belt and furrowed her brow at the screen. 'Hmm. Well, this is interesting.'

'What? What is interesting?' The device was showing green and purple waves spiking up and down. Peregrine reached out for it without thinking.

Rowan tapped her hand away. 'Don't touch that!' She hugged the device towards her. 'The spectrometer is *very* complex CosTech.'

Peregrine rolled her eyes. 'Whatever,' she muttered.

Rowan looked up at Peregrine, her gaze softening a smidgen. 'Every immortal leaves behind a Cosmic signature. B-Class immortals like Daedalus should leave behind a trail for at least an hour . . .' Rowan's forehead crinkled as she stared at her spectrometer. 'But these CosRays – they're coming from . . . the plant.'

Peregrine hugged the plant pot closer. 'From Bernadette?'

'Yes.' Rowan reached out and, reluctantly, Peregrine handed the plant to her.

'I need to keep moving.' Rowan prodded one of Bernadette's leaves tentatively. 'I could maybe take the AquaPod . . . It's old, though, a few centuries at least.' She brought Bernadette closer to her face. 'I should take the plant. Daedalus seemed to imply that it was important.'

'What? No!' Peregrine reached forward. Bernadette was *her* responsibility. 'Bernadette is mine! Well, Daedalus's. Anyway, you wouldn't know how to look after them.'

'Kid, I'm a *dryad*.' Rowan looked at Peregrine pointedly. 'I'm approximately 16 per cent chlorophyll, I *know* how to look after a simple housepl— Yeoow!' Rowan dropped the plant, which Peregrine caught deftly. 'It BIT me.'

Peregrine smirked, hugging Bernadette to her. 'It's just a *simple houseplant*, Rowan,' she sang mockingly while stroking the leaves. 'Looks like you need my help after all?'

Rowan sucked her throbbing finger. 'I don't believe this!' She shook out her hand. 'Fine.'

Peregrine's smile wavered as she gazed down at Bernadette. How did this strange little plant fit into all this? There must have been a reason why Daedalus had told Rowan about them.

'What are you not telling me?' she whispered.

Rowan brushed down her coat. 'So, do you or the *plant* have any ideas on how to get us out of here before the BogBrethren come back?'

Bernadette reached out a leaf to tickle Peregrine's nose.

'Achoo!' When she opened her eyes again, she was looking straight at the rusted submarine in the corner. 'Rowan, what's an AquaPod?'

10

HEKATE

**Location: HekTek Laboratory, Level Seventeen,
Olympus Inc., the Mountain
CosDate: 300.23.241**

The end of Hekate's nose quivered as she sniffed the potion. She detected notes of rattlesnake, pufferfish and an undertone of rotting knotweed. All excellent. Her nose was telling her that there was something not quite right though, and she trusted her nose. Hekate's nose was small, pointy and slightly upturned. It was also excellent at its job. Many credited Hekate's hyper-functioning, potion-sniffing nose with her nomination for Grand Architect. Others, less flatteringly, put her success down to her hexing most of her competitors with molypox. Both theories, as it turned out, were correct.

Pungent green spirals curled their way into the nymph's

nostrils. 'I smell –' she sniffed the vial again – 'I smell –' the corners of her mouth twitched – '*failure*.'

BANG! The rock goblin who was assisting her dropped his clipboard on the ground. 'B-but I followed the instructions –' he stammered as he scrambled to pick up the pieces of paper, which crumpled and tore in his thick, gravelly fingers.

'How much porcupine spine did you add?' Hekate asked as she shook the vial and peered into the murky liquid.

The rock goblin, who was called Hemlock, examined his list with shaking hands, knowing that, unfortunately, there would be no right answer. 'T-two and a half centimetres. Just as it says here –'

'Idiot!' Hekate screeched. She snatched the clipboard and scratched out the line, which clearly stated *two and a half centimetres of porcupine spine, stirred twice*. 'You have clearly taken the spine from the shoulder of the porcupine, it should be taken from the buttocks. The BUTTOCKS!'

Hemlock stared at her, then picked a piece of gravel out of his nose.

Hekate sighed. She needed a proper assistant. Someone she could mould in her image and teach the Craft to. Someone who had *style*. Someone who didn't, both literally and metaphorically, have rocks for brains.

She emptied the vial back into the top of a glass tube that spiralled down so the liquid dripped into a shimmering glass orb. Hekate clicked her fingers.

'Yes, mistress?'

'Bring me the adder venom. The good, *really* poisonous stuff. And the hair of puppy dog's tail. Spaniel. Spotted if we have it.'

Hemlock lumbered towards the supply cupboard. Hekate watched him go, then let her gaze rest on the bubbling mixture in front of her. She liked her laboratory. The position of Grand Architect that she had inherited from Daedalus came with lots of perks: an office on the twenty-seventh floor, limitless resources to develop her HekTek, and also, rather wonderfully, access to confidential communications.

She tapped the crystal pendant hanging at her throat so it clinked against her purple-painted fingernail. Not that Olympus Inc. was her end goal. No, there were limits to what even the Cosmics would allow her to do.

Hemlock skidded back into the room, arms laden with deadly (and potentially explosive) ingredients, which he dropped clumsily onto the table.

Hekate shuddered. Finesse was lost on these stony creatures.

She selected a few hairs, and a bottle with a label that read *Serpa*. 'Yes, this will do.' She sprinkled the ingredients into the glass tube and turned up the Bunsen flame to an electric blue. The liquid bubbled. Hekate watched as the potion turned from the colour of pond to a glowing purple, then to a lurid acid-green. After one minute exactly, she pipetted out the liquid back into the vial.

'Perfection,' she drawled. 'You see, basalt-for-brains, potion-making is about *initiative*.' She took out one of her golden hairpins – long, sharp and deadly – and dipped it in the acid-green mixture. The glittering pin sucked it up like smoothie through a straw.

Her CosPad buzzed. The noise made her hand falter slightly, and a drop of the liquid fell onto the lapel of her tailored lab coat. She narrowed her eyes at the stain, then at Hemlock, who gulped loudly.

'I need three more vials of this.' She tapped the glass. 'Take it to the lab technicians. NOW.'

The rock goblin nodded and took the vial. 'Thank you, mistress.' He bowed deeply, then stumbled out of the room backwards.

Hekate speared her coiled bun with the hairpin and looked down at her CosPad. She pressed a button, and two figures fuzzed onto the screen.

'She's not answering. Does that mean we don't have to tell her?' Stan whispered to Earl.

'Ahem.' Hekate coughed deliberately. 'Tell me WHAT, gentlemen?' Her voice was sweet, the kind of sweet you could choke on.

Both men whipped towards her. Stan, the squatter, denser of the two, and Earl, the shrewder, taller one. Their lizard eyes blinked in surprise.

Hekate peered at them over her platinum-rimmed glasses.

Stan and Earl were part of a gang of BogBrethren who were doing time in Olympus's Sewage Detail, sent there because of the toxic nature of their crimes, but also because BogBrethren did very well in the sewers. It was their webbed feet and ability to hold their breath for days at a time.

'I have been trying to get hold of you boys. You did not check in at Alexandria,' she purred. 'Should I be worried?'

'You said that the Librarians would all be locked up! We weren't expecting –' Stan began.

'WHAT?' Hekate snapped. Heat flooded her cheeks and her nostrils flared.

Earl grabbed the CosPad from Stan. 'It is a minor hitch. For some reason, this Librarian wasn't caught in the CosPort like the others.' His eyes darted to something off the screen. 'But she's trapped in one of those old Olympic safe houses. There's no way in, but –'

'But no way out neither,' Stan finished, smiling at his own cleverness.

Hekate stroked the bridge of her nose; she found the sensation deeply relaxing. 'Gentlemen, do you know what I need?' She stopped stroking and jabbed her razor-sharp nail at the screen. 'What I need is *information*, what I *need* is results.' She narrowed her eyes. 'Do you know what I *don't* need?'

Stan looked genuinely stumped. 'Er . . .'

'An Olympus official running around finding out my secrets and ruining my plans!' Hekate screeched.

'Ooh, right.' Stan nodded, then paused. 'What about the girl?'

Hekate put her fingers to her temples. This was getting very trying. 'Girl?'

'She's a *Terran*.' Earl shuddered. He swiped his fingers across the CosPad so that a gangly, angry-looking figure appeared on Hekate's screen. 'She's listed as one of the Architect's known associates.'

'Associate?' Hekate spun the holo-figure with her thumb and index finger. This was new. Since when had Daedalus been in the habit of collecting *associates*? This might actually turn out to be to her advantage. She looked at the other screen, where Daedalus, her former mentor, was spinning, trapped in a vortex of her magi-mist like a wrinkly rotisserie chicken. He was safely secured in Alexandria, just waiting for her to visit. It wouldn't hurt to give him a little more . . . *incentive* to answer her questions.

A smile spread across Hekate's delicate face. 'When you catch the girl, bring her with you to Alexandria, would you?' She touched her hairpin, lightly. 'I think we might have found our leverage.'

'Leverage!' Stan whooped, as if he knew what it meant (which he almost certainly did not).

'And the Librarian?' Earl asked.

'I do not like loose ends, gentlemen.' She tucked a stray hair behind her ear. 'Please tidy that one for me.'

11

ROWAN

Location: Keep Nine, Magpie Lane, Oxford, England

'Open.' Rowan tapped the bronze-coloured door of the *River Run 4000*. Nothing happened. 'It's voice-activated,' she said in mumbled explanation to Peregrine, who was peering over her shoulder. 'It's voice-ACTIVATED,' Rowan said again, this time louder and with an angry slam of her palm against the door.

The AquaPod seemed to sense her no-nonsense tone. A green light appeared around the doorframe as the hatch slid open with a dull sucking sound.

'That's better,' Rowan muttered as she squeezed through the door into the cosy cockpit. Peregrine followed.

Rowan noticed that the girl didn't need to duck – unlike herself, who had to fold her long dryad limbs uncomfortably to step inside. Annoyingly, all pods were sprite-sized as standard.

'Ow!' Rowan said as her hat banged against a copper pipe.

Peregrine sniffed. 'Er, what's that smell?'

Rowan wrinkled her nose and picked up a moulding cup of coffee sitting in the cup-holder by the pilot seat. 'AquaPods *always* smell like this, it's the sealant,' she lied as she held the cup with two fingers and quickly deposited it in the recyclone, where it vaporised immediately.

Though she wouldn't admit it, this AquaPod really *was* a hunk of junk. The CosPorts were updated every few hundred years or so, and Portal Tunnel 9 was always the last to get any of the new CosTech. Portal 3 had a Cloud Buster Mark IV, for Hera's sake! Rowan had seen it in the catalogues that Basst, the chic weather sprite who manned the Bologna desk, had shown her at last year's CosCon.

'Runs like a dream, I tell you,' Basst had drawled, pointing lazily at the lilac leather pod interiors. 'There's nothing like it, darling – flying over the Colosseum by moonlight. You miss *all* the traffic.'

Rowan tucked herself into the tattered pilot's seat and patted an arm rest, which promptly fell off in her hand. Without looking, she hurled it over her shoulder.

'Hey!' Peregrine yelled from behind her. 'That almost hit my head!'

'Sorry,' Rowan lied. This was *supposed* to be a simple mission: find Daedalus, fix the portals, go home. And now, what? The Cosmic Realm was being attacked? This Search and Retrieve was rapidly becoming an adventure – or, worse, a *quest*. She felt a little vomit rise, and gagged. She was unprepared for this and, more importantly, she was *unqualified*.

'Don't touch *anything*,' she called from the cockpit. 'The place is filthy enough without having grubby mortal fingerprints over everything.' She looked up at the switches above her head. 'Now I just have to remember how to start this thing . . .'

'This is so cool!'

Rowan turned to see Peregrine opening up a copper wall panel. She stared open-mouthed as Peregrine began pulling out wires, admiring each one in turn.

'What does this run on?' The girl held a wire up to her nose and sniffed it. 'Some kind of solar power fusion?'

'What are you –? I said, don't TOUCH anything!' Rowan jumped out of her seat and slammed the panel shut. 'Go sit down.'

'My fingers aren't *that* grubby,' Peregrine mumbled mutinously as she went to sit in the co-pilot's seat, but Rowan held up a hand.

'No, NOT there.' Rowan indicated one of the passenger seats behind her. '*There*. And don't forget to put your seat belt on,' she snapped.

Peregrine rolled her eyes and fell into one of the chairs.

'Oh, and you should use this.' Rowan unhooked a grey jumpsuit from its peg on the side of the pod and threw it to Peregrine. 'It will fit. Probably.' She glowered as she took off her hat – the top of her head was still smarting – before turning her attention back to the U-shaped steering wheel. She knew she was being a bit mean, but what had her sisters told her when she left for the Academy? Fake it till you make it, right? Act brave and you will be brave. Act like a heartless harpy, and you will be a . . .

'Do you know what you're doing?' Peregrine called, her voice muffled as she pulled her school jumper over her head.

'I am an Academy-trained Librarian, so *yes*.' Rowan nodded slowly, climbing back into the pilot seat and staring at the controls. 'I know *exactly* what I am doing . . .'

Peregrine hopped on one foot as she slid her other leg into the jumpsuit. 'It's just that –'

'What?' Rowan snapped. '*Please* tell me how to drive this machine that you didn't even know the *name* of ten minutes ago –'

'You have the handbrake on.' Peregrine zipped up the front of the suit.

'I *know*.' Rowan did not know, but she *had* read the AquaPod manual and passed all of the Academy simulation drills, so how hard could it be? The wiser, more sensible part of her told her firmly that it could be hard – really, really hard. She cracked her knuckles. The simulation drills *had* been on much better models: shinier, more up-to-date and . . . Rowan looked down at the gear stick.

'*Flooharght!*' She slapped the wheel. That's it. They were absolutely, completely doomed. They were going to fail in this mission, and probably die, because she – Rowan Strong – hadn't completed her Academy training. How could she have been such a flittertwit to think that *she* could guard the portal, even for a single day? She was nowhere *near* ready!

'What's wrong?' Peregrine called.

'I never learned how to drive a manual,' Rowan whispered.

'Oh.' Peregrine was strapping a quietly squeaking Bernadette into the passenger seat. 'I know how.' She vaulted nimbly over the back of the chair next to Rowan. 'Daedalus lets me drive the tractor when we collect the seedlings.' She slid calmly into her seat. 'It can't be that different.' She grabbed the steering wheel.

Rowan reached out a hand. 'NO! Wait!'

Peregrine grinned, clearly excited that she got to ignore another reasonable request. She flicked the ignition switch above their heads, and voila! The AquaPod started to rumble. 'There we go.' She glanced at Rowan. 'You should probably put your seat belt on now.'

Breathe, just breathe. Rowan exhaled loudly. 'OK, but *I'm* navigating.' She looked at Peregrine, who gave her an overly formal nod.

'So,' Peregrine began, 'where exactly are we going?'

'Er ...' Rowan did not have an answer. Luckily, at that moment, her CosPad beeped. *'INCOMING CALL! INCOMING CALL!'*

Rowan clicked the CosPad screen and a bearded, pixelated face appeared.

'Cal!' Peregrine punched the sky. 'You're back!'

The faun was on a swivel chair that was turning slowly clockwise.

'Where in Hera's name have you been?' Rowan snapped.

'I'm so sorry, the holo-comm failed.' Cal swivelled the chair back the other way with a *tap-tapping* sound that Rowan assumed was his hooves. 'We are suffering huge power outages here. Sibyll has got her best sprites down at the Cor trying to boost the signal.'

'Humph.' Rowan huffed.

'I've only just found your signal again, Agent, but I *did* get your messages. Let me see . . .' He peered down his nose at his clipboard. '"Help, help, they are after us".' He paused to flick over the page. 'And then three minutes later, "Pick up the phone, you lazy, good-for-nothing goat boy" and *then* a further two minutes later "I will stuff that sandwich down your – oh no, wait my mistake – *up* your –"'

'Yes, yes, I'm sorry about that.' Rowan *was* a bit sorry. 'But they *were* chasing us, and not all of us can just disappear.' She clicked her fingers to illustrate her point.

'All right, all right.' Cal took his glasses off and squinted at his screen. 'Well, I have *also* been busy. I checked the portal logbooks,' he continued before Rowan could cut in, 'and there is no sign of any BogBrethren having been granted visas recently. Are you sure they're –' he gulped – 'gone?'

'Yes, we lost them.' Rowan paused. 'We think. We're in the AquaPod.'

Cal tipped his head to the side. 'You're going to use the *AquaPod* to search for Daedalus? Can you even drive one of those?' Before Rowan could reply, he sighed. 'And Pear-grinn, you are sure you're all right?' He put his glasses back on at a slightly wonky angle, and they slipped down his nose. 'All limbs still accounted for?'

'Hi, Cal!' Peregrine was leaning sideways to get a better look at the screen. Rowan put her hand on the side of Peregrine's bubble helmet and slowly pushed her back.

Cal paused his flustering. 'You're not intending to take Pear-grinn *with* you, are you, Agent?'

'Well, I couldn't exactly leave her in the safe house with all that CosTech, could I? It would be against regulations.' Rowan directed her gaze down to the navigation panel.

Cal's face regained its reddish tinge, then changed to a kind of purplish plum. 'You are taking a twelve-year-old Terran *child* on a top-secret potentially fatal mission?' His face turned a sickly puce. 'That is at least *fourteen* code violations!' He narrowed his eyes further. 'Fifteen, if you include the jaunty angle of your hat.'

Peregrine put up her hand. 'Er, fatal?'

'We'll have to deal with that later,' Rowan snapped, quickly readjusting her hat inside her helmet. 'Daedalus seemed to imply that she was useful . . . somehow.'

'Somehow?' Peregrine stared at Rowan. 'I answered the riddle –'

'Yes, well done.' Rowan gave her a thumbs up.

Peregrine's face darkened.

Cal sighed and took his glasses off, wiping them on the sleeve of his cardigan. 'Any other major Cosmic-altering events that have happened in the last –' he checked his CosPad – 'seventeen minutes that I should be aware of?'

'No.' Rowan thought that was *probably* true. 'I'm heading after Daedalus, as ordered.'

'Excellent.' Cal nodded. 'So where do you think he is?'

'Er . . .' Rowan scratched her ear.

Peregrine put her hand up again.

'Yes, Pear-grinn.' Cal nodded to her.

Rowan rolled her eyes as Peregrine shuffled over so she was firmly back in Cal's eyeline. 'The BogBrethren – they mentioned Alexandria. That *must* be where they've taken Daedalus, right?'

'Alexandria, of course. That is where we're going.' Rowan nodded enthusiastically.

Cal raised an eyebrow.

'Anyway –' Rowan turned to Cal – 'you don't think they've taken him to the library, do you? We were told at the Academy that Portal Tunnel 1 was decommissioned years ago?'

'*Two thousand* years ago, to be exact.' Cal began typing something into his console.

Peregrine put up her hand again.

Rowan sighed.

'I've read about the Library of Alexandria,' Peregrine said. 'The famous one, the one that burned down.'

Cal and Rowan looked at her blankly, but Peregrine pressed on. 'But a portal? There is a *portal* in the Library of Alexandria?'

'*Was* a portal, yes.' Cal put his glasses back on. 'It is one of the first things that we learn about Cosmic lore. Where there is an ancient library, there is a portal. It's sort of a chicken-and-egg situation, except much, *much* more complicated.'

'Shocking,' Peregrine muttered under her breath.

Rowan readjusted her hat a couple of degrees. 'The Library of Alexandria was the first. The first library and –'

'The first portal!' Peregrine finished.

Cal nodded. 'The Alexandrian portal was taken off the Portal Tunnel Network after the library fire collapsed the entrance. The Librarian was terribly upset, of course – no one has seen him since.' Cal shook his head. 'The Alexandria piece is interesting, though. Let me see what I can find out for you.'

Rowan nodded. 'Update us – I mean, *me*.' She coughed. 'Update ME when you know anything.' She relaxed her grip on the seat and forced a thin smile at Cal. 'It is going to be fine.'

'If you say so.' Cal shrugged. 'I have to go and let Sibyll know that you're still alive. She will be thrilled.' He took one more appraising look at Peregrine and disappeared.

Rowan glanced sideways. 'Stop smiling,' she barked. 'You're here because of a plant.'

Peregrine's smile widened even further. She was still grinning as Rowan pressed a button and a radar display popped up over the console. 'This –' Rowan prodded at the holo-screen – 'will take us to the river Isis, and then we can ride the riverways until Dover.' Rowan forced herself to sound confident, but in truth she had no idea how this antique AquaPod would fare in the open ocean. The *River Run* was designed for short-range trips to London and the occasional jaunt to Hadrian's Wall to check if the giants were still sleeping – definitely not for travelling to decommissioned portals thousands of miles away.

'And then?' Peregrine clutched the gear stick and looked at her.

Rowan bit her lip. 'And then we pray Poseidon is feeling generous.' Or better yet, she thought as she pulled the ramp-release lever, that he just doesn't notice us. 'Let's go.'

PEREGRINE

Location: AquaPod Cockpit, Keep Nine, Magpie Lane, Oxford, England

Peregrine manoeuvred the pod jerkily onto the ramp. There was a loud creak, like a branch snapping, as the backside of the pod was lifted up. She sneaked a glance to her right. Rowan seemed calm enough – so this was normal, then? Well, about as normal as sitting next to an immortal nature sprite – sorry, *nymph* – on an antique magical sub.

A door opened in front of the pod and Peregrine could see runners, like train tracks, heading straight through to the entrance, lit with blinking blue dots. She recognised the *thunkety-thunk* as the sound that a rollercoaster makes before it hurtles down into water or swoops around a loop-the-loop or simply drops down into nothing. Peregrine had always liked rollercoaster rides, and she felt the familiar thrill of adrenaline charge through her fingertips as she gripped the steering wheel. The AquaPod was the perfect size for her: on the tractor, Daedalus had to be the one pressing the pedals most of the time, but even though her feet touched the floor, there were no pedals here.

Hang on, there were no pedals. 'Rowan, where is the brake – ?'

WHOOSH. Peregrine's stomach dropped into her shoes as the soft warm glow of the room was swallowed up by the darkness of the tunnel. They were getting faster. Peregrine switched to second gear. Third gear. Fourth. The lights in the pod flickered. Peregrine turned to check on Bernadette, still strapped tightly into their seat. Their leaves were shaking in time with the juddering machine, but they seemed happy enough.

'Keep the speed!' Rowan shouted over the rattling. 'We should be at the river in seconds.'

Peregrine could see the blue runners stretching out in front of them, flashing like Christmas lights. Until they stopped flashing. 'Rowan, the lights!'

Just when Peregrine was sure they were going to slam into something solid, splattering mortal, dryad and plant into oblivion, a door slid open and dark water rushed around them and swallowed the pod whole.

Peregrine blinked into the blackness and put her hand to her nose. It felt damp and clammy, but at least it was still attached to her face. She scanned the buttons in front of her. 'Aha!' She clicked a picture of what looked like an Olympic torch and two beams of light shone out in front of them, illuminating the riverbed.

Even with the headlights, there wasn't much to see through

the murky water. From the hovering holo-map, it looked as if they were somewhere near Christ Church College.

'We'll follow this river pretty much the whole way.' Rowan leaned forward, scrunching her eyes up at the map. 'We'll have to watch out for rowing boats until we get to the Thames, and even then –'

Grrrrrrrrrr. A loud rumbling filled the cockpit.

'What was that?' Rowan snapped her head towards the viewscreen. 'Kraken larvae? Selkies?'

Peregrine shook her head and pointed to her stomach, her face reddening. 'I guess I'm a bit hungry.' When was the last time she had eaten? So much had happened in the last couple of hours, she couldn't remember whether she'd actually had breakfast. Then she remembered Daedalus's half-finished plate of toast, the half-full cup of coffee. Was Daedalus also hungry, wherever he was? Was he conscious, was he . . . OK?

Rowan had unclicked her seat belt and was rummaging in the compartment above her head. She pulled out two bars wrapped in iridescent leaves and thrust one at Peregrine, who accepted gratefully. 'They're CSI rations.' Rowan screwed up her face. 'Pretty basic, but we should eat something, keep our energy up.' She unclicked her bubble helmet. 'The oxygenator seems to be working too. I think we can risk taking these off, just while we eat.' She popped off the helmet and shook out her curls.

As soon as Peregrine unwrapped the mother-of-pearl style packaging, it disintegrated in her fingers, leaving just a sticky toffee-coloured slab in her hand. 'What is this?' She held it up, her mouth already watering.

Rowan shrugged. 'Standard-issue SolarBar: walnut, stardust

and dates wrapped in CosFilm. Not the best.' She took a bite and spoke while chewing. 'But one bar can keep you going for an entire solar-cycle.'

Peregrine bit into the bar and almost choked – it felt like a tiny fizzing firework was whizzing around her mouth. 'WHOA!' She took another bite and this time the popping went all the way down to her stomach. 'It's like I've just eaten a sparkler!'

'That'll be the stardust.' Rowan chewed slowly, apparently used to the sensation. 'Or possibly the walnuts.'

The third bite tasted of . . . was that chocolate? But a specific kind of chocolate. It tasted like the kind of airport chocolate that Mum would bring home when she returned from one of her archaeological digs. It felt warm and comforting and sort of sad, all at once.

'It's supposed to fill you up. Physically, but also emotionally.' Rowan spoke through her last few mouthfuls, then picked a bottle of sanitiser from her belt and squirted her hands with it. She rubbed them together aggressively. 'A little bit for the body, a little bit for the –' she waved her newly sanitised hands around in the air – 'you know, "soul".'

Peregrine side-eyed the dashboard. It looked like they were going at a steady pace: the river had widened now and they'd dropped a few metres in depth. She swivelled the chair so she faced Rowan, and tucked her legs in. The SolarBar had filled her up: now it was time to get some answers.

'So –' she leaned in – 'are there lots of immortals like you here? On Earth, I mean.'

'No way.' Rowan shook her head. 'Most left the Terran Realm centuries ago because, you know –' she took another bite of her SolarBar – 'the Cosmic Realm is so much better.'

Peregrine felt a prickle of envy at the casual way Rowan said that, like it was a fact rather than just an opinion. 'But what about Daedalus?' she countered. '*Daedalus* is an immortal and *he* lives on Earth.' She bit her lip. She *had* always wondered why her godfather was still on Earth if he could live somewhere as exciting as the Cosmic Realm.

'Yes, that's always been a mystery.' Rowan scratched her ear. 'You know, Daedalus was the Grand Architect for a *millennium* – that's almost unheard of.'

No, Peregrine *didn't* know. The prickle of envy was growing spikes. She knew Daedalus's sandwich preference (quince), and how he liked his tea (green), but how much did she know about him *really*? She looked back to Bernadette, whose leaves were waving as if to music. How much did she know about *anything*?

'What's a Grand Architect?' she asked, finally, through gritted teeth.

'Oh, I forgot you didn't know –'

Peregrine's envy was now a full-blown porcupine prowling in her chest. She narrowed her eyes.

Rowan continued, oblivious. 'It *means* he was a Big Deal. Sort of Head Inventor, basically in charge of *all* Cosmic technology,' she explained. 'And then, just like that –' she snapped her fingers – 'he left. Nobody knows why. Now we have Hekate, who by all accounts is a bit of a psycho –'

'*WARNING. WARNING.*' The computer's shout filled the pod. The lights above them flickered, then switched to red, then blue, then red again. It was as if a dozen police cars had suddenly surrounded them, demanding to know why a CSI operative was telling a Terran a whole bunch of Cosmic secrets.

'Emergency lights!' There was an urgency to Rowan's voice. Her fingers flew across the control panel.

The holo-map was flashing too. A red dot had appeared on the screen and was moving towards them at speed, like a red ant racing hungrily towards a sugary doughnut. And they were the doughnut.

'*WARNING. WARNING. Unidentified object on collision course.*' Even the computer sounded stressed.

'We should go faster now, right?' Peregrine was looking at the red dot, which was getting closer by the nanosecond.

'Yes, yes, absolutely, yes!' Rowan shouted. 'Let's go! NOW!'

Peregrine pressed the accelerator and clunked the AquaPod down into second gear. A growl like a disgruntled pug waking from a nap welled up from deep inside the machine. 'Come *on* . . .' She gritted her teeth and pressed the accelerator button again. Then again. The revs rattled the steering wheel but she clung on, willing their speed up, up and up. The pod gave a final mechanical yawn, then stopped making any sound at all. Their speed was dropping, slower and slower. Peregrine gasped. Shards of sunlight sliced through the murky water: they were floating up towards the surface.

'What is going on?' Rowan was wide-eyed and panicked. 'We need speed, we *need* to get out of here!'

'*WARNING. WARNING,*' the computer repeated. '*Impact imminent.*'

Peregrine turned to Rowan. 'We've stopped.' Her voice was a whisper. 'We're dead in the water.'

13

ROWAN

Location: AquaPod, River Thames, London, England

'*Impact imminent,*' the computer repeated.

Think, Rowan. We can't move and there is an unknown entity hurtling towards us. What are we going to do? She squeezed her eyes shut, trying to move past the chaos of the moment and into a state of clear, calm decision-making.

'*Impact VERY imminent.*'

Her eyes snapped open. No, this was not working.

'Could it be Stan and Earl?' Peregrine asked, her voice barely audible over the rattling, wheezing pod. 'Could they have followed us here?'

'BogBrethren *can* swim underwater ...' Rowan raked her hands through her curls, then cast an apologetic look at Peregrine. 'But they've got GlamPasses on, so I don't know. I just don't know.' As a career Librarian, Rowan found the lack of adequate information on the situation particularly stress-inducing.

Ach-CHUG. The AquaPod shook, as if it had sneezed, then let out a little fart noise.

'What was that?' Rowan's eyes widened.

'Well, it wasn't me!' Peregrine yelled back. 'And anyway, how should I know? It's your submarine!'

The engine wheezed.

'It's not a *submarine*, it's an AquaPod –'

Ach-CHUG.

'Aargh!' Rowan and Peregrine screamed simultaneously. A pair of huge grey-green eyes in goggles had emerged from the gloom and were now staring in at them through the viewscreen.

Peregrine recovered from her shock first. 'It's a woman!' And then, 'An *old* woman.'

Rowan felt her staccato heartbeat slowing to a more predictable rhythm. *This* she could deal with. At least they were not being attacked – not yet, anyway.

Bubbles appeared from the woman's mouth. Was she laughing at them? Silvery hair danced around her crinkled face and she seemed to be wearing some kind of . . . boiler suit?

'*And* she doesn't have a helmet on.' Peregrine moved her head to the side, squinting. 'How is she breathing?'

'Nyad.' Rowan shook her head.

'Nyad?' Peregrine paused, chewing over this new highly classified morsel of information. 'A water nymph?' Her voice was laced with awe. 'I've read about them. They live in rivers, right?'

'Uh-huh.' Rowan pulled her CosPad from her belt and brought it up to where the nymph was doing a graceful somersault in the water. 'Did you *also* read that they are renowned show-offs?' She blew a curl off her forehead. 'At least *dryads* know how to follow the rules. Don't be seen by humans. Really, it's not that hard. It's not like they are particularly observant.'

Peregrine turned sharply, but Rowan shrugged. Everyone knew it: Terrans were famous for ignoring the mystical, even when it was right in front of their mortal faces; the moon was a great example.

The nyad blew a kiss, and a heart-shaped bubble hovered in front of the windscreen. Rowan clicked a photograph.

'I wish I could swim like that!' Peregrine pressed her nose against the glass.

'You probably could if you had gills,' Rowan muttered. She bashed the side of the CosPad. 'Call Cal.' She spoke loudly and clearly.

Nothing happened. 'Call CAL!'

This mission was so far over her head – so far that she could hardly see it (and what she *could* see was very unpleasant). She bashed the CosPad again. It's not like Rowan didn't know what she should do. Her training had been very clear: she should wait, and be *told* what to do. Except it was hard to get instructions when no one in the Cosmic Realm actually knew exactly where they were, or what *exactly* they were doing . . .

The CosPad fuzzed a bright, hopeful blue, then nothing. Rowan groaned.

The nyad had finished showing off and was now pointing

towards two chains that were attached to the pod. That must have been what those sneeze-sounds had been.

'She's going to tow us!' Peregrine was giving the woman a thumbs up while nodding enthusiastically.

Rowan looked up from her still-blank CosPad. 'She's going to WHAT?' Her eyes widened.

The nyad had spun around and was swimming in strong, fluid movements towards an antique AquaQuad that Rowan could just see through the grey-green murk. Were those green flames painted on the side? Oh boy. She felt the rumble of the AquaPod vibrate through her body, making her wobble.

'We're moving!' Peregrine yelled as they picked up speed.

'Get back into your seat!' Rowan barked.

Rowan watched the green dot of the AquaPod whizz across the navigation screen. They were indeed moving fast: past a Terran air travel port and a large amphitheatre called Wembley. Where in Hera's name were they going?

The pod lurched forward then was dragged sharply upwards, throwing them back into their seats. They must be moving towards the surface.

Rowan leaned forward; she couldn't see the AquaQuad any more. Her mother had always warned her that nyads could be slippery – where *was* she taking them?

Upwards, upwards, upwards – and then *plop!* The AquaPod broke the surface.

'Wow,' Peregrine whispered, for at least the second time that day.

Rowan whipped to face her. 'Not *everything* is wow, Peregrine. *Some* things are bad, really, really –'

Peregrine leaned over and gently turned Rowan's face towards the viewscreen.

'Oh.'

A huge domed greenhouse loomed before them. Mist hung low from the roof and snaked around the dozens of plants that grew across the floor, up the walls and around the spiral staircase that led up to a gallery. A faded wooden sign leaned up against one of the doors. In looped handwriting it read:

Notice: Greenhouse 72 is closed for renovation between 2nd August and 24th November 1842

Rowan brought out her spectrometer. After a few false starts and a worrying whirring sound, it started to scan. She was done with surprises. What she needed now was cold, hard, reliable data. The spectrometer showed that the room was fifteen metres wide, a balmy 23 degrees, and home to one B-plus immortal female and one other small warm-blooded vertebrate. There were no other life forms with spines, as far as she could tell.

She scratched her left ear underneath her hat. This was new territory for her. Section 22C of *The Librarian's Handbook* made some reference to 'being inside enemy terrain', but that was on land and within the Cosmic Realm. She pulled *The Handbook* out of her jumpsuit pocket and placed a shaking hand on its comforting green cover.

'We both just need to breathe.' Rowan closed her eyes and inhaled slowly as she traced *The Handbook*'s delicate border of interweaving gold branches. 'To breathe, and take things one calm, calculated step at a time.' A scuffling sound made her turn, eyes wide with annoyance. '*What* do you think you are doing?'

'We don't have time to be calm.' Peregrine had hoisted herself out of her seat and was fiddling with the pod door seal. 'And we *definitely* don't have time to calculate.'

Rowan's voice rose in panic. 'But this is not part of the plan!'

'We don't *have* a plan,' Peregrine bit back, then stuck her tongue in between her teeth in some kind of show of concentration.

'The *plan* is that we need to wait for official instructions,' Rowan explained slowly, as if to, well, a child. 'We have no idea who this woman is!' She turned back to her CosPad, pressing buttons in the hope of getting through to Cal, to Sibyll, to *anyone*. 'She might be in league with the BogBrethren, she might be –'

The door opened with a sound like a plunger being pulled from a sink, and Peregrine was yanked through by her jumpsuit before Rowan could yell 'Evil!'

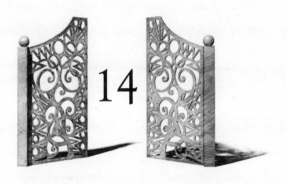

PEREGRINE

Location: Greenhouse 72, Royal Botanic Gardens, Kew, London, England

'Oofle.' Peregrine spoke into the nyad's muscular shoulder as she was pressed into an iron-tight hug. 'Oofle moofle.'

Peregrine did not like hugs. She did not like them in general, and she especially didn't like being hugged by strangers. But, she had to admit, she did not hate *this* hug. The nyad smelled like pine needles and crisp, damp mornings; *this* hug felt strangely familiar.

Finally the nyad released her and Peregrine took a big gulp of fresh, cool air. It was the kind of air that her mum said made you more alert and ready for action.

Action!

Penelope Quinn's aikido lessons snapped into place and Peregrine struck her defensive stance: feet wide, fists up, and eyes fixed in a well-practised I-will-END-you glare.

'Are you going to *fight* me, Peregrine?' the nyad cackled. Steam was rolling off her wetsuit in waves. 'Just like your mother, eh?' She snapped her goggles up onto her head and grinned.

'Huh?' Peregrine lowered her fists, then raised them again. This could be a trick, a way to get her off balance without even throwing a single punch. 'How do you know who I am?' Her gaze darted around the greenhouse, then back to the nyad. 'And how do you know my mum?'

'Daedalus and I taught your mother when she was at school.' The nyad shook out her wave of glamorous silver hair, which dried instantly. 'Clever, scrappy wee thing she was. Daedalus tells me you're that and then some, eh?' She went to punch Peregrine lightly on the arm, but Peregrine swerved to the left. 'Oh, very good!' The nyad's face crinkled into a smile that made her look like a very old, very kind tortoise.

Images swirled around like smoke inside Peregrine's brain, intangible and half-formed. There *was* a memory, but it was gone before she could pull it in closer to examine it properly. She lowered her fists.

'Maybe this will help.' The nyad pulled a business card from her overall pocket and handed it to her. 'You can call me Nim, dear.'

Peregrine read the card out loud.

They were at Kew Gardens! Of course! Peregrine had been here with Daedalus, when he was lecturing for the Royal Horticultural Society, and then again for the Bi-Annual Botanical Convention . . . Come to think of it, Daedalus visited Kew a *lot*. Peregrine peered around at the many vibrant exotic plants: her gaze fell on a pink-flowered vine that was climbing over a hat stand. Wasn't that the wisteria that Daedalus had been struggling with six months ago?

'Hero support?' An emerald-faced Rowan clambered out of the bobbing pod behind them, pondweed clinging to her coat.

Nim put her hands up. 'I know it's a little old-fashioned. I mean, who talks about *heroes* any more?' She sighed. 'It's all questing-by-committee now.' She lowered her voice. 'Trust Olympus to squeeze the fun out of it.'

Rowan sneezed.

'I think you have some things to tell me, but I want us to eat first.' Nim walked over to a table in the shape of a shell which was laid as if for high tea. Lots of little sandwiches, cupcakes covered in pink icing and sugared buns were piled high on a multi-tiered cake stand. 'Bad news is best served with butter, wouldn't you agree?'

Peregrine's stomach gurgled in agreement as Nim buttered a sweet-smelling crumpet. 'Bad news?' Peregrine didn't know how much more bad news she could take.

'Have a scone, dear.' Nim picked up a swirly-blue-patterned plate and offered it to Peregrine, who took it cautiously. 'It's taken me three hundred years, but I think the recipe is very *nearly* perfect. The jam is strawberry, and the scones are . . .'

Peregrine took a bite.

'. . . seaweed.'

Peregrine choked, spluttering seaweed-scone crumbs across the floor. 'Thank you,' she said, recovering.

'The *bad* news is that I lost contact with Daedalus a couple of hours before I found you.' Nim sighed. 'And that can only mean one thing.'

Peregrine inhaled, anticipating the worst.

'Well, actually it can mean one of six, possibly seven, things. In all likelihood he was –'

'Kidnapped,' Rowan cut in. 'He was . . . kidnapped.'

Peregrine exhaled. Clutching the crumbly scone, she tried to squeeze out the memory of Daedalus lying unmoving on the shop floor, but she couldn't stop herself remembering. She swallowed hard.

'A kidnapping?' Nim repeated, tapping her finger on her chin. 'It's been a while since we've had one of those.' She shrugged. 'When you've been around for as many years as Daedalus, you do tend to collect the odd nemesis or two.'

Peregrine took another shaky bite of scone. 'Or *twoff?*'

Nim eyed Peregrine's trembling hands. 'Let me get you some tea. Arthur, could you bring some extra cups?' Nim called.

A duck appeared from one of the doors out of the dome and waddled towards them, carrying two porcelain teacups in his beak. He flapped up onto the table, dropped the cups and kicked the teapot with an aggressive quack.

'Don't mind him.' The nyad sighed. 'He's just grumpy because I didn't tell him I was leaving.' She addressed the duck. 'It was an *emergency*, Arthur.'

The duck kicked the teapot again, then stuck his beak up in the air and sat down on the table, refusing to look at anyone.

Peregrine blinked. She had met a faun, she had run away from lizard men, she had driven a submarine, but somehow it was the duck kicking a teapot that might just break her brain. She closed her eyes, opened them again and gasped.

The duck was staring straight at her, its eyes narrowed.

'As soon as I lost contact with Daedalus, I came to find you. *Immediately.*' She eyed Arthur, who gave a low quack and pecked at some scone crumbs.

'Hang on.' Rowan had not touched her scone. 'Sibyll told me the TraxTech isn't working. How did you find us?'

Nim's eyes twinkled. 'I followed Daedalus's tracking device.' She looked at Peregrine.

'Daedalus was *tracking* me?! The sneak!' Peregrine felt a sudden torrent of rage at her godfather. Rage at keeping this secret, rage at getting himself kidnapped. Rage, rage, RAGE. She patted her hair, trying to locate some kind of bug.

'Oh, we wouldn't tag *you*, Peregrine, don't be ridiculous. No, Daedalus said he put the tracker on one of his plants.' Nim took a sip of tea. 'Just in case.'

Peregrine jumped up. 'Oh no!' In all the kerfuffle, she had

forgotten to water Bernadette! 'Excuse me,' she said as she grabbed a glass of water and sprinted back to the pod. The plant was there, of course, just as she'd left them. 'Sorry, Bernie.'

Bernadette's leaves fluttered in greeting as Peregrine unclicked the seat belt and tipped a little water into their soil. She stroked a leaf in apology. Standing there in the AquaPod, she could hear the clinking of teacups and the soft mumblings of Rowan telling Nim that Peregrine had 'this thing' about a plant.

'Don't we all?' Nim muttered back.

Peregrine chewed her lip. Bernadette let out a soft squeak and wrapped a leaf around Peregrine's finger.

'We'll find him, don't worry,' Peregrine whispered. 'We've got help now.' Smiling weakly, she tucked Bernadette back into her rucksack and stepped out of the pod and into the watery light of Greenhouse 72.

Rowan raised her eyebrows to Peregrine as she sat back on her chair. She nodded in response, in what she hoped was an everything's-cool-I'm-fine-don't-worry way, and picked up another scone.

'So, seeing as the feds are involved –' Nim dipped her teacup at Rowan – 'I'm assuming there is some other kind of wider Cosmic crisis at hand? It's not like Olympus to care much about what we immortals get up to here in the Terran Realm.' She stiffened a little. 'Apart from that new chap at Terran Communications – he's terribly good. What's his name? Cally—?'

'Cal,' Peregrine offered.

Nim nodded. 'I see. So, what is it? Wait, don't tell me. The giants – are they unionising?' She took a sip of tea. 'About bloody time, if you ask me.'

Peregrine looked again at the wisteria twining over the hat stand. Daedalus had trusted Nim enough to ask her for help, and she *had* rescued them from their sinking AquaPod. Peregrine exchanged a look with Rowan, who nodded solemnly.

In between bites of seaweed scone, which actually weren't all that bad once you'd removed the jam, Peregrine started talking. Rowan joined in and soon they had told Nim all about their journey from Oxford and the BogBrethren who were probably still following them.

When Rowan described the events before meeting Peregrine, Nim almost spat out her tea. 'The portals are broken?!' Her eyes widened. 'This is much more serious than I thought.'

'And then Daedalus disappeared!' Rowan finished, shooting her hands up into the air as if miming an explosion.

'Disappeared?' Nim raised an eyebrow. 'Now that *is* new.'

Peregrine nodded her head, fast. 'Yes. And there is one other thing.' She ignored Rowan's glare. 'We think they have taken him to Alexandria –'

Nim dropped her teacup with a clatter and stared at her. 'Alexandria? Are you sure?'

Peregrine nodded slowly, then wiped crumbs from her mouth. 'Yes.' Interesting. She'd thought that Daedalus being kidnapped would have been the bit of the story that got the reaction.

'Why didn't I think about it before?' Nim stood up so swiftly she almost knocked Arthur off the table. She dashed over to a huge clock on the greenhouse wall, which Peregrine hadn't noticed as it was hidden by two huge plants with leaves the size and shape of elephant ears. Nim pushed the glossy green leaves aside, squinted at the clock and swore. *'Flooharght!'*

The clock was made of seven interlocking circles, all in different shades of blue, from a dark midnight to a vibrant turquoise on the outside rim. Around the edge were phases of the moon etched in silver. And instead of just two copper dials, the clock had seven, each turning at a different rate. One was even turning backwards.

Peregrine had never seen anything so beautiful. *'Wow.'*

Rowan sighed loudly.

Nim traced her fingers around the clock, then tapped her finger at a point where two of the dials met over a symbol of what looked like a whale. *'Flooharght!'* She inhaled. *'Flooharght, flooharght, floochety-floo –'*

'What,' Rowan interrupted, 'is going on?'

Nim scooped up her teacup and brandished it so wildly that liquid sloshed over the sides as she talked. 'Eris rises!' She shook her head. 'Why didn't he *tell* me? What a clattering Cosmic calamity!' She started to pace. 'We'll have to help him, and that means getting *you* there, of course.' She pointed to Peregrine. 'But how?'

Peregrine and Rowan looked at each other.

'I'm sorry, but –' Peregrine began.

Nim stopped pacing and turned to face them, her eyes sparkling with a wild green fire, like glowing algae on a garden pond. 'It appears the quest is on!'

15

PEREGRINE

Location: Greenhouse 72, Royal Botanic Gardens, Kew, London, England

'Come.' Nim beckoned them over to a corner of the greenhouse.

Peregrine glanced sideways at Rowan. The dryad's mouth was moving silently, as if listing all of the reasons that this was a Bad Idea. Even Peregrine could think of a few, but what choice did they have?

'Quack?' Arthur jumped off the table and waddled after Nim, hopping over some trailing vines. Peregrine's gaze followed the duck. Amid a tangle of ivy, tropical ferns and hibiscus stood a shallow stone dish filled with water. Nim was pushing some of the foliage out of the way. 'Sorry,' she muttered. 'It has been a while.'

Peregrine tugged at Rowan's sleeve, breaking her from her reverie. They edged closer to the bowl and peered in. Four reflected faces blinked back at them: two nymphs, one human and a duck.

Nim reached up to a sky-blue buddleia bush that hung over the water and tapped it, so a shower of the tiny petals fell into the bowl. 'Hmm.' She dipped in a finger and traced it around the pool, twice clockwise, once the other way. 'Let's see, shall we?' A half-smile cracked Nim's serious expression.

A faint blue light glowed from the depths of the pool, mixing with the flower petals as they swirled.

'Have you heard of Discord?' The smile had vanished from Nim's face. The air around them seem to crackle with cold at the very mention of the name. *Discord.*

Peregrine felt Rowan shudder next to her. 'The goddess of chaos,' Rowan said quietly. 'Everyone knows about her.'

'I don't.' Peregrine sniffed. She crossed her arms over her chest, yet again feeling the sting of not knowing something that was obvious to the immortals around her. 'Who is she?'

'She *was* OPS's enemy number one,' Rowan explained, her voice still quiet below the whispering of the branches. 'For centuries she wreaked havoc, death, destruction. Sort of her MO.'

Nim nodded slowly. She swirled the petals one more time and Peregrine watched in amazement as they hovered above the water. 'You say you haven't heard of her, Peregrine, but I think you have. As happens with many of these things, what starts as truth, morphs into myth, then finds its echo in stories – even Terran ones.'

Peregrine gasped as the petals arranged themselves into a row of tables. It was a banquet! Tiny people made of petals sat at the tables, laughing and toasting each other. 'Discord survives in your folk tales and bedtime stories. The original bad fairy.' A shadow covered the feast and the people stopped moving. The petals dropped back into the bowl.

'But she is no fairy.' Nim stirred the bowl again. 'Discord is a primordial, one of the Old Ones. She emerged at the beginning of creation, before even the Cosmics stepped into existence.' The petals hovered once more, gathered themselves into a tight ball and suddenly scattered, as if the ball had exploded. The petals hung in the air, waiting for Nim to continue. 'She is void, darkness, nothingness. She is the . . . abyss.' The petals formed the shape of the Earth, spinning slowly.

'But she's *gone*, and always will be.' Rowan spoke the last word with a tone of finality, as if she was slamming a book shut.

'I hope so, dear. I hope so.' Nim sighed and the blue petals danced in the air, moved by her breath. 'Let an old nymph tell you a tale . . .'

Rowan's eyes widened slightly, and Nim swept a hand once more over the pool. 'Many, *many* years ago, not at the beginning, but close enough –' she paused to take a deep breath – 'the Cosmics were very involved in Terran affairs. They couldn't help themselves, and they didn't want to. They meddled a *lot*.' The petals swirled around each other until they had formed the shapes of giant-sized figures striding through a mountainous landscape.

'The realms erupted into chaos.' The petals split into two groups, like an ocean divided. 'War, treachery, destruction.' The petal waves crashed towards each other: people, weapons and animals leapt and swirled in the chaos. 'Discord fed on all of it, feasted on our pain. She became stronger while we became weaker, more separate.'

Peregrine's jaw dropped as she saw a huge mouth appearing above the petals: blue petal lips, a blue petal tongue. Slowly the petal creatures were sucked in, their mouths open in silent screams.

'When everything was thought lost, the Cosmics decided to work together to keep the peace. A treaty was agreed.'

'The Apple Accords,' Rowan whispered. She was staring at the pool as the petals formed the shape of an apple that bobbed on the water.

Peregrine turned to her. 'Accords? What were they?'

Rowan shook her head, so Nim spoke. 'The Apple Accords was the treaty the Cosmics signed when they *finally* agreed to stay out of Terran affairs.' She prodded the apple as it floated along the surface. 'Discord did not approve of the Accords. She thrived on chaos, and on death; she *needed* it. So she rallied her demons and fought back. Many lives were lost.' Nim sighed and the petals fell away and dropped to the bottom of the bowl.

'She evaded capture for many centuries. But finally she was caught and banished to the Fourth Realm, from where *no one* has ever returned.'

'Zeus banished her.' Rowan had stopped looking at the pool and was looking straight at Nim, her eyes clear and focused. 'Zeus *saved* us.'

Nim nodded slowly. 'What you won't know, Rowan, is *how* they banished her. That, only a few people know: the Cosmics, the Olympus Council and those who were there.' She turned to them both now. 'They used a portal – the most powerful, the first. The portal located in –'

'The Library of Alexandria.' Peregrine sucked in air. That was where Daedalus was!

Nim sighed. 'Daedalus warned them – tried to stop them even.' She ushered them back towards the table. 'Daedalus knew that if Olympus could use the portals to banish Discord, then her followers could use them to bring her back. He left Olympus after that, but he kept his eye on the portals, and asked a few others to help him.' She smiled softly.

'What are you saying? That the BogBrethren, they work for, for . . . *Discord?*' Rowan's face paled to a sickly green colour.

'They *might* work for Discord, or for somebody who is helping her, yes.' Nim's voice was grim. 'There is a small window where the veils between the realms are thinnest, a window that opened at midnight last night.' She looked back at the clock. 'Midnight . . . ish.'

'So that was why Daedalus was checking the portal in the Bodleian!' Peregrine clicked her fingers.

Rowan's hand flew to her hat. 'The Bodleian Library? My library?'

'Yes,' Nim interrupted. 'I think somebody, I don't know who, is using this window to their advantage.'

Rowan had taken off her hat and was staring at it. 'And they're trying to open up that portal, the one in Alexandria, to . . . to . . .'

'To bring Discord back, yes,' Nim finished for her. 'If Alexandria is where they are taking Daedalus, then I can only think that that is what they plan to do. They might try to make him help them – he was instrumental in Discord's downfall, after all.'

'We have to stop them –' Peregrine's mind raced – 'and *before* they open the portal!'

'Yes, there is no time to lose!' Nim bounded over to the shell table and poured herself another cup of tea.

16

CAL

Cal sat staring at his CosPad, his horned forehead resting in his hands. In front of him he had everything he'd gathered on the Library of Alexandria. There wasn't much, just a few holo-pics and a case file. And even getting that had been a mummy's worth of red tape.

Pear-grinn's hope-filled face floated into Cal's mind. She was counting on him! He raised his weary head, slid his CosPad towards him and typed 'the fire of Alexandria'.

'*INFORMATION CLASSIFIED.*' The computer's steely voice echoed through his office.

'WHAT?' Cal shouted back. '*Everyone* knows about the fire – there's even a CosPlay about it!' He let out an exasperated sigh and pushed his glasses up his nose. 'What about "the Alexandrian portal"?' He typed, hopefully.

'*Information VERY classified.*'

Cal smacked the CosPad down on the desk. 'That is VERY unhelpful!'

Taking a deep breath, he clicked to open another file and, after flicking through a number of redacted images, a holo-screen appeared in front of him. A blue-tinted holo-pic of a curly-haired, stern-looking centaur wobbled into view, paired with a rectangle of text.

'The Librarian,' Cal whispered. The text read:

Missing immortal: Tyron Grey

Case file number: 56253431

Last known location: Portal One, Library of Alexandria

CosDate: 287.952.30

Case status: Paused

Officers in charge of case: Captain Suleiman Prim, Captain Tobias Hedge, Lieutenant Hansel Pine

'Pine!' Cal ground his teeth.

There was a hefty knock at the door. Cal had approximately three milliseconds to turn off the holo-screen before Sibyll stormed in. He managed it, but only by the breadth of a beard-hair.

'Report?' Sibyll crossed her arms over her vast leathery

bosom. Her eyes, always hawk-sharp, looked tired, with blue half-moons hanging beneath them.

Cal slid the CosPad under a pile of papers. 'Can I offer you a coffee, Chief Inspector?' He tapped his mug.

'Caffeine is for the weak, Cal.'

Cal stopped his tapping. 'Absolutely.' He slid the mug off to one side.

'As I have not *heard* from you –' she raised an eyebrow – 'I am assuming that Rowan has not managed to locate our former Grand Architect?'

'No, not quite.' Cal hopped up and brought over two chairs. One faun-sized seat didn't seem quite enough for Sibyll's giant-sized backside, and he wanted her to be comfortable. 'Agent Strong is on Daedalus's trail as we speak.' He gestured to the chairs. Sibyll glared at him, and then sat down with a giant-sized creak.

'She has liaised with Daedalus's assistant and has enlisted her help.' Cal went back to behind his desk and clasped his hands in front of him. 'Memory-wipe is, I'm sure, imminent.'

'Hmm.' Sibyll tossed her tangled wave of silvery-grey locks, and a spider as big as Cal's fist dropped onto her shoulder. 'I suppose these are extenuating circumstances. Any other leads?' She flicked the spider back into her hair, saving it for later.

Cal tugged at his cardigan sleeve. 'Are you sure I can't offer you anything? A sandwich, perhaps? I have pickled goat's cheese . . .'

'Cal.' Sibyll leaned forward. The chair creaked dangerously, as if it too was asking a question. 'Is there something you are not telling me?' She spread her giant hands on the desk and glowered down at him.

Cal felt his face grow hotter. 'There appears to have been some kind of . . . some kind of . . .'

'Spit it OUT!' the giantess yelled. 'That's an order!'

'Kidnapping.'

The look that Sibyll gave Cal was one that *is* usually reserved for people who have just spat something at you. 'KIDNAPPING?!'

'Yes.' Cal glanced at the console screen, where the words *'LOCATION UNKNOWN'* were still flashing red over Daedalus's smiling face.

Sibyll's face was not smiling. 'You are telling me that a former Grand Architect of the Cosmic Realm, an immortal who has designed nearly *90 per cent* of our CosTech, has been kidnapped by *unknown hostiles?'*

Cal shrank further into his chair. 'Yes, it would appear so. Yes.'

Sibyll let out a sound that was somewhere between a lion's roar and walrus mating call. It started in her throat and reverberated through her whole mouth, making her lips shake. She began to pace; her giant footsteps made the office quake so much that piles of paperwork slid sideways into one another, like skyscrapers in an earthquake.

'This is bad news, Cal. As if we haven't got enough going on.' She shook her hair again and a few more spiders took the opportunity to make a dash for freedom. 'I'll *have* to report it to OPS.' She slammed her hand down on one of the slower spiders that hadn't quite made it off the desk. 'They'll *love* this.' She wasn't really talking to Cal at this point. 'And we won't be able to protect Daedalus if they find him –'

'Do we *have* to tell OPS?' It didn't sound as if OPS thought they needed Daedalus as much as Sibyll did. Cal imagined Pear-grinn's face again – this time glaring at him – and gulped.

'A kidnapping confirms an external threat, which means this falls outside CSI's remit. My hands are tied.' Sibyll sighed. 'Anything else?'

Cal's hand hovered over the pile of papers where his CosPad was hidden. 'No.' He shook his head. 'Nothing.'

Sibyll lifted an enormous eel-like eyebrow. 'OK, keep me updated. OPS will want to know everything, on Agent Strong, Daedalus and –' she pushed herself off the desk and stormed out the door – 'everything else!' she shouted over her shoulder.

'Yes, absolutely!' Cal called after her.

When he was sure that Sibyll had left, he pulled out his CosPad and slid his thumb across, shutting down his open tab on Tyron. He exhaled loudly.

Maybe Rowan and Pear-grinn would find Daedalus before OPS did, and then *no one* would need to get blown up. Yes, that was a very good thought. He gulped. Because if they didn't, and OPS got there first . . . who knew if there would be much left of Daedalus to find?

PEREGRINE

Location: Greenhouse 72, Royal Botanic Gardens, Kew, London, England

'Could we fix the AquaPod?' Rowan asked.

Nim shook her head. 'It will take too long. You need a complete overhaul of the electrics and a new fuel pump.' Then she added, 'And I don't have a vessel big enough or fast enough to get you across oceans.'

'Why don't we take a plane?' Peregrine asked.

Rowan made a face.

'Don't be such a snob!' Peregrine huffed.

'I'm not being a snob! I have read about these "planes".' Rowan air-quoted. 'Held up by human ingenuity and tree-burning fossil fuels? I'll pass, thank you *very* much.' She waved a hand airily.

Peregrine rolled her eyes and took her phone out of her

pocket. 'There's a flight that leaves in about eight hours from Heathrow. That would get us to Alexandria at –' she thought for a moment – 'around one o'clock tomorrow afternoon local time.'

Nim shook her head. 'That would be too late. If someone is opening up a portal to the Fourth Realm, we need you there yesterday.' She turned to the duck. 'Bring the car, would you, Arthur?'

Arthur dipped his beak, flapped off the table and waddled towards the door.

'Don't worry.' Nim had seen Rowan's concerned expression. 'It's on auto-drive,' she whispered. 'It just makes him feel important.' She took a final sip of tea. 'Quite a quest you've got for yourselves, hmm?'

Rowan had taken off her bowler hat and was turning it nervously around in her hands. Peregrine gulped and nodded. Nim seemed to be the only one who was actually excited about this. 'OK, so we're not going by plane, and the AquaPod is broken, so . . . how do we get there?'

'There is one way.' Nim lowered her voice to a conspiratorial whisper. 'But it's dicey. Deadly, even.'

'*Deadly*?' Peregrine leaned in. Something fizzed in her chest. Is this what Cal had meant by 'fatal'?

The room fell into hushed silence. Nim looked left, and then right. Peregrine screwed up her face. Who was Nim thinking was going to overhear them? They were in a greenhouse, for goodness' sake, and she seemed to trust the duck.

'You could go through the . . . *Under Realm*,' Nim whispered.

'The *underwhelm*?' Peregrine asked, loudly.

Nim sighed in exasperation. 'Not "underwhelm", Peregrine. Under *Realm*.' She walked over to one of the bookcases at the edge of the dome and, moving some banana plants out of the way, began rustling through papers. 'Most of the entrances have been sealed, but I know a way in.' She moved to a filing cabinet, opened a drawer and began flicking through its contents. 'Now where did I put it?' she muttered. 'Aha! There you are!' She spun around, flourishing a small white leaflet about the size of a sandwich in her hand. She held it out to Peregrine.

Peregrine peered at it. 'Er, Nim . . .' She didn't want to be rude. 'That is a . . . Tube map.'

'Yes, yes.' Nim sighed again. 'Well, open it up then!'

Peregrine took the map and unfolded it slowly. There. It was exactly as she was expecting: multicoloured squiggles on white paper, showing the various stops on the London Underground. Except, wait. Some of the lines were disappearing and the white background was becoming murky, now grey, and then finally a deep midnight blue. Silver lines overlaid the multicoloured ones, then travelled straight off the page, reaching out into the air around the paper so the space in front of Peregrine was shot through with crackling lines of light.

'Now *that* is a Tube map,' said Nim smugly. 'Don't lose it, it's my only one. Actually, come to think of it, it's *the* only one.' She picked a remote control out of a holster on her belt. 'Now, let's get you kitted out, shall we? Peregrine, please move two steps to your right.' Nim gestured with the remote. 'Yes, that's perfect, thank you.'

'What do you mean, kitted out?' Rowan asked suspiciously, just as Nim pointed the remote upwards and the panels of the dome dimmed, blocking out the sun. The whole room was plunged into darkness. Rowan clutched Peregrine's hand, then let go before Peregrine could squeeze back. 'W-what is going on?' Rowan stuttered.

She was interrupted by a series of pneumatic hisses as a dozen glass cases, the kind that you might see in a museum, rose out of the floor. Each was lit with an iridescent blue glow.

Peregrine's eyes widened. Every case was filled with weapons: axes, spears and gold-plated armour gleamed in the blue-tinted light – and was that a Samurai sword? Mum would be in heaven – she *loved* sharp, dangerous things.

At the thought of her mum, something pulled behind Peregrine's ribcage. Her mum had taught her to fight as soon as she could make a fist. It was important, she said, to be able to defend yourself, but her lessons had come with the strict understanding that Peregrine would not fight for fun, and would definitely *not* throw herself into unnecessary danger. Peregrine pinched her lips together. The Under Realm *did* sound like the textbook definition of danger, but it was also necessary, and probably wouldn't be that much fun. And she was hardly throwing herself into it, more like casually walking . . . backwards.

Nim who was now – somehow – under a spotlight, grinned. 'Welcome, *heroes*, to your armoury!' She opened her arms wide.

'Heroes?' Peregrine looked sideways towards Rowan, who had turned very pale. 'Nim, this *isn't* a quest, and we're not really heroes, we're just –'

'Hush now!' Nim was clearly enjoying herself. 'Here you have your basic hand-to-hand weaponry.' She pointed to an array of axes. 'Your long-range . . .' She nodded to a wall of archery equipment that had sprung up in front of one of the bookcases. 'Your high-tech, CosTech and your magical. It's all here.' She leaned forward, her eyes bright. '*Now* tell me you don't like a good quest!'

Something metallic had caught Peregrine's eye. She reached for the lid of a case marked *Laser Death 360*.

'No weapons!' Rowan slammed her hand onto the lid and shot Peregrine a piercing look. 'Thank you.'

Peregrine glared at her. A laser would be useful for LOTS of reasons. Opening panels, welding doors, melting the brains of the BogBrethren. Lots and LOTS of reasons.

'Are you sure?' Nim looked concerned. 'The Under Realm is a dangerous place. You'll want to be prepared . . .'

'She's TWELVE.' Rowan still had her hand on the laser case.

Peregrine eyed up a case full of bejewelled swords. She could feel Rowan watching her like some kind of nosy hawk, ready to pounce if Peregrine touched anything fun, shiny or interesting. Still with one eye on the case of swords, Peregrine asked, 'What *is* the Under Realm, Nim? Is it really that dangerous?'

The sparkle faded from Nim's eyes and her expression shifted. 'It wasn't always. The Under Realm used to be a safe place for the immortals who lived on Earth to gather, and travel between magical sites via the UUG.'

'The UUG?' Peregrine asked.

'The Under Under Ground,' Nim replied. 'That's what your map is for – look.'

Peregrine opened the map again and read the title printed at the top.

The Under Under Ground:
Immortal Transportation to Sites of Significant Cosmic Interest

Nim pointed out a few of the stops: Stonehenge, Lourdes, Angkor Wat, Shangri-La. 'The Under Realm was abandoned around the time of the Industrial Revolution,' she continued, her voice steeped in sadness. 'The amount of toxic waste that ended up in the Styx, it was disgusting. Human refuse and Cosmic Magic combined . . .' She shuddered. 'Well, it was a killer combination. Quite literally.' Nim clicked a button on her remote control, and a console lifted out of the ground. 'Hybrid monsters started appearing.' She clicked another button and an image of a dinosaur-sized creature sporting fangs the size of shovels appeared. 'We called them chim—'

'What are you *doing?*' Rowan waved her hand through the image so it flickered and disappeared. 'We don't have to tell her EVERYTHING!' She lowered her voice. 'She's a *Terran*, remember?'

Lava-like fury rose up in Peregrine, but before she could open her mouth to spew it at Rowan, Nim coughed. 'There is time enough for that, I suppose. Well –' she clucked her tongue – 'unless the world ends in a fiery tornado of chaos and destruction first, of course.'

Both Peregrine and Rowan looked at her, their eyes wide.

'*Anyway*,' Nim continued, unperturbed, 'eventually the deaths became too frequent and too gruesome for even Olympus to cover up any more, so they shut the Under Realm down.'

'I'm sure Olympus didn't cover anything up without a good

and proper reason.' Rowan's voice was fast and squeaky, like she'd inhaled helium. 'It makes sense to protect the public, and not cause panic.'

Nim looked at Rowan, her face kind but stern. 'My dear, Olympus Inc. is all the things you think it is. It is magical, and grand *and* good. But –' she held up a finger – 'it is *also* clever.' Another finger. 'Calculating.' A third finger. 'And occasionally cruel.' She balled her hand into a fist. 'It will not hesitate to crush those that get in its way.' She pressed her fist into her other palm. 'Not all those who live in the clouds are the good guys. I need you to think about that, OK?' She uncurled her fist and patted Rowan's shoulder.

Rowan narrowed her eyes.

Nim shrugged and turned back to the cabinets. 'No one dares use the UUG any more, unless you are a smuggler wanting to shift something *extremely* illegal.' She paused. 'You're very *sure* you don't want any weapons?'

Peregrine moved her hand slowly back towards the *Laser Death 360*.

'We're SURE.' Rowan side-stepped between Peregrine and the blue case. 'Do you have anything less . . . extreme?'

Nim pressed another button on her remote control. 'Suit yourself,' she muttered as the cases sank back into the floor.

Peregrine watched helplessly as the cases vanished beneath the floorboards and sunlight once again streamed into the dome. They were about to adventure into what was essentially the Under World. What had Nim called it? Deadly? Her mum had always taught her that nine times out of ten, all you needed to defend yourself was a witty one-liner – and, if that failed, a strong left hook. But surely, if someone offered you a laser, you *took* a laser, right?

'What have we got for you instead . . . ?' Nim tapped her chin with the remote control. 'Aha!' She started pressing buttons, and cases rose up and disappeared around them apparently at random. 'Was it this one?'

Flames erupted from the floor.

'Aargh!' Rowan ducked.

'Maybe not . . .' Nim put the remote control to her ear and shook it. 'It's been such a long time since I've had a hero visit. Makes me quite giddy!' Something clicked. 'Ah!' She stuck her tongue between her teeth and pointed the remote at the floor. 'Here we are!'

A wooden chest lifted from the ground in a spiral. It had a dozen drawers and on its top the word *Stealth* was inlaid in swirly silver writing. Nim walked over to the chest and opened a drawer, then reached inside and picked out two pairs of bronze-rimmed goggles. she handed one to Rowan, and one to Peregrine. 'These –' she tapped the rim of Peregrine's goggles – 'are CosGogs. Blink three times for night vision, twice fast for X-ray, and once *very* slowly for thermal imaging.' She closed her eyes, then opened them in demonstration. 'There are also some other settings you can use with the dials here.'

Rowan was turning the goggles over reverently in her hands. 'Are these what OPS use?'

'The *Olympic Punitive Squad* prefer to get their gear from HekTek at the moment.' Nim sniffed. 'The CosGogs are my own design.' She indicated the leather strap of her own goggles, where the words *Lake Designs*™ had been embossed.

Peregrine grinned and snapped the goggles onto her head. 'They are brilliant!' She blinked twice. 'Whoa.'

Rowan's skeleton glowed. It looked very almost human, but with a few extra bones here and there that might have been branches.

'Er, *rude!*' Rowan put her hands on her hips.

Ignoring them, Nim slid out the next drawer and beckoned to them. 'You'll need these too.'

Peregrine had seen drawers like this in the Natural History Museum when she'd visited with her mum. There, lifeless bugs, beetles and butterflies had been neatly pinned to boards, their wings paper-thin and shimmering. It had made her sad to see them, all dusty, dead and forgotten, but the bugs that Nim was showing them *weren't* dead; they were . . . moving.

Nim tickled a bright blue mechanical scarab beetle. 'Wake up, sleepy.'

The bug whirred lazily, rubbing its front legs over its eyes.

'You too!' She tapped a glittering purple dragonfly until it – finally – flickered its wings open and stretched its six delicate legs, clicking as it did so.

The two bugs hovered whisper-quiet off the case and landed neatly on Nim's palm. She leaned in and spoke in a voice so quiet that even though Peregrine strained to hear, she could only catch the words 'hero', 'quest' and 'no, best not tell her yet'.

After a few moments, the purple dragonfly flew towards Rowan, who stood as stiff as an icicle while it attached itself to her coat.

'That, Rowan dear, is FlutterBug, and this, Peregrine, is GrumBug.' Nim tipped the scarab beetle from her hand onto

Peregrine's jumpsuit where, after a few chirps and a bit of wriggling, it stilled. 'These are CosBugs. They are wired for sound and video surveillance and synched to your CosGogs. I only made a few in the end as they can be . . .' She waved her hand in the air, as if searching for a word.

'Temperamental?' Peregrine offered.

'No . . .'

'Unpredictable?' Rowan eyed FlutterBug warily.

Nim clicked her fingers. 'Volatile.'

Peregrine stared down at her CosBug; it glittered like a beautiful bejewelled brooch. She touched it lightly and could feel the soft beat of a mechanical heart underneath her fingers. 'Nice to meet you, GrumBug,' she whispered. A feeling of warmth flickered deep in her chest. If she and Rowan had this much help – Nim, Arthur and the CosBugs – maybe the Under Realm wouldn't be so terrifying after all.

Nim looked at her watch. 'We really *should* get going now. Arthur will have packed us some food.'

18

CAL

'Oh. My. Gods.' Hansel Pine's tanned blond crew-cut head poked around Cal's door. 'It's Scruffers!'

Cal froze, mid-sandwich, to stare up at the handsome nymph. No, this couldn't be happening. Not now. Not ever.

Cal's CosPad bleeped. *'YOU'VE GOT MAIL.'*

He looked down. It was a CosMail from Sibyll:

Captain Pine is taking over the Daedalus case. OPS orders.

Hansel strutted through the open door and pounded on Cal's desk with a large muscular fist. Cal could see the veins popping on the back of Hansel's hand. He gulped.

'You know, when Admiral Prim asked me to take over this investigation, I said, "Admiral, I am so *busy*. I have training" –' he counted on his perfectly manicured fingers – '"and patrolling on my new CosQuad".' He paused, as if trying to think of something else he did. 'And, if I'm not out there, guarding the perimeter, then WHO –' Hansel blew a gust of hot air at Cal's face – 'is going to keep the Cosmic Realm safe? I mean, WHO?' Hansel waved his arms around as if looking for an army of Cosmic protectors and finding just empty, unarmed air. 'But then he told me WHO –' another gust of air – 'had messed up this case. Do you know WHO it was, Scruffers?'

Cal opened his mouth to speak, but no words came out, just a faint wheezing sound.

'YOU.' This gust of air was so strong it steamed up Cal's glasses. Hansel lowered his voice to a gravelly growl. 'I hear the Investigation Unit actually allowed a Cosmic citizen to be *kidnapped*?' He sucked air in sharply. 'And as ever, it's up to us at OPS to clear up CSI's mess.' He tutted. 'Not good, is it?' He slammed his hand down again on the desk. 'Is it?'

No. The answer was *clearly* no.

Hansel sighed. 'Well, let it not be said that Hansel Pine doesn't look out for the little guy, hmm?' He sprawled over the two chairs that were still there from Sibyll's last visit and looked down at his fingernails. Cal shook his head. Hansel's golden uniform shone, making him look like some kind of polished awards statue. Hansel had plenty of those. Maybe Cal could give him one more, for being the Cosmic Realm's biggest –

'When was the last time I saw you, Scruffers? Graduation, was it?'

Yes, graduation, when you pushed my head down the Amphitheatre toilet, Cal thought. He should say that. Yes, he should. That's what you should do to bullies: you should stand up to them, let them know they can't boss you around. Cal readied himself. 'Baaaaaa,' he bleated, then coughed. 'Hello, Hansel.'

Flooharght!

'No point just lying around here, Cal!' Hansel swung his legs off the chairs. 'We have got an important meeting to attend in –' he looked at his CosPad and jumped up – 'four minutes.'

'We?' Cal asked, confused. Was that a royal 'we', as in Hansel and his massive ego?

Hansel brushed down the front of his uniform, then picked at it as if removing hairs. This was an action that Cal took as a personal affront. Fauns do *not* moult; they are *not* huskies.

Hansel was already at the door. 'NOW, Scruffers!' He clapped his hands, twice.

'But ... But I could stay here?' Cal gestured to his office meekly. 'Please?' Then he could continue his investigations without Hansel sticking his perfectly formed, hyper-performing nymph nose in.

Hansel strode out of the door. 'NO.'

Cal rushed to catch up with Hansel's loping strides, while at the same time doing up the buttons on his cardigan. 'Where is it that we are going?'

Hansel nodded smugly at a handsome receptionist who was flicking through a magazine. It had Hansel on the cover in his signature pose – laser blaster pointed up as he crouched, superhero-style, smouldering at the camera.

Hansel halted in front of the lift. Cal scooted to a stop, almost bumping into Hansel's muscular buttocks.

'To the Council Chamber!' Hansel pressed the button labelled *UP*.

The Council Chamber? Cal gulped. That was on Level Fourteen, he had never even been allowed past Level *One*.

'*Lift arriving. Please wait,*' chimed a sweet, lyrical voice.

'Captain Pine does *not* wait,' Hansel whispered, his voice low and menacing, his expression determined.

Cal started. He recognised that phrase: it was a line from Hansel's recent smash-hit movie, *Cosmic Cowboy*, from when he was facing down the mechanical many-headed hydra. He groaned. He really needed to stop watching that garbage. 'What does that even *mean*?'

What it meant was that, thirty-one flights of steps later, a red-faced Cal stood in a damp, sweaty cardigan outside the Council Chamber. So this was Level Fourteen. The walls were shinier, the air was sweeter, the marble floor was obviously polished daily, and there were fresh floral arrangements in terracotta vases lining the halls. There was even a long window that looked out onto the Pegasus fields. Cal gasped. He would have to tell Nanny Goat about this. She would be so impressed that *Cal* – faun and feeble – had trotted these hallowed halls.

Hansel knocked once, decisively. The door shook.

'Come in, Hansel.' Cal recognised Chief Inspector Sibyll's voice.

Hansel waited for Cal to push open the door for him, then sauntered through. Cal hovered at the threshold and peered inside. At a gold-plated wooden table sat Chief Inspector Sibyll,

Admiral Prim, Grand Architect Hekate, Magistrate Attica and Magistrate Helena. There was an empty seat at the end of the table. That must be for Hera who, as President of Olympus Inc., was also, by default, Head of the Olympic Council.

All five looked towards the door as it opened. Cal waved at Sibyll, who rolled her eyes and rested her head in her palm. Grand Architect Hekate wrinkled her nose and edged her chair backwards.

Cal had the sudden urge to sniff his cardigan.

'Wait for me here,' Hansel said as he slammed the door shut.

Cal blinked. He had only just noticed that Simon was there too, obviously waiting for Sibyll. He waved a turquoise hand at Cal then went back to playing on his handheld CosGame™.

Cal edged towards the door and flicked his ears towards it. Nothing. There must have been some kind of magical soundproofing, because fauns have excellent hearing.

Twenty-five ear-twitching minutes passed before the door swung open once more and Hansel strode out. His face was stormy. Clearly something had not gone to plan.

'A *Thunderbolt*?!' Sibyll roared behind him, pushing the door open so fiercely that it clanged against the wall. An amphora filled with sunflowers crashed to the ground and Simon swiftly pocketed his CosGame™. Sibyll's cheeks flared red. 'How could you even suggest such a thing? Are you completely MAD?'

Captain Pine crossed his arms over his chest, but before he could reply, the Head of OPS, Admiral Prim, walked through the door and stood beside him, glowering at Sibyll. 'I agree with Captain Pine. We need to act decisively and, most of all, *violently*.'

'Um.' Cal put up his hand. Everyone turned to him. 'W-what is a Thunderbolt?'

'Excellent question, Cal!' Hansel pointed to him, and then to his CosPad, where an image of a bullet-shaped torpedo was spinning. 'THIS is a Thunderbolt.'

'Agent, this is hardly the time –' Sibyll began.

The other Council members were streaming out of the Chamber, giving the gathering a wide berth. Everyone knew about the grudge between OPS and CSI, and no one, not even the Council, wanted to be caught in that particular crossfire.

Grand Architect Hekate smirked as she wafted past. 'I *must* get back to my laboratory.' She glanced sideways at Sibyll. 'These portals will not fix themselves, after all.'

Cal could almost feel the heat emanating from Sibyll's livid face as Hansel pressed another button on his CosPad. He seemed unperturbed by the giantess's boiling anger. 'Designed using Zeus's own vulcanised bolts, this highly sophisticated weapon has a Boggart-built titanium hull and an inbuilt navigation system.' A holo-clip of lightning being pounded in a forge appeared on the screen. 'We have reserves stored in a facility under Mount Etna.'

Sibyll huffed, unintentionally mimicking the smoking volcano. 'The fact that they are made partly from Zeus's bolts is *exactly* what makes them so dangerous!' she cut in. 'They are fickle, vengeful, unstable and –' she counted on her giant fingers – 'indiscriminately destructive.'

Admiral Prim waved his hand, brushing off any such minor concerns. 'The targeting system can be controlled from the Command Hub, allowing for zero Cosmic casualties –'

'Apart from Daedalus, you gargling flittertwit! The very person *my* CSI operative is trying to retrieve, *you* are willing to aim this Thunderbolt at and blow up! We *need* Daedalus to fix the portals, for Hera's sake!'

'Grand Architect Hekate said that –' Hansel began.

Sibyll exhaled so loudly that Hansel stopped talking, which was incredibly rare. Then he began again. 'You said it yourself in the Council meeting, Sibyll – the timing *is* suspicious. Daedalus being kidnapped at exactly the same time as the portals are broken? Terribly convenient, isn't it?' Hansel tutted. 'Either Daedalus is mixed up in this somehow –'

'No!' Cal shouted. Then immediately he put his hand over his mouth. 'Sorry,' he mumbled. 'I mean, he probably isn't.'

Hansel glared at Cal. 'OR somebody is trying to use him to get at our secrets.' He shook his head. 'Either way, it doesn't look good for our former Grand Architect.' He swept his hand over his crew cut so it crackled. '*No one* is more important than the safety of the Cosmic Realm. NO ONE. We at OPS know that, and are willing to make . . . sacrifices.'

Hansel narrowed his eyes at Sibyll, who, after uttering three or four unrepeatable swear words, turned and stalked back along the corridor with Simon fluttering closely behind.

Admiral Prim turned away from Cal to converse quietly with Hansel.

Cal's heartbeat quickened. *Sacrifices?* Did that also mean Rowan, and Pear-grinn? What if they got in OPS's way? A feeling that wasn't fear, or anxiety, and was therefore quite unfamiliar to Cal, bubbled in his chest.

He clenched his fists. He needed to warn them, and fast.

19

ROWAN

Location: Nim's Mini Cooper, Temple Station, London, England

Nim was a terrible driver. Rowan thought it and, judging from the barrage of beeps they'd gotten on the way here, so did everyone else in this mad Terran city.

Though she now officially worked on the Mountain, Rowan was a forest girl at heart, and she stared open-mouthed at the shining red buses and the buildings with elaborately carved stone facades. There was even a brass band! She couldn't look for very long though, as her seasickness had now transmuted into carsickness, which was possibly even worse.

Her stomach flipped, then promptly flopped as Nim hurled the Mini around another bend. 'Why does the DUCK get to ride in the front?' Rowan asked in between deep breaths into the brown paper bag that Nim had given her, on the tiny off-chance that she felt like vomiting.

'He's navigating,' Nim shouted over the honking traffic. 'Good call on the A40.' She nodded to Arthur. 'That traffic would have been a *nightmare*.'

Arthur quacked, smugly.

Peregrine was fiddling with her CosGogs, scanning objects out of the window, and was quiet apart from occasional exclamations of 'Oooh' and 'NO WAY!' Rowan watched as Peregrine's CosBug travelled from her shoulder to above her ear, using Peregrine's plait as a kind of ladder.

SCREECH.

Nim spun the wheel so sharply to the right that two of the Mini's wheels lifted off the ground. The car came to a final, juddering stop. 'And we're here!' Nim yanked up the handbrake and honked the horn in triumph.

'Aach!' Rowan hurled the car door open and breathed in a giant gulp of fresh, heavily polluted air. Hundreds of Terrans were rushing around her, all hunched over and talking to themselves, this suited army all seeming strangely eager to disappear down a flight of steps into a long dark tunnel.

'The entrance to the Under Realm is . . . the London Underground?' Peregrine moved her goggles back onto her hair. '*Oh!* The UUG map makes much more sense now.'

'Humph.' Rowan wrapped her tartan scarf around her face so only her eyes could be seen glaring out from underneath the brim of her hat. She was not impressed. Dryads were chlorophyllic creatures and therefore needed sunlight to survive, even more than their Terran ancestors. Being underwater was bad enough, but now they were going *subterranean*? She closed her eyes for a moment. Soon she would be home, resting in the Enchanted Forest, in her parents' glade, with starlight sprinkling her face. Soon.

'You'll want to take a few minutes to stretch your legs and gather your strength.' Rowan opened her eyes to see Nim step gracefully out of the tiny car. 'Not too long, mind.' Nim straightened up and plucked a silver pocket watch from her jumpsuit. *'Tempus fugit.'* She shook the watch at Rowan.

Rowan saw Peregrine pull her rucksack from the car and meander over to an ice-cream van. It was almost midday and the Terran sun was climbing to its peak, warming the concrete pavements and wafting a grotesque bouquet of smells towards Rowan's ultra-sensitive nose: tarmac, sun cream, grease and sugar. Delightful.

A small child was licking a pink swirly kind of confection by the van, getting it all over its tiny face. Rowan wrinkled her nose as an older female, presumably the child's guardian, bent down and dabbed at the child with a tissue.

'All better,' the woman said as she wiped one last pink blob from the child's cheek. Peregrine was also looking at this scene, her head cocked to the side as if analysing it. After a few moments, she reached into her jumpsuit pocket and pulled out her phone. Over the commuter traffic Rowan heard snippets of her conversation.

'Mum, I'm fine, but when you get this . . .' Peregrine whispered.

Rowan ducked behind a nearby bus stop. Her heart twanged. Penelope must be so worried. But maybe after this mess, perhaps Peregrine could introduce her? Maybe Rowan could even get her autograph? And ones for her sisters too.

Hazel would be thrilled! She'd always been such a big fan.

Thinking of her sisters made Rowan's heart twang a second time. She pulled her own communication device out of her pocket and screwed up her face. What would her sisters do in this situation? She sighed. She knew what they would do. They were Librarians. They would do their job.

Like her sisters, Rowan had been brought up with a strong sense of duty to do *exactly* as she was told. That was the reason she had excelled at the Academy, the reason she had been offered this job in the first place. Nim's words swam across her mind: *Not all those who live in the clouds are the good guys . . .*

She *knew* she should check in with Olympus and give them a full and accurate report, but for some reason telling them about Discord – about the chance that she could be involved in the kidnapping – made her . . . hesitate. The information hadn't been confirmed, after all, and events were already so out of control.

FlutterBug clicked on her collar, making Rowan jump. Her eyes snapped open and she looked down at the CosPad. She had *seven* missed calls, all from Cal. They must have only just stepped back into reception. Sensing her anxiety – or, more likely, her rapidly rising heart rate – the CosBug buzzed off her collar and landed on the CosPad. Its mechanical antennae angled towards the screen, then towards Rowan, then back to the screen. It flicked its wings once.

'All right, all right,' Rowan muttered. 'I'll ask the faun.'

Thumbs fumbling over the keypad, she dialled in. No answer. On the fourteenth buzz, just as she was about to hang up, Cal's worried face appeared in front of her.

'Finally!' Rowan scraped her hand through her curls. 'Cal, something has happened, and –' she inhaled – 'I don't know what to do.'

'Rowan, I've been trying to get hold of you –'

'I know. Look, I'm sorry, but some really strange stuff has been going on here.'

'Here too – this isn't the best time to talk.' Cal looked like he was about to shut down the communication.

'Don't even think about it, goat boy!' Rowan snapped. 'I NEED to talk to you!'

'Agent Strong?' Cal's anxious features were replaced with a chiselled, familiar face. Rowan inhaled so quickly she coughed. That was Captain Hansel Pine. He seemed to have snatched the CosPad away from Cal.

'Hey! Give that back!' Cal yelled.

'I – as I'm *sure* you know – am Captain Pine.' The famous nymph appraised Rowan with his even more famous steely-blue gaze.

'I-I do know,' Rowan stammered, and immediately blushed a rich emerald. Not only was Hansel Pine on almost every billboard in Cosmopolis, a movie star *and* the most brilliant OPS soldier of his generation, but Rowan's mum had bought her a membership to the Hansel Pine Fan Club last Michaelmas. She even had a poster of him on her bedroom wall. Her blush deepened to a dark forest green.

'What is it that you wanted to tell us, Agent?'

Rowan hesitated. 'Um . . .'

Captain Pine's eyes glinted. His gaze was much sharper and much less charming than it looked on the big screen. 'OPS is in charge of the hunt for Daedalus now, Agent. You report to me on this matter.'

'*Hunt?*' Rowan squirmed. Something felt very wrong about this conversation. Very wrong indeed.

'Do I need to remind you of the seriousness of this situation?' Captain Pine continued. 'If there is anything you can tell us, anything at all . . .'

'Discord.' The name stumbled out of her mouth so fast that she gasped. She hadn't meant to say it. 'I didn't –' She caught Cal's gaze in the corner of the screen, his eyes wide with fear.

'Discord?' Captain Pine repeated. 'As in –' he lowered his voice – 'Cosmic Enemy Number *One*?'

Rowan nodded, words tumbling out before she could stop them. 'Yes, we have reason to believe that she is involved in the Daedalus case. There may even be an attempt to open the portal at Alexandria. We're going there now, actually. We think we've got a good chance –'

But Captain Pine wasn't listening. He had thrown the CosPad back at Cal and was now talking to someone through an earpiece. 'Admiral, he's at Alexandria. Yes, exactly. We have a target. Converge the Council.'

Cal looked at Rowan with sad, scared eyes.

Had Captain Pine just said 'target'? A cold, gnawing feeling tugged at her stomach and spread all the way to her throat. 'What are you going to do?' Rowan asked quietly.

'That is not your concern, *Agent*. We'll send orders to you soon.'

'But –' Rowan caught one last glimpse of Cal, his mouth open as if about to say something, before Captain Pine reached out and turned off the communication.

All the chlorophyll drained from Rowan's face. She felt sick, and it wasn't down to the car this time. She had just told an OPS officer where to find Peregrine's godfather. *Breathe, Rowan, just breathe.* Perhaps 'target' was an official OPS term she just didn't know about yet? They couldn't mean . . . they *wouldn't* . . .

'Rowan?' Nim sang. Rowan emerged from behind the bus stop to see Nim rootling around in the car with one hand and waving with the other.

Rowan walked over slowly, her breath becoming calmer with each step. She looked over at Peregrine, who was still by the ice-cream van, and her stomach lurched. Maybe nothing would happen. If Rowan and Peregrine got to Daedalus first, then they – *she* – could still fix everything. It would all be *fine*.

'Ah, there you are, dear.' Nim plucked something from the depths of the glove compartment. 'Found it!' She wiped whatever it was on her boiler suit, picked some chewing gum off the back, then presented it to Rowan, beaming.

'Thank you?' Rowan took it cautiously. It was a rectangular piece of gold metal with a Thunderbolt embossed on it.

'It's a railcard. It's a bit old, obviously, but it should work –'
BEEP. BEEP.

Arthur was honking the car horn with his beak.

'Ugh!' Rowan put her hand to her head. A headache had emerged to do battle with her nausea for ultimate sick-making domination.

'What is it, Arthur?' Peregrine was running back from the ice-cream van, a half-eaten wafer in her grubby hand, chocolate sauce smeared over her mouth.

Having gotten their attention, Arthur hopped onto the roof of the car and gestured with his wing. *'Quack!'*

Rowan's headache disappeared immediately as adrenaline flooded her nervous system, steam-cleaning her neural pathways. Two figures were moving towards them through the bustling London traffic. One was tall and slight, the other shorter with the approximate muscular girth of a swamp pig.

'It's the BogBrethren!' Peregrine gasped. 'They've caught up with us!'

Stan was in front, ploughing a path for Earl to stalk through, aloof and unimpeded.

'Go now, girls!' Nim snapped her goggles down onto her face. 'Just follow the lightning bolts!'

Peregrine was locked to the spot. 'No, we need to stay.' She looked at Rowan pleadingly, her eyes wide and, for the first time since they had met, confused. All confidence was gone from her voice. 'We need to help!'

Rowan's words caught in her throat. She wanted to tell Peregrine everything – about the conversation with Cal, about what she'd said to Captain Pine . . .

'NOW!' Nim nodded to Rowan over Peregrine's shoulder, and in that moment the nymph seemed to pass on the baton of responsibility for Peregrine, for the mission, for everything. 'RUN!'

No, Rowan couldn't tell her, not now. She wouldn't understand, and anyway, there was too much at stake – for both of their realms. She grabbed for Peregrine's hand. It was smaller than hers, and sticky. Instead of pulling away, Peregrine's fingers gripped hers tightly.

Rowan dared a look back as she tugged Peregrine forward and saw Stan shoulder-barge a commuter out of his path.

'Hey!' The man blustered to his feet, dusting off his phone. 'Watch where you're going, mate!'

Rowan turned her head back just long enough to see where she was going. She heard a snapping sound. Please, for Hera's sake, let that have been the man's phone. She looked back one last time to see Nim, crouched like a cat, ready to pounce as the men moved closer. Nim's back was towards them. Peregrine's refusal to leave had lost them vital seconds; Nim was giving Peregrine and Rowan a shield, she was giving them *time*.

As Rowan and Peregrine reached the top of the stairs, Nim ran towards the men, her biker boots thudding on the pavement while Arthur flew straight at Stan's face. Stan stopped in his tracks and waved his arms wildly, trying to smack the duck away.

Earl looked past the chaos and caught Rowan's eye. She felt her blood freeze. His gaze was cold, calculating, and said two things. One: I see you. And two: I *will* keep chasing you.

Rowan gritted her teeth and pulled Peregrine down the steps.

20

PEREGRINE

Location: Temple Station, London Underground, London, England

Peregrine's breathing was hard and fast as she jogged down the stairs and into the foyer of Temple Station. There were people all around them, going about their ordinary lives – a couple of teenagers laughing and shoving each other, a man pushing a buggy, a woman leaning against a pillar reading a book. None of them had any idea what was happening above them, what danger they were all in.

'Rowan.' Her voice cracked, and she tightened her grip on the dryad's hand. 'What about Nim, Arthur . . . ?' Tears pinched at her eyes. Nim had looked so sure, so ready to help them. Peregrine had only just met the nyad: was this the last time she'd see her? Ever?

Peregrine pulled her hand away from Rowan's to rub at her

nose. She felt a line of snot streak across her face like a snail trail, mixing with the chocolate sauce. She reached out again for Rowan's hand.

'Eew!' Rowan looked at Peregrine's outstretched slimy fingers and pulled her hand away. 'Seriously? We've got to focus! Nim said to follow the old lightning bolts, like on this UUG card.' She took a shiny card out of her pocket. 'But I can't see any.'

Peregrine turned so she was back to back with Rowan in the middle of the station foyer, both of them scanning for any sign of the jagged symbols.

'Are you girls all right?' The security guard had turned from his post and was walking towards them.

Peregrine blinked the tears from her eyes. No, they *weren't* all right. Nim had bought them some time, but it was running out fast. The BogBrethren could be here any second.

Something whirred next to her ear. She looked sideways to see GrumBug on her shoulder, its mechanical wings beating, as if it too was anxious to get going.

'I wonder,' she said out loud. 'Rowan, give me the railcard.'

'OK . . .' Rowan handed it over reluctantly.

Peregrine lifted her palm up. 'GrumBug, can you see that? Can you find those symbols?'

'What are you –' Rowan began, but stopped as she saw the CosBug hover, give a click of agreement and buzz straight over the ticket barrier.

'GrumBug's found one!' Peregrine whooped. The lightning bolt was small, about the size of a fifty-pence piece, and was pulsing behind a poster advertising a West End musical, right there in the middle of the witch's hat. GrumBug paused then sailed on, this time to a tile where a tiny golden bolt had been scratched into the floor.

'Are you lost? Do you need any help?' The security guard was just a few feet from them.

There was a bolt on the top of the tunnel leading to the Circle Line. 'Hold tight, Bernie,' Peregrine muttered. Then, hugging her rucksack to her front, she dashed towards the barrier and vaulted over it. Rowan was close behind her, except she didn't so much vault as tumble.

'Hey!' the security guard called behind them.

'Oh, leave them be, Paulo!' Another guard chuckled jovially. 'Looks like they're playing one of those computer games, you know –' she mimed punching buttons on her palm – 'where you try and find things?'

'*Scrabble* is a game, Irene,' the guard grunted. 'Fare evasion is a *criminal offence.*'

Irene blew a raspberry at him.

Peregrine looked over her shoulder. What if she asked the security guards for help? Maybe they would get the police involved? Or they could call the army, and maybe mobilise some kind of specialised SWAT team, like in the movies?

Then she remembered the man who Stan had knocked into earlier. She remembered him toppling like a skittle, and that crack. No, this wasn't a movie and it wasn't a game. No one else should get hurt because of her.

GrumBug led them further and further into the belly of the London Underground. The crowds thinned; no one seemed to go down this far any more. Breathing hard, they followed a trail of lightning bolts down some steps.

'Oh, it smells, it *smells*!' Rowan whined. 'I can smell fifty-two different brands of hair gel. FIFTY-TWO!'

'You can smell all of that?' Peregrine was impressed.

Rowan tapped her nose. 'Nymphs have heightened olfactory systems.' She sighed. 'It's both a blessing and a curse.'

At the end of an empty station platform, they ducked under a dusty neatly printed sign: *Closed for maintenance.*

'I see it!' Rowan pointed.

There it was. The lightning bolt was printed, neatly this time, in the centre of the 'O' of the word 'Coke', which looped across the banner of a rusty vending machine squatting next to the door to the station toilets.

They stepped closer. The bolt pulsed invitingly.

'*Welcome, immortals, to the London Central Under Realm entrance.*' The vending machine glowed green as it spoke. '*Please insert your Under Under Ground railcard.*' Everything dulled except for the credit-card slot, which glowed an even brighter green.

Peregrine stepped back as the CosBug landed safely back on her suit. 'Nice work, GrumBug.' The bug clicked as she tapped the top of its head in thanks.

Rowan snatched the railcard from her and shoved it triumphantly into the machine. 'There!'

'*I'm sorry. By order of Olympus Inc., this Under Realm entrance has been closed until further notice. Have a Cosmic day!*' The slot glowed for a moment, then spat the railcard back into Rowan's glowering face.

'WHAT THE –'

'It's locked.' There was a flushing sound and a man appeared with a newspaper under his arm. He wore a grisly expression that arranged itself around an unkempt beard, beady bloodshot eyes and a slightly wonky nose. On his head was a battered navy-blue guard's hat with a golden apple embroidered on the front. Probably didn't work for Transport for London then.

'Yes, we can *see* that it's locked,' Rowan said huffily. She drew herself up to her full very-almost-six-feet and put her hands on her hips. 'I am on *top*-secret Olympus Inc. business, and I demand that you open it for us.' She faltered. 'If you wouldn't mind.'

'Nope.' The man flopped down in a plastic chair and picked up a flask that was propped against it. A waft of something sharp and pungent stung Peregrine's nostrils. As he opened his paper, Peregrine read the title printed on the top, *The Muse Letter*, and the headline: *Cosmic Sprite Investigation Unit Slips Up Again.*

'There must be a way . . .' Peregrine picked up the card from where it had fallen on the ground and put it in the slot again.

'*I'm sorry . . .*' the clipped, haughty voice began again.

'I will not.' Rowan kicked the vending machine. 'Have a.' Kick. 'Cosmic.' Kick. 'Day.'

'Please stop that.' The guard did not look up as he turned a page of his newspaper.

Rowan stared at him, then spun towards Peregrine. 'Could you, maybe, you know . . . ?' Rowan flailed her hands at the machine. 'Help?'

'With the kicking?' Peregrine grinned a wide impish grin. She walked up to Rowan and rolled up the sleeves of her jumpsuit. 'I thought you'd never ask.' Peregrine's grin widened. She wished her mum was here; she *loved* kicking things.

'Hey, do you know those guys?' The guard didn't look up from his newspaper but nodded behind them.

'Hello, girls!' It was Earl. He and Stan were standing at the end of the platform. Stan was holding his right arm close to his chest, and Earl had a huge rip up his right trouser leg.

Peregrine gulped, cold dread pumping through her veins. If this is what *they* looked like, then what had happened to Nim and Arthur?

'Peregrine!' Rowan's panic was etched on her face.

Keep focused. Her mum's voice echoed in her mind. *Don't look at them, don't look at Rowan – look at your target.* Peregrine could hear the BogBrethren striding towards them, but she inhaled deeply. An image of her mum's face flashed into her head, eyes fierce and determined under her wide-brimmed hat. Peregrine nodded grimly, then side-kicked the vending machine. 'Ha!' Peregrine's sharp exhale, though quiet, allowed her to clench her abdomen and therefore protect her lower vertebrae. While she suspected the mechanism only needed a little force to dislodge, her mum had taught her to kick from her gut, and there was little point in breaking form now.

Peregrine's grin reappeared. The kick was perfect. Something inside the machine pinged.

'Railcard accepted. Have a Cosmic –'

A trapdoor opened up beneath them, and Peregrine just had time to grab the UUG card before both she and Rowan dropped down into darkness.

21

HEKATE

Location: Portal One, Archive Room 17, the Basement, Bibliotheca Alexandrina, Egypt
CosDate: 300.23.241

'What am I *missing*?' Hekate paced back and forth, her boot heels clacking on the library floor. Her eyes half-closed in concentration, she waved her hairpin through the air like a conductor's baton.

'Mmmm,' a mumble came from the corner.

'Look, if you don't have anything *useful* to say, I would appreciate it if you could at least let me think.' She sighed. 'So rude.'

The gateway crackled next to her. She had opened the portal between Alexandria and Olympus temporarily to have this little chat. While she was here in the Terran Realm, Hemlock was guarding the Olympus entrance in Grand

Central Library, with the excuse that Hekate was conducting experiments in order to fix it. She wasn't too worried; Sibyll and her CSI minions were busy enough tying themselves in highly amusing knots trying to figure out how to release their Librarians from the locked CosPorts.

'*Do* you have anything useful to say?' She opened her eyes and turned to Daedalus, who was spinning in a vortex of magi-mist – a useful trick she'd learned from Discord.

'Mmmmuffle,' Daedalus repeated.

Hekate flicked her hand to remove the mist from his mouth. 'What was that?' She snapped her hands to her hips. 'Well?'

'Bleergh!' Daedalus wriggled his jaw around. 'You couldn't let me out to use the facilities, could you, Hekate, dear?' His voice was irritatingly calm. 'I had quite a bit of coffee before I was kidnapped by your ruffians, and my bladder is not *exactly* what it once was. Old age, you know. Happens to us all.' He paused. 'Eventually.'

Hekate rolled her eyes. Time was running out. As incompetent as they had proven themselves to be, it would only be so long before Sibyll's sprites figured out how to open the CosPorts and release a horde of cranky Librarians into the Terran Realm. One was proving meddlesome enough. She needed to know how to clear the way to the Fourth Realm, and she needed to know *yesterday*.

She tapped the end of the pin on her fingers. *This* was the moment that Hekate had been waiting for, ever since Discord's banishment and her own appointment as Grand Architect: a chance to finally free her mistress! Her eyes narrowed. And if *she* could wait for over two millennia, then

Daedalus could wait another few hours to urinate. 'I'm sure I have the right star window . . .'

Daedalus looked as if he might say something, but she put up a hand. 'And *don't* try to convince me otherwise. I know that this is the correct astrological phase because *you* were snooping around the portals.' She smiled. He was so pathetically predictable. 'Didn't think anyone else knew about that, did you?' She turned swiftly, so the silk of her extra-long lab coat swished loudly along the ground. She had been very specific with the designer about that. 'You never recognised my brilliance.' She pouted.

'You were always a *bright* student, Hekate,' Daedalus said slowly.

Hekate's eyes flashed. She *was* bright: bright, beautiful and dangerous, like a lightning strike. You see, ever since she was a child, Hekate had possessed a certain . . . talent: the capacity to hop between the realms. It was unpredictable and unrefined, but still *completely* unique for an immortal who was not a Class A Cosmic. It had taken just one (perhaps two) teeny-tiny inter-realm transportations for Hekate to be promptly packed off to the Academy. She had been only nine years old. And even there, among the 'great' Cosmic minds, her extraordinary gift had never been celebrated as it should have been. Instead of proper praise and instruction, she had been told to forget, to pretend to be *ordinary*. Imagine? All of that glorious, untapped, unpolished potential left to wither by fearful, small-minded –

'You just never wanted to do the work.' Daedalus sighed.

Hekate's attention boomeranged back to the present. 'Don't

talk to me like I'm still your *pupil*, old man,' she snapped. 'We are not in the Academy any more!'

'No, no, we are not.'

Hekate walked over to the portal. She put the pin back into her bun and placed a hand on the metal rim. Once her rock goblins had finally unearthed the portal, it had been an easy enough job to get it working again. But to use it as a gateway to the Fourth Realm – *that* was the challenge. *That* was what she was struggling with.

'The truth is, I was always disappointed in you as a teacher.' She sighed dramatically as she traced her fingers down the wires. 'I thought you were going to be my guide, my *mentor*. Oh, I remember the thrill at receiving the news! Apprenticed to the famous Daedalus! *Surely* he would be the one to show me the means to *real* magic? But, alas.' She shrugged and looked back towards her former teacher. 'No. You were just like the rest of them: dulled by fear and limited in your imagination, in your scope for invention.' She sighed as she hovered her fingers over the green light of the portal. 'I thought I was doomed to an eternity of mediocre instruction, but then SHE arrived!' Hekate's eyes glazed over as she remembered first meeting her mistress all those years before. Discord, the only one who hadn't been afraid of her gift. 'SHE understood.' Hekate pulled absentmindedly at a portal tendril. 'She taught me that there is creation, but there is *also* –' she snapped the tendril off – 'destruction.' The tendril fell, its glowing green flesh turning brown and brittle before it hit the floor.

She pouted again. 'I'm already using the other eight portals' life force, and I am sucking the Cor dry diverting power to this one, but it's not enough, is it?' She waved a hand at the wires wrapped around the portal. 'I've tried to retrofit, but it's just *archaic*. I mean, relying on organic matter for transport between realms?' She shuddered. 'Barbaric. So what is it?' She stomped over to Daedalus. 'Do I need more energy?' she snapped. 'More power?'

She paused Daedalus in his spinning. He looked at her with his grey, serious eyes. 'It's not always about power, Hekate.'

'WRONG!' She jabbed a purple fingernail at him. '*Everything* is about power.' She looked down to the pendant at her throat. The red drop suspended in the crystal was slowly bleeding to the edges. The crystal, which had been clear just hours before, was becoming redder and redder. She was done waiting.

'Perhaps you need an example.' She brought out her CosPad and pressed a button. One of the hooked-up computer screens flickered on. 'This is Terran CCTV footage taken just thirty minutes ago.' The screen showed the Peregrine girl vaulting over a ticket barrier at a London Tube station, the dryad following clumsily behind. 'Recognise the short one, do you?' She raised an eyebrow.

Daedalus didn't flinch; he was giving nothing away.

Hekate's left eye twitched. Time for some hardball. 'My men haven't quite caught up with her yet, but they will.' She clicked the CCTV footage off. 'And when they *do* catch her, I will spare one of her limbs for every piece of information that you give me. How does that sound?'

Daedalus was silent for a moment. When he spoke again, his voice betrayed an unfamiliar steely edge. 'Excuse the cliché, my dear –' he smiled grimly – 'but you will have to catch her first.'

22

PEREGRINE

Location: The Acropolis Arcades, Under Under Ground, the Under Realm

'. . . rrgh!' Peregrine left half of her scream on the platform as the trapdoor slid closed above her with a heavy, decisive hiss.

Whoosh! She was sliding swiftly down a slippery, blue-lit metallic chute. A cold stream of air shot up the tunnel, making her plaits flap about her ears.

Below her, Rowan put both her hands on her hat and held on tight. 'OW!' Her elbow banged the side. 'How did this ever pass safety checks?'

The chute turned a corner and Peregrine's stomach flipped.

Rowan made a kind of whimpering sound. 'Don't be sick, do *not* be sick.'

The lights changed from blue to a lurid green. Then a bright orange. Then green again. Peregrine moved her rucksack to her front and, feeling for Bernadette, hugged them to her as the tunnel turned another corner so fast that she rolled all the way around the chute.

'Just breathe,' Peregrine heard Rowan mutter. 'Imagine that you are not *illegally* entering a forbidden realm through a decades-old rusted and decommissioned pipeline. No, instead you are on a . . . water slide. A fun, recently serviced water slide.' Rowan's breathing grew only slightly calmer. Peregrine somehow couldn't imagine Rowan enjoying water slides either.

The lights flickered and changed back to orange. Were they going *faster*? The cool air had gone now, and the back of her throat felt dry and papery. That made sense, as they were presumably getting much closer to the Earth's core, but surely the Under Realm would still have some kind of protective shield or oxygen supply or –

'Don't forget to visit the Very Hot Springs while you are here,' a sugary-sweet voice echoed around the chute. The projected face of a sprite with a purple bob wobbled into view. 'Find us in Lava Pool Five.' She giggled and, batting her eyelashes, disappeared in a shower of pink bubbles.

Rowan sighed. 'A warm bath and a willow bark scrub *does* sound tempting . . .'

'Seriously?' Peregrine yelled.

'Mystery. Danger. EXCITEMENT!' A hooded face with a wide lipsticked grin floated into her vision. 'Three credits have been automatically added to your UUG card, courtesy of the Acropolis Arcades.'

Peregrine heard her railcard bleep.

'Join us –' the hooded eyes glinted – '*if* you're feeling lucky, lucky, lucky, lucky.' The face winked repeatedly as it glitched, until it finally blinked out in a starry blue dot.

Mystery. Danger. Excitement? All that time she'd spent begging Daedalus to tell her more about the Cosmic Realm – was this what she'd wanted? Peregrine squeezed her eyes shut as the chute veered steeply down, so fast that her bum lifted up from the side. Maybe a bath and a bark scrub *wasn't* such a bad idea. 'Ow!' She landed back down with a clang.

Her eyes shot open. A pinprick of light had appeared at the end of the chute. Finally!

'*Under Under Ground station coming up: The Acropolis Arcades.*' The same mechanical voice from the vending machine filled the chute. '*Please be reminded that Olympus Inc. is not, I repeat, NOT, liable for any loss of personal items, body parts or cherished memories. Have a Cosmic Day and . . .*' the voice paused as the circle of light grew bigger and bigger, then added, '*Mind the gap!*'

And with that, Peregrine flew out the end of the tunnel. The aforementioned 'gap' turned out to be about four feet of warm, thick air between the end of the chute and the ground. Well, not quite the ground.

'*Flooharght!*' Rowan swore as Peregrine slammed down on top of her.

She stared upwards. They had arrived in a huge, warmly lit, grand station hall.

'Er, get *off*, please!' Rowan jabbed at her leg.

Peregrine coughed as a thick cloud of orange dust erupted from the concrete-coloured cushions that had softened their fall. 'Sorry.' She shuffled forward so she could roll up, blinking as the dust cleared.

The cavernous station sparkled above them. Polished stalactites dripped artfully from the cave ceiling, each studded with diamonds that made them glitter like disco balls, scattering light across the hall.

A huge statue of Zeus loomed before them. He held his two-tonne lightning bolt high as he looked imperiously down at the rows of fussy, colourful little shops and cafes, ready to smite any sprite who dared steal a croissant. A statue of Hades looking at his CosPad stood off to the left, the weave of his tweed suit expertly rendered in obsidian. There was a gold engraved sign under the figure: *Don't forget to book your UUG tickets early – save time and dinars!*

Peregrine's smile faltered when she saw four deep-cut lines in the hem of Zeus's tunic. Claw marks. And a very dubious-looking stain. She gulped. What had Nim said about monsters?

Behind the statues was an imposing temple complex perched on a small hillock. 'I can see the platform!' Peregrine yelled. A neon-pink sign flickered: *The Arcades.*

'Wow! That building!' She pointed. 'It looks like the real Acropolis – you know, in Athens?'

'Uh-huh,' Rowan said vaguely. She was breathing into the paper bag Nim had given her for travel sickness. To be fair, the dryad did look greener than usual. 'The Boggart who designed the Arcades still claims full artistic originality.' Rowan took another breath into the bag. 'HE says the Terran architects stole his idea.'

The envious porcupine uncurled in Peregrine's chest, and

growled. Of *course* the Cosmics got there first. She peered around the vast marble station. 'But it looks like a ghost town,' she whispered.

'*Actually*, most ghost towns are quite lively places.' Rowan took one last breath and put the paper bag back in her pocket. She shrugged as she took Peregrine's outstretched hand and scrambled up. 'The undead love to party.'

Peregrine stared. Her mythology books had definitely *not* mentioned that.

'Welcome to the Acropolis Arcades!' a voice boomed. The red-lipped, hooded holo-figure suddenly appeared in front of them.

'Aargh!' Rowan screamed, then slapped a hand over her mouth. She looked at Peregrine, who had stepped forward and was peering curiously at the hologram.

'Your one-stop shop to all the wonders of the Under Realm. What do you need, little girl?' The hologram smiled down at Peregrine. 'An aura-seeking amulet? A choco-charm bracelet? A Caspar Cream Tea?'

'I'm all right for bracelets.' Peregrine cocked her head to the side. 'But I *do* need to get to Alexandria.' Then, remembering her mum's strict policy on manners, she added, 'Please.'

The hologram fuzzed, then flickered back, this time holding a tray of coloured bands. 'Are you sure? They come in an array of fascinating flavours –'

'Whoa . . .' Peregrine waved her hand through the figure so it rippled. 'This is a recording, right? Not a transmission, like with Cal?'

'Can you *please* stop poking things?' Rowan checked the time stamp on her CosPad. 'We don't have time for this.' She glared at the hologram. 'The kid's right, we need to get to Alexandria. So, where do we go?'

The bracelets disappeared as the hologram lifted up his hands. 'The Under Under Ground does not *go* to Alexandria, I'm afraid. Have a C-Cosmic D-Day.' The hologram bowed, flickered again, then blinked off.

'What do you mean, the UUG doesn't go to Alexandria?' Rowan shouted at the space where the hologram used to be. 'Absolute centaur droppings!'

A sudden gust of wind blew through the hall and knocked Rowan back down towards the cushion. Orange dust flew upwards.

'Hey!' Peregrine had also been blown backwards, but had somehow managed to stay upright. 'What was that?' She snapped her CosGogs down, and GrumBug, clicking loudly, began circling her head, scanning for danger.

Rowan scrambled up again for the second time, her face stormy. '*That* was weather. The Under Realm has its own weather system.' A hollow moan echoed in the far corner of the hall. 'Watch out!'

Peregrine and Rowan ducked their heads as another powerful gust of wind flew over them.

'And since there are no sprites down here to control it any more, it's obviously gone a bit . . . feral.' Rowan stood up and dusted down her coat. 'That is the last thing we need, a rogue weather system!' She shook her fist at the cave ceiling, but was distracted by a curl of smoke wafting from her overcoat. FlutterBug buzzed off her collar, clicking angrily.

'Damn magma moss!' Spores were settling on her overcoat and erupting into tiny fires. 'Hot, hot, hot,' she muttered as she batted at the flames.

Peregrine's gaze was flicking from the cave wall to the flames and back again. 'Magma moss?'

Rowan pointed at the fiery swathes covering the walls of the station. 'Looks like the weather is not the only thing out of control.' She grimaced.

She wasn't kidding. Carpets of luminescent algae floated in the fountains, glowing golden-leafed vines trailed the statues, and curled ferns sprouted from each crack in the marble flooring.

'Those –' Rowan pointed – 'are fire ferns. Careful, they have a tendency to explode. And those –' she pointed at a gaggle of furry winged creatures hanging above them – 'are lampfire bats.'

'Dangerous?' Peregrine asked, zooming in with her CosGogs.

Rowan shook her head. 'No, just annoying.'

The lampfire bats, apparently not used to being disturbed, were leaving their upside-down perches on the cave ceiling to investigate the commotion. The tiny bioluminescent creatures swarmed in and out of Peregrine's eyeline, squeaking and breathing violet-coloured fire.

Rowan waved her hands above her head, scowling. 'But as a nature nymph I am obligated to respect *all* living things.' She looked pointedly at Peregrine. 'No matter *how* annoying they are.'

Peregrine was about to reply, but just then something cold and wet fell on her nose. 'Is it *snowing*?' She put her hand out and peered at an ice crystal that settled on her palm before melting. 'This is so cool! How is it doing that?'

'Cool? *Cool?*' Rowan elbowed past Peregrine so now *she* was in front. 'No, this not *cool*, Peregrine.'

Peregrine looked up into the icy air. 'Actually –'

'No, *this* –' Rowan flicked another snowflake off her nose – 'is just the kind of unpredictable chaos that can happen without *strict* sprite regulation.' She wrapped her scarf around her throat and tightened it with a tug. 'I'll be sure to make a thorough report when I get back.' She paused. '*If* I get back.'

The blizzard spun and moaned.

'Oh, behave!' Rowan growled as she put her hand on her hat and strode onto the platform. 'Let's go.'

Marble steps had been cut into the rock in between two unmoving escalators. With the snow swirling around them and wind whipping at their cheeks, Peregrine and Rowan trudged up the escalators towards the Arcades.

The pillars loomed above them like great redwood trunks as they stepped through into the Acropolis foyer. Peregrine stamped her feet to get the snow off her trainers, the noise echoing in the cavernous space. 'These suits must have some kind of th-thermo-regulation s-setting.' She had her hands squeezed under her armpits, but was still shivering from the cold.

Rowan blew into her own hands and nodded. 'You can adjust the temperature here.' She tapped a band over her left arm and turned it ninety degrees to the left. 'Although you've got a reserve suit, so it might be a bit glitchy. I don't know when the AquaPod was last serviced.'

Peregrine copied her and Rowan saw her suit shimmer.

'Thank you! I can feel my legs again.' She jumped up, crunching her knees in towards her chest. 'Is it kinaesthetically charged?' She spun around, looking at her arms.

'It's very complicated,' Rowan snapped, then exhaled slowly. 'To be honest, I have no idea. We haven't covered that yet at the Academy.' She paused, thinking. 'You'd better take this too, in case the suit fails.' She ripped a swathe of magma moss from a pillar and tore it into pieces. After stuffing some in her own suit, she offered two pieces to Peregrine. 'Put them in your pockets.'

'No way!' Peregrine shook her head. 'Isn't that the stuff that burned your coat?'

'It's OK, it'll warm you up. It only catches fire when you blow on it, or –' she flicked her gaze upwards – 'the wind does.'

Peregrine cautiously took the moss and shoved it deep into her jumpsuit pockets. Immediately she felt the warmth travel up her legs and down her arms. 'So –' she patted her cheeks to get the feeling back in them – 'what do we –'

A metallic clang echoed through the cave. Then another. It sounded like a giant was stamping on the roof.

'Fee, fi, fo, fum,' muttered Peregrine.

'*Shhh!*' Rowan glared at her.

Peregrine ignored her. It wasn't *her* fault that these maniacs were chasing them. 'It's Stan and Earl,' she whispered. 'They're trying to get into the chutes!'

Rowan squeezed Peregrine's elbow. 'As long as we can hear banging, we know they haven't got through. Let's hurry.'

But hurry where? The moaning wind hurtled over their heads as they jogged past the intricately carved shopfronts and the flickering neon signs advertising Lava-roasted Lampfire Bat, Fresh Algae Burgers and Steamed Cave Fungus. She saw Rowan wipe a smidgen of drool from the side of her mouth.

Peregrine pointed to the statues. 'There!' There was a huge placard that looked like some kind of tourist information sign underneath Zeus's statue. 'That might show us where we need to go.' She scooted over to the map. GrumBug hovered off her suit and scuttled onto the placard, casting light from its butt onto the map. 'Alexandria is . . .' Peregrine screwed up her face in concentration as she moved her finger down the list of stations. '. . . not here? Do you think Olympus deleted it after it burned down?' She looked at Rowan, puzzled.

Rowan looked as confused as she was. 'No, Olympus wouldn't do that! I-I don't think they would, but I don't know, I –' The last drops of conviction seemed to leave her as she turned away. 'I don't . . .' Peregrine heard her sniff. 'I don't know whether we can do this.' Her voice was barely audible over the clanging.

A cold empty feeling began to spread in Peregrine's belly. 'We can't give up! There *has* to be a train!' That was why they were here: to get to Alexandria to find Daedalus and rescue him. What other option was there, other than the UUG? To wander around the tunnels until they were either eaten by monsters or Stan and Earl caught up with them? And she knew deep in her bones that they *would* catch up with them.

Rowan let out another sniffle.

Peregrine reached out and touched Rowan's back. 'Nim thought that we could do this,' she said softly. 'She thought that *you* could, so we can't –' She grabbed hold of Rowan's shoulder and shook it. 'THAT'S IT!'

'OW!' Rowan yelled, spinning around and shoving Peregrine's hand away. '*What's* it?'

'Nim's map!' She must have given it to them for this exact reason! Peregrine pulled her rucksack off her shoulder and, gently nudging Bernadette to the side, rummaged around. 'Got it!' She unfolded it, and once again the slender lines of sparkling light grew from the centre, making the air around them glow a soft twilight blue.

Rain was now lashing down from a flock of clouds that were scudding across the cave ceiling, disturbing the lampfire bats.

'Peregrine –' Rowan was wringing out her scarf, her voice rising in panic. Rain pooled in the rim of her bowler hat.

'So, to get to Alexandria, we need to –' Peregrine paused as she read the scrawled text that sat below a shadowy expanse of grey on the map – 'take the Scorpio Line. That's great! We've got this! We've –'

'Peregrine!'

'What?' she snapped.

'*Listen.*'

A high whistling sound sliced through the air towards them. Stan and Earl were coming down the chutes. How long did they have? Three minutes? Four? Peregrine thrust the map into her pocket. Mr Alkhaki's voice boomed in her head. *Time equals distance divided by –*

With a loud click, GrumBug hovered off the placard and whirred through the pillars. Lesson temporarily forgotten, Peregrine raced after the CosBug, her school shoes splashing through the puddles. As she ran, she noticed the gold symbols carved into the Acropolis pillars that framed various tunnels: an arrow, a ram, a crab, and –

Peregrine pointed; the furthest tunnel from them had a small golden scorpion over its arch. 'That one!' She whooped. 'We've found it!'

23

PEREGRINE

Location: The Scorpio Line, Under Under Ground, the Under Realm

The whistling sound from the chute stopped suddenly, as if somebody had pressed pause on a music player. From the silence, a bone-shaking laugh rattled through the cave. Peregrine almost fell over her own feet as she looked over her shoulder at the scene below them.

Stan roared as he left the chute, sending orange dust and raindrops flying. Peregrine gasped. He had seen her, and as soon as his feet hit the floor, he hurtled towards the escalator like a boulder: just as unstoppable, just as thick.

Earl dusted off his brown suit with sharp, efficient movements, then turned his head like a compass needle towards Peregrine. The rain was coming down more heavily now and water flowed off his long nose onto his ugly silk tie in a steady stream.

Even at this distance, Peregrine was sure she saw his beady yellow eyes narrow.

She ripped her gaze from his and turned back towards the platform. There she saw the train. She could see that it had once been sleek and shiny, but now its windows had been smashed, some of the copper panelling had been prised off, and somebody had even slashed a red line over the lightning bolt emblazoned on the side.

Willing her legs to keep moving, Peregrine leapt onto the Scorpio train, tugging a stumbling Rowan after her.

Rowan's ears had turned a bright lime green. 'He's so close!'

'Helpful, thanks.' Peregrine gritted her teeth as she scanned the dashboard. There were three buttons – forward, back and stop – and a series of levers. The steering wheel had to just be for show.

'The vents,' Rowan called from her lookout. 'You'll need to clear the vents.'

Peregrine grabbed the nearest lever and pulled it down, and was rewarded by a piercing screech as the wheels started to move. Steam billowed through the open window onto her face, along with a bucketful of rainwater. Peregrine pushed her wet hair out of her eyes. She could feel her heart thumping.

'Peregrine . . . look!' Rowan ushered her over to the window and pointed.

Through the clouds of steam, Peregrine could just make out Stan sprinting up the escalator, his thick arms pumping at his sides like pistons. A thought flew into her mind unbidden – if Stan and Earl were henchmen, then was it Discord who was giving them orders? Her gaze flicked back to

Stan. Could Discord really be more terrifying than *him*?

Shoving the thought away, Peregrine hurried back to the dashboard. She pressed the forward button. And then again. The train was not going any faster. They *needed* the train to go faster.

'We just need to make it through the tunnel,' gasped Rowan, ducking her soaked head back into the carriage. 'They can't follow us there . . .' She squeezed her eyes shut and started to shake so much that droplets of water flew from her curls and onto Peregrine's nose.

'Just to the tunnel,' Peregrine repeated, wiping her nose with the back of her hand. She turned back to the steering wheel, gripping it so tightly that her knuckles turned ghostly in the moss-light. Rain lashed the windscreen as the mouth of the tunnel got nearer, and nearer. She risked a look into the side mirror. Stan was definitely closing in on the last carriage. He stretched out an arm.

'Please, *please*,' Peregrine whispered, digging her nails into the fabric cover of the steering wheel. Rowan slumped down onto the floor, hugging her knees to her chest.

And then suddenly the twinkling lights of the cave ceiling disappeared.

Rowan's eyes sprang open and she stared at Peregrine. Without the sound of the rain or the thudding of footsteps, everything seemed eerily quiet.

'Do you think. . . ?' she began.

'*Coming up on your left, the Abyss of Eternal Despair. Please close all windows,*' a computerised voice trilled. '*And whatever you do . . .*'

Ach-CHUG. Peregrine wobbled and . . . she couldn't help it. She looked sideways out of the open window. There was the tunnel ceiling, rocky and glittering with stalactites, and then beneath it – darkness, a complete, all-encompassing void.

'. . . *don't . . . look . . . down.*'

Air sucked at Peregrine's ears. A silence that was fuller and heavier than before filled the air around her. It was like dipping her head into a swimming pool: all she could hear was the dull thud of her heart and the muffled chugging of the engine. Her breath spiked. *You're all right.* She heard her mum's voice echoing in her head. *Breathe, Peregrine. You're all right.*

She stumbled back. The train juddered and Peregrine slammed against the side of the train, her ankle twisting. 'Aaargh!' White-hot pain shot up her leg.

'*You are now leaving the Abyss of Eternal Despair. Next stop, St Michael's Mount.*'

'Peregrine!' The last thing she saw before she blacked out was Rowan springing up and slamming the window shut.

24

PEREGRINE

Location: The Scorpio Line, Under Under Ground, the Under Realm

'. . . *Change here for the Temple at Tunis, the Oracle of Delphi and the Pyramids of Giza.*' A lilting voice rang out in the carriage. '*Have a Cosmic Day!*'

Peregrine jolted. Had she fallen asleep? To be fair, the carriage was incredibly comfortable: soft purple silk cushions lined every booth, all embroidered with the Olympian gold lightning bolt and scented with what smelled like lavender. Cascades of serene lyre music flowed from the speakers above her head, willing her to rest, relax, enjoy the ride. She shook her head, trying to shake off the fuzzy underwater feeling.

Rowan was in front of her, spraying a can labelled *Ice It Now* onto Peregrine's ankle which, she now realised, was throbbing painfully.

'You're awake. Good.' Rowan paused in her spraying and shoved a SolarBar into Peregrine's hand. 'Have this. Don't just stare at me – EAT!'

Peregrine bit down dutifully. With the first chew, a warm, tingly feeling trickled down her oesophagus. Images flashed into her mind: Bernadette curling a leaf around her finger; Nim squeezing her in a pine-needle-scented hug; Rowan asking for her help to kick down a door. She sighed.

'That's better.' Rowan nodded approvingly.

'Mmmmf.' Peregrine chewed happily. This carriage was much more comfortable than the driver's compartment. A midnight-blue crushed-velvet carpet stretched across the floor, and crystal chandeliers tinkled on the ceiling, casting rainbows on the wall.

She sniffed her jumpsuit. It was starting to smell, and *not* of lavender. She giggled. She was hilarious. 'Any sightings of Stan and Earl?' she asked, pushing herself up.

'Nope.' Rowan shook her head and readjusted her hat. 'We've been travelling for about an hour –'

Peregrine swallowed a bit of SolarBar and hiccupped. 'An *hour*?' How long would it be until Discord found a way to open the Alexandrian portal? She shuddered, then hiccupped again.

Rowan eyed her warily. '*And* according to Nim's map, we've still got four stops before we get to Alexandria.'

'*Four*?' Peregrine took another nibble of the SolarBar, giggled, then immediately became serious. 'Yes.' She took another bite of her bar and burst out laughing again.

'OK, that's it.' Rowan put down the *Ice It Now* and held out her hand. 'I'm cutting you off.'

'What?'

'The SolarBar. Hand it over. Only non-mystical seaweed scones for you from now on.'

'But I'm *injured*.' She pointed to her ankle which, to be fair, *had* swollen to the size of a very small moon. 'Oh, all right!' Peregrine scowled. 'So *serious*.' She took the half-chewed bar out from between her teeth and handed it to Rowan. Then giggled, and slapped her hand over her mouth.

'Thank you.' Rowan screwed up her face and flung the soggy bar straight into a bin labelled 'recyclone', where it vanished with a whizz. She picked out her hand sanitiser from her belt. 'We should think about our next steps,' she said as she sprayed and scrubbed.

Peregrine leaned over to rub her ankle. 'Uh-huh.' She hauled her leg off the cushion so she was sitting upright and put her CosGogs back on. She twisted the right dial halfway clockwise, then twisted the left dial two clicks counter-clockwise. 'At this speed –' she said as she turned the left dial a further click – 'we should get to Alexandria in less than an hour.' She leaned back into the purple booth, trying to look a lot more confident than she felt. 'And then I guess we get to the library, free Daedalus, shut down the portal and, you know –' she gave Rowan a thumbs up – 'save the world?'

'That's your plan?'

Peregrine dropped her thumb. 'In outline, yes.' She closed her eyes, trying to fill in the many, *many* gaps in the 'plan' on the inside of her eyelids. A faint impatient squeak made her open them. Bernadette!

She pulled her rucksack towards her and, unscrewing her water bottle, tipped some liquid into Bernadette's pot.

Bernadette ruffled in thanks, their leaves shaking with the shuddering of the carriage. 'Sorry, Bernie,' she whispered. 'We'll be home soon, I promise.'

Rowan coughed. 'So, when we *get* to Alexandria –'

'*Warning. End of the line imminent,*' the electronic voice chirped over the loudspeaker. '*All change here, all change.*'

The train juddered. 'End of the line? What does that mean?' Peregrine pulled herself up and hobbled to the window. All she could see was the darkness of the tunnel and some marks that might have been soot on the cave wall. Were they . . . scorch marks?

'Put the high beams on.' Rowan rushed up next to her and punched a button on the dashboard. The tunnel was immediately filled with light. They looked at each other.

'*Flooharght!*' they said simultaneously. A huge boulder was blocking the tunnel. The same tunnel that they were still hurtling down.

'*You are reaching the end of the line. This train will terminate here.*'

Peregrine imagined Mr Alkhaki in front of her, tapping the steering wheel with his board marker. 'The *speed* at which the boulder smashes into you is determined by its *distance* divided by . . .'

The train screeched to a sudden, violent halt – throwing Peregrine and Rowan backwards so they tumbled onto the floor – then let out a low, extended hiss.

'*All change here. All change.*'

'We're not dead.' Rowan's tone was one of complete surprise as she patted Peregrine on the shoulder and helped her up. 'N-not dead,' she repeated, before leaning, exhausted, against the carriage wall.

Buzz. Buzzzzz. Rowan's CosPad vibrated, making both of them jump and Bernadette squeak, loudly. *'INCOMING CALL. INCOMING CALL.'*

Rowan hastily pushed herself upright and took the CosPad from her belt. 'Thirteen missed calls?' she muttered. 'From Cal!'

Peregrine edged closer so she was next to Rowan as she pressed the button to receive the call. Cal's face appeared, though his usually rosy cheeks were pale and his eyes looked a little puffy.

'Cal, what is it?' Peregrine peered at the faun. 'Are you OK?'

Before he could answer, another figure – much taller, much blonder and with a much more confident expression – entered the frame.

'Captain Hansel Pine,' Rowan hissed under her breath, then added, even more quietly, 'As soon as I'm home, I'm going to *rip* that poster down.'

'OK . . . ?' Peregrine whispered. 'Who is he?'

Rowan scowled. 'He's from OPS.'

Before Peregrine could ask what Rowan meant by *OPS*, Captain Pine's voice sliced through the conversation like a sabre. 'You haven't been answering your CosPad, *Agent*.' His statement was almost a snarl.

'I've been a little busy,' Rowan snapped. She turned back to Cal, concerned. 'What is it? What's happened?'

'Olympus wants *you* back at your library.' Captain Pine smirked.

'Back at the Bodleian?' Peregrine couldn't keep the confusion out of her voice. 'But why? We've come so far!'

Rowan nodded. 'She's right. The mission was to find Daedalus, and that's what I'm – what *we're* – doing.' She paused. 'Sort of.'

Cal sighed. He took his moss-green handkerchief out of his cardigan sleeve and, taking off his glasses, began to clean them with it. 'We're under new orders now, Rowan. Given the degree of . . . threat, OPS have taken over the investigation, and they are sending in –' he put his glasses back on and stared at her solemnly – 'a *Thunderbolt*.'

Peregrine put her hand up. 'What's a Thunderbolt?'

'It's a kind of missile,' Cal explained.

Peregrine gasped. That could only mean only one thing. One really, *really* bad thing.

Captain Pine checked his watch. 'We are arming one in Mount Etna now. The Bolt should be at Alexandria within three hours.' He sneered. 'I would stay far, *far* away if I were you.'

Blood roared in Peregrine's ears. 'WHAT?' she shouted at the screen. She'd been chased, shot at, catapulted through an underground labyrinth – and all so some kind of messed-up Olympic military could launch *missiles* at Daedalus? No. This was *not* happening. 'You can't blow up Alexandria! First of all, it's an *actual* city, you know, where *actual* people live? And also, don't you know that Daedalus is there? I thought you wanted to *find* him, not kill him!' She turned to Rowan, who had turned a sickly green, and was backing into the oak-panelled wall.

Realisation struck Peregrine like a lightning bolt. 'What did you tell them?' She shook her head in disbelief. 'After what Nim said about not trusting Olympus?' Her voice shook with anger. 'What did you tell them, Rowan?'

Rowan started to speak, but Captain Pine cut in. 'Who is this?' He pointed his thumb at Peregrine.

'She's Daedalus's . . . associate,' Rowan said sniffily.

Peregrine pulled herself up to standing. 'Actually, I'm his god-daughter.'

'Well, Daedalus's *god-daughter*. It's very complicated. You are a mortal child, a Terran. You have no idea what's at stake.'

Discord. They mean Discord. Peregrine inhaled. *That* was what Rowan had told them. She jutted her chin forward, but Rowan made a sound that was sort of a squeal and sort of a whine. 'Don't,' she hissed.

Peregrine bristled. She wanted to yell that she *did* know what was at stake, and then maybe smash that stupid CosPad screen for good measure. Calm had never been her forte; that was her mum's speciality. What would *she* think about all this?

Be careful, pumpkin. Her mum's voice rang in her ears. *Be very careful.* Emotion lodged in Peregrine's throat. It was as if Penelope was in the room with them. Peregrine swallowed hard. She wished she *was* in the room with them.

Captain Pine glared at Rowan. Maybe *he* was the one who was in charge of memory-wipes? 'You must appreciate that the safety of the Cosmic Realm comes first. Even a *Librarian* knows this.'

Peregrine bunched her hands into fists. How should she be careful, exactly? They were speaking like she wasn't even there! 'You can't go around blowing people up just because it suits you!' She was yelling now. 'I'm only *twelve* and I know that.'

Captain Pine looked genuinely confused, like he'd never *not* considered blowing people up just because it suited him.

He looked as if he was about to say something else, but Cal grabbed the CosPad and moved it towards him.

'Listen to me.' He looked more serious than Peregrine had ever seen him. 'That Thunderbolt will be at Alexandria in less than *three* hours. It is made from Zeus's bolts, the most powerful substance in all the three Realms. That means this bolt will destroy *everything*.'

Peregrine inhaled. 'No.' The word resonated around the carriage. These might be adults, magical mythological immortal beings or whatever, but no one, not *even* a bunch of ancient gods, was going to tell her there wasn't any hope for Daedalus. And if they weren't going to do anything, then *she* would. She grabbed her rucksack with Bernadette's leaves still sticking out the sides, and turned towards the carriage doors.

'Peregrine, wait!' Rowan glanced between Peregrine and Cal. 'Cal, I have to go.'

'But Rowan –'

Rowan punched the CosPad, ending the call so that she and Peregrine were left staring at each other in the eerie, empty silence of the carriage.

'You *told* them about Discord,' Peregrine said finally. 'Even though you knew it would put Daedalus in danger.'

Rowan scraped her fingers through her curls. 'It's my *job*, Peregrine. I'm a trainee agent, a CSI operative. I can't keep information from Olympus. That's insane!'

'But Nim –'

'Olympus Inc. . . . it's my life.' Rowan paced the carriage. 'I've worked so hard for this!' Her face was getting hotter, and greener. 'I can't throw it all away for . . .' Her words puttered out. She stopped pacing and put her hand over her mouth. 'I'm sorry, I –'

Peregrine glared at her. Had she really been about to say that her *job* was more important than all the people in Alexandria, than Peregrine's *family*? 'Is this how you think of us mortals? Of Terrans?' She bunched her hands into fists. 'Do you *really* think that you are that much better than us?'

Rowan's stiffened. 'I didn't mean . . .' She let out an exasperated sigh. 'Hera's sake, you're just a *kid*. You wouldn't understand!'

The words stung like a slap across Peregrine's freckled face. 'Being older doesn't mean you know everything.' Peregrine sniffed.

'I know, I'm –' Rowan began.

Peregrine wiped her nose with her jumpsuit sleeve. 'Daedalus taught me that.'

Rowan sighed. 'This is such centaur droppings, but we *still* don't have a choice,' she said quietly. 'Peregrine, we need to go back.'

'No, YOU need to go back. You and your precious rules.' Tears were shining in Peregrine's eyes. 'It's Daedalus. I can't just leave him in Alexandria to be blown up by this –'

'Thunderbolt,' Rowan finished for her. 'Look, they *need* to destroy Alexandria to save the Cosmic Realm . . .' Her sentence hung in the air, incomplete, as if even she didn't believe it.

'I don't care about your stupid realm!' Peregrine roared as she hit the exit button with her fist. Immediately the doors slid open, revealing a wall of thick grey mist. 'Daedalus is my family. I can't leave him.'

Rowan's eyes widened. 'But the tracks have ended!' She

pointed out of the door. 'What are you going to do? *Walk* down the tunnel? There is NOWHERE to go!'

'BLEEP. BLEEP.'

Tendrils of the grey mist snaked their way steadily into the carriage, making it harder to see.

'Return to your designated library and await orders,' the CosPad trilled.

Peregrine was already half-swallowed by the train's steam, with one foot out of the door.

'Peregrine, we need to be calm about this. Maybe –'

'Do NOT follow me,' Peregrine growled, hoisting her rucksack onto her back. 'I don't need your help. I can do this ALL by myself.'

And with that, she turned and ran lopsidedly into the mist.

25

HEKATE

Location: HekTek Laboratory, Level Seventeen, Olympus Inc., the Mountain
CosDate: 300.23.241

'Ugh.' Hekate pushed her cat-eye glasses up her famous nose, and peered down at the acid-green stain on her lapel in pure disgust. 'This just won't do.' She sighed as she rubbed at the splodge with a delicate, razor-sharp fingernail. She tapped the stain once. *'Eklepio!'* The stain sparkled gold around its edges, then vanished. Poof. Gone!

Except it wasn't *really* gone, she knew. It was just hidden. *Disguised.* This ordered Cosmic Magic was basic, crude, inefficient. Hekate shuddered. She itched for the Chaos Magicks, the skill to open and close the void at will. Discord had only shown her a smidgen of this artistry before she had been unfairly ripped from her by Daedalus and the wretched Cosmics that he served.

She wanted her teacher back NOW. Anger fizzed inside Hekate like a tonic. She adjusted her collar, pulling it away from her throat. She could almost *feel* the potential clawing at her insides. She *had* the power – it was right there, at the tip of her manicured fingertips, but alas – she pulled again at her collar – it was fleeting, unpredictable and, as yet, untamed. If she'd just been given just a little more time . . .

Soon, her mistress's calm, cold tones hissed in her mind. *Soon I will be free and we will have all the time in the world . . .*

Hekate let go of her collar and pulled out her pendant, bringing it up to her eyeline. The red had bled almost to the edges. 'Soon.' She let the crystal swing from her fingers.

Smoothing down her lapel, she returned to the recording of the call between the Librarian and the faun that she had been reviewing. She rewound slightly and paused it. The blonde Terran child looked deliciously *angry* at the dryad. Her eyes were filled with such sadness, such mistrust. Hekate tried to mimic the child's devastated expression. 'Oh, stop!' she rebuked herself, wiping tears of laughter from the corners of her eyes.

There had been a flicker of worry that these two might have somehow affected her plans, but this mortal and the dryad Librarian were no more than mosquitos – a little irritating, to be sure, but easily squashable. Even if Stan and Earl hadn't managed to eliminate them just yet. She restarted the recording, and her eyes widened.

'What –' Hekate looked over her glasses and zoomed in on the bag the Terran child was carrying – 'is *that*?'

No. It couldn't be. She swiped her finger through the air, and the edges of the vivid, spade-shaped leaves – just visible through the sides of the bag – were magnified to the width of the viewscreen. 'It's not possible.' She shook her head at the plant.

Daedalus had told her they were extinct. He had told *everyone* they were extinct.

She flicked to another screen and brought up a map of the existing portals. Eight little red dots scattered across the Terran Realm, like a particularly nasty case of octopox. All dying nicely. And then her own portal, the one in Alexandria, was there, a pulsing purple dot. She sighed. That tired old portal was sucking all the remaining life energy from the Portal Tunnel Network and, as it happened, the Cor of the Cosmic Realm too. She hadn't quite factored in *that* little hiccup. But even with all that, her portal was still at only 42 per cent power: *42 per cent* towards opening a portal to the Fourth Realm and freeing her mistress. Her fingers scrambled back to the crystal at her throat. She was running out of time, the pale crystal bleeding to red. As soon as it reddened completely . . .

No, she had time. And more importantly, she had *this*. She flicked her gaze back to the girl's bag and the leaves sticking out of it. *This* could be the key to her plan, to everything. And it was right there, in front of her perfect nose. Daedalus, that old scoundrel, had been holding out on her.

Well, once she had that plant, she wouldn't *need* Daedalus. She wouldn't even need the little Terran brat as leverage. That plant would be practically *dripping* with power.

Hekate cracked her neck to the side, flexed her fingers and

withdrew a vial of grey liquid from her pocket.

Discord hadn't had the time to teach her everything, but she *had* taught her a lot. Hekate hummed to herself as she watched the smoky mixture writhe inside the bottle, as if straining to be free. She had even been able to smuggle out a few potions before OPS had ransacked Discord's strongholds. So many sacred dark artefacts had been destroyed by that horde of bumbling Olympic idiots in their shiny gold onesies.

She clasped the crystal at her throat. Soon. As the edges of the realms burned, the Mountain would crumble and the Olympic Punitive Squad would be helpless to stop it. But for now, all she had to do was get rid of this one tiny little Terran child – and retrieve that precious plant in the process.

Her smile spread to her high, sculpted cheekbones. And to think she had thought this afternoon was going to be dull.

26

ROWAN

Location: The Scorpio Line, Under Under Ground, the Under Realm

Rowan stared into the mist. She was shocked. Gobsmacked. Well, that sorted it. She knew exactly what she should do now.

Her chin wobbled.

'No!' She rubbed her eyes. 'No, no, NO!' Why did Peregrine have to make everything so *difficult?*

She stamped her foot, making the carriage shake feebly.

She was a *Librarian*, for Pan's sake, *not* a hero! You had to have *very* specific training for that, and then get committee approval for each heroic act at least a month in advance. There was a *system*. What she *should* do was somehow turn this train around, get back to her precious, predictable library, have a few more of those jelly beans and wait for the OPS professionals to sort this whole thing out. Yes, that was it. Rowan pressed the button of the door. 'Peregrine!' she called, but the short, reckless human had stormed off impressively fast. Rowan couldn't even hear her footsteps any more.

'*Flooharght!*' The curse echoed around the empty tunnel, bouncing off the walls and somehow getting louder and louder until even Rowan was offended by it. 'Sorry,' she muttered. Then, just in case Peregrine had heard, she shouted, 'I am NOT sorry!' into the tunnel, before letting the doors slide shut.

OK, maybe she was a *little* sorry.

Time for some calm, rational thinking. She sat down on the cool train carriage floor, placed her hands on her knees in a meditation stance and closed her eyes. Finally, a little quiet.

She had been told – no, *ordered* – by a superior officer to return to her post and await retrieval. Fact. She wiggled her fingers. And that was all she had wanted in this whole messy situation, wasn't it? Clear, *direct* instructions?

So that was what she should do.

Her nose twitched. She couldn't SERIOUSLY be thinking about going after the girl who was, at this very moment, running as fast as her short, injured legs would carry her towards almost certain death . . . could she?

Her nose twitched again. Messing with Olympus Inc. went against every single thing Rowan had ever been taught; it *should* go against every plant fibre of her being . . .

Rowan opened her eyes, scratched her nose and sighed. She pulled her CosPad from her belt and redialled. By some Cosmic miracle, there was signal and the call connected.

'Cal, I need you to do me a favour.'

She was *definitely* going to regret this.

27

CAL

Cal clopped quietly along the corridor of Level Fourteen. A favour was switching shifts, maybe even agreeing to babysit a friend's cute, curly-coated kid. A favour was *not* breaking into a government facility to try to deactivate a magic-infused missile.

'Oh *sure*, Rowan, what a great *idea*, Rowan, yes, I would *love* to commit a felony for you, Rowan,' Cal muttered under his breath. He poked his head around a corner. Empty. He exhaled, and readjusted his satchel strap over his shoulder. In his satchel he had everything he might possibly need for a mission of this magnitude: CosPad, laptop, toolkit, sandwich-making equipment. His mouth watered. This spy stuff was ravenous work.

At that moment, Hansel's irritating and authoritative tones floated along the corridor. 'What I'm *saying*, Admiral, is that I'm concerned we are not throwing *enough* firepower at it.'

Cal flattened himself against the wall, then side-clopped towards the next corner and pricked up his radar ears.

'Zeus used just one bolt last time. And look where we are now – the portal is *still* there.' Hansel's voice fizzed with rage.

Last time? What did Hansel mean, last time? Cal edged forward to the corner, where there was a collection of amphora-shaped plant pots filled with daisies. He crouched behind them and peered between the petals. He could see Admiral Prim and Hansel huddled in conversation by a windowless steel door.

Hansel growled. 'And to make things worse, that fool Daedalus was *right*. She's now using it to return. We need to destroy it! Completely!'

Opposite Hansel, Admiral Prim, looking very fine in his shiny gold jumpsuit, stroked his neat white beard. He had the look of a fierce armoured badger. 'The Council has sanctioned the use of *one* bolt.'

'One.' Hansel laughed, a short bark of a laugh.

'Shh!' Admiral Prim looked around. Cal ducked.

'I understand your concerns,' Prim continued. 'That's why I asked you to meet me here.' He indicated the door. 'Magistrate Helena does not yet understand the gravity of the situation. She's too easily swayed by the chief inspector.'

Both agents took a moment to growl in sync.

'This is why we are going to have to take things into our own . . . hands.' Prim took out a key card from the front pocket of his uniform.

'And what's this?' Hansel crossed his muscular arms over his shiny chest.

Admiral Prim smiled through his striped beard. 'Only the magistrates *officially* have access, but these are extenuating circumstances.' He waggled the card. 'I think three bolts and a full CosCannon spread should do it, don't you?'

A grin like that of an unhinged hungry tiger spread across Hansel's face. 'That will flatten half the continent, sir.'

'Would you like to do the honours?' The Admiral swiped the card through the door's card reader.

'*ACCESS GRANTED.*'

Admiral Prim clapped Hansel on the back and they walked through.

Cal sat as still as a hare caught in chariot headlights. He blinked, making the daisies quiver. OPS were going behind the Council's back to destroy the portal! It wasn't just Daedalus's *kidnappers* they were after. Cal felt a bead of sweat trickle down the side of his face and into the curls of his beard.

And this wasn't the first time OPS had been involved in Alexandria! Cal thought back to the information he'd found on Tyron, the missing Librarian. Captain Pine and Admiral Prim had been among the officers assigned to that case over the centuries, though Pine had only been a lieutenant then. Surely there was a link?

The door clicked open and the two men strolled out.

'Good work, Captain.' Admiral Prim held out his hand. Hansel shook it vigorously. 'You'll get a medal for this, I'm sure. Time to celebrate, don't you think?'

Hansel looked at his CosPad. 'The time to celebrate will be

in two hours and twenty-five minutes, Admiral. I have a bottle of St Elmo's Fire ale somewhere. I'll ask the faun to collect it. Then we shall toast together!' He saluted.

'Indeed.' The Admiral nodded and turned to walk away in the opposite direction.

Hansel was about to do the same, when he sniffed the air. Cal held his breath. He had almost forgotten that Hansel was a nymph! Hansel wrinkled his nose and looked towards Cal's hiding place.

Cal squeezed his eyes shut and crouched down. He heard Hansel's footsteps slow as they walked towards him. He sent up a silent prayer to Pan, promising to dedicate an entire half of his next sandwich to the forest god.

The sound of Hansel's footsteps stopped and then suddenly – perhaps hearing something – he sped up and marched briskly down the corridor.

'The *whole* sandwich,' Cal whispered.

28

PEREGRINE

Location: Abandoned Tracks, the Scorpio Line, Near the Necropolis, Under Under Ground, the Under Realm

Peregrine paused for breath. Her lungs hurt and she wasn't crying exactly, but her eyes prickled and her face was damp. She squeezed the magma moss in her hands to warm herself up, but had to stop herself from automatically blowing on them. Wind howled somewhere along the tunnels – or at least she *thought* it was the wind.

Stuffing the moss back in her pockets, Peregrine pressed her warmed hands to her face. She'd been waiting years to go on a proper adventure. But she'd assumed, when it was time, that Daedalus would be with her. She looked around. Instead she was on her own in a dark, potentially endless tunnel, miles underground, with no plan and only Nim's seaweed snacks for food. She rubbed her hands over her eyes.

At least she'd made some friends. OK, so Cal had disappeared, she'd abandoned Nim, and Rowan had betrayed her. She sighed. Was Candice right? *Was* she a freak? An image of Raj sorting through his fossil collection flashed into her mind. Despite the sadness of her immediate situation, she smiled. When she got back – if she got back – she would try to be a much better friend to him.

GrumBug clicked its front legs together on her jumpsuit, and she patted it affectionately. Yes, even Mr Alkhaki's maths class was sounding pretty appealing right now.

Perhaps not wanting to be left out, Bernadette wriggled in her rucksack. 'All right, all right.' Peregrine unzipped the top of the bag and let the plant's leaves uncurl and stretch towards the orange moss-light that dappled the ceiling of the tunnel. At least Bernadette was on her side. 'What did Rowan think I was going to do?' She addressed the plant, who was now playing with the light that was bouncing off their leaves. 'Just let Daedalus to be blown up by some kind of weaponised lightning bolt?'

Bernadette squeaked.

'Exactly.' Peregrine nodded. It was nice to hear that they were on the same page. Bernadette wasn't going to give up on Daedalus either. Peregrine blinked some wetness out of her eyes. No, there was no time for that now. What had Captain Pine said? Just three hours until the Thunderbolt struck?

'You will never find him. You know that, don't you?'

Peregrine froze. It was a woman's voice: harsh, piercing and cold. She pushed Bernadette back down into her rucksack.

'Who said that?' Peregrine looked around, but the voice

was ricocheting off the tunnel walls like a bullet. Where was it coming from? She peered down the tunnel. There *was* something there . . .

She gasped. A wave of thick mist was rolling towards her over the tracks, hugging the ground. Except that it wasn't moving like mist, it moved like a creature – like a lot of creatures – slinking towards its prey. As she watched, she could see shapes forming.

'Who are you?' Peregrine called towards the mist. 'What do you want?'

'You're quite *nosy*, aren't you?' A high-pitched laugh echoed off the walls of the tunnel, repeating like a pod of psychotic dolphins. '*What? Who? Why?*' The voice imitated Peregrine's questioning tone, then cackled. 'Daedalus always found that kind of . . . curiosity . . . so *noble*, so *charming*.'

Peregrine could see the mist clearly now. It was made up of dozens of snake-like tendrils, writhing and slithering forward. She took a step back. 'Daedalus?' Her breath puffed out in ragged clouds. 'Do . . . do you know where he is?'

The mist flashed purple, like a shock of lightning in a cloud. A rumble rolled through the tunnel.

'This is not your story, Peregrine *Quinn*.' The word reverberated around the tunnel. 'You have arrived at the end, at the very last page of a *very* long book where you – a girl, a *mortal* – are a slip of a pen, a mistake, a . . . *smudge*.'

As the mist rolled forward, a wave of molten anger cascaded through Peregrine. *Run, Peregrine.* Her mum's voice rang in her ears. *Run, now.* She clenched her fists, but she couldn't fight mist. No one could, not even her mum. She took another step back, then another. Then she turned on her heel, and ran.

'They always run . . .' The mist crackled.

Maybe she could get back to the train, to Rowan. Peregrine glanced over her shoulder. The mist was gaining on her.

'There is nowhere to go, little girl.' The voice pressed at her ears, her face, her eyes. 'Chaos is climbing out of her pit.'

Peregrine hurtled forward. Her lungs hurt, her legs were screaming. *Just keep running.*

'All of your efforts, and all you are doing is stepping closer to her *teeth.*'

The mist hissed and crackled again, the snake-tendrils snapping at the air. Peregrine could feel it pressing at her back like a wall of ice. *Don't stop, Peregrine, just a little further.* In front of her, the tunnel split into two branches. She daren't slow down, but which fork had she come from? Which way would take her back to the train? To Rowan?

BLEEP BLEEP! GrumBug gave an excited buzz, hovered off Peregrine's jumpsuit and whirred forward.

'GrumBug!' Peregrine hissed. 'Get back here!'

What was it doing? GrumBug had switched on its blue LEDs and sped up, darting down the left-hand tunnel.

'Well, I guess we're going this way then!' Peregrine gritted her teeth and hurtled after the CosBug. The mist was almost on her; she could feel the chill biting at her ankles.

Suddenly, the tunnel opened up onto a marble platform. Hope drained from Peregrine's limbs. She was sure she hadn't passed this before. GrumBug must have taken them the wrong way . . .

SLAM.

The sound was so loud it shook the ground. Peregrine stopped running and spun around. The mist was swirling around the entrance to the tunnel. It had stopped. For some reason, it couldn't follow her. She was safe, but for how long? She needed to get out of here.

Cautiously, Peregrine turned back towards the platform.

But where *was* here? The platform was a simple one. It was made of marble, like the Acropolis Arcades, but this marble was a heavy grey, the colour of a sword blade.

She pulled Nim's map out of her back pocket. As she opened it, the now familiar blue light ebbed into the space around her as the silver Under Under Ground lines grew out of the sides.

She traced her finger along the Scorpio Line until it split. She must be here. 'The Necropolis,' she whispered. Underneath it, in smaller letters, was written. *Warning: dead zone.*

'What's a dead zone?' she whispered.

GrumBug bleeped.

Peregrine looked up. She was sure she had seen something. She blinked. There! It was a woman: she was shimmering, like a rainbow seen through mist, but she was becoming more and more solid.

The woman wiggled her pointed ears, and flicked her long, silvery hair over her shoulder.

'NIM?' Peregrine lowered the map, a smile shining from her face. 'You're all right!'

GrumBug buzzed towards the nyad, chirping excitedly before landing on her shoulder with a contented click. Nim stroked the CosBug's bronze wings and looked up at Peregrine, smiling her kind tortoise-smile. 'A little behind schedule, aren't we?' She took a ghostly pocket watch out of her boiler suit and raised an eyebrow through her CosGogs.

Peregrine didn't know what to say. She looked down again at the map. 'But, how are you –'

'And you've got your plant still. Good, good.' Nim put the watch back in her pocket. 'Could have told me about *that* little puzzle piece, couldn't you?' Nim muttered. Peregrine got the distinct impression that she wasn't talking to her.

'What do you –'

'Well, we best make this sharpish.' Nim snapped up her CosGogs. 'Even in the Necropolis I can't keep corporeal for long. The magic is terribly exhausting and – between you and me – *incredibly* complicated.' She winked.

That word again – *complicated*. Peregrine sniffed. 'What –'

Nim held up a hand. She shimmered, disappearing for a moment. 'Even as an outsider I'm bound by the rules, I'm afraid. Darn frustrating, if you ask me!' She glared up towards the cave ceiling. 'You'd think they'd cut me a little slack, hmm?' Her form paled and flickered. She sighed and shook her head. 'You get one question.' She held up a finger. 'Only one. So, what will it be? Hit me.'

Peregrine was clearly lost, and in a hurry, so the obvious choice would be to ask the fastest way to get to the library. 'I want to know how to –'

'Ahem!' Nim coughed. She held up her hand as she bent down and hacked something out of her throat. 'AHEM.'

Peregrine screwed up her face then, remembering her manners, unzipped her bag and brought out her water bottle. 'Would you –' She stopped herself before finishing the question, instead she shook the bottle so the last few drops sloshed around.

Nim stood up and grinned, darting her eyes from side to side as if she'd just got away with something. She stuck out her tongue. 'Nope, nope. Very kind, but I'm as right as a rainy Thursday in Thebes.' She patted her chest, then moved her hand to the marble wall. 'Now, where were we?'

Peregrine opened her mouth to speak, but before she could, Nim slammed her hand against the wall.

Peregrine stared. Right by the nyad's hand was a sign scratched into the wall: *Alexandria*, and an arrow pointing along the platform.

Nim grinned. 'So, what was it you wanted to ask me, dearie?'

Was it a trick of the light, or was Nim getting fainter?

'Er . . .' Peregrine now knew how to get to the library, but what would she do when she got there? They – *she* – needed all the time she could to find Daedalus and escape. She took a deep breath. There really was only one question. 'How do we stop the portal being opened?'

Nim's friendly grin vanished and was replaced by a fierce, hard line. She blinked once, and when she opened her eyes they were white – not just the whites of her eyes, but her irises and pupils too. Peregrine gasped, and her skin skittered with that sensation she now recognised immediately: magic, and lots of it.

Nim tilted her head to the side and spoke in an eerie, sing-song voice.

Let it flicker, let it die,
For realms in earth, in sea and sky.
This is a magic held by few,
Prune it now, to grow anew . . .

Nim was getting paler by the moment – so pale Peregrine could hardly see her.

'Let it . . . *die?*' Peregrine stepped forward. 'What does that mean? Nim? What needs to die? You can't mean Daedalus! I can't –'

A flicker of a smile played on Nim's lips.

Girl with wings who soars so far
You do not know yet who you are.

Girl with wings. Was that *her?* 'Wait!' Peregrine reached out her hand. 'I . . . I don't know if I can do this!' The words escaped her before she could catch them.

The colour returned to Nim's eyes, and they crinkled at the corners. 'You were born for adventure, Peregrine Quinn.' Her smile widened. 'That is why your mother gave you a name with *wings.*'

'But –'

'*Tempus fugit.*' Nim shook her shimmering grey hair once and was gone, faded away to nothing.

29

ROWAN

Location: The Scorpio Line, Under Under Ground, the Under Realm

Rowan stood by the train door, her finger hovering over the button. As soon as she stepped out of this carriage, she would be stepping into Hera only knew what kind of trouble. Inside the carriage, she had a plan. Outside, no plan, no plan at all.

Rowan coughed, wrapped her scarf around her mouth and nose, and put one hand on her hat. She grimaced and pressed the button. This was a TERRIBLE idea.

She stepped cautiously into the tunnel and, squinting through the mist, surveyed her surroundings. The overhead lights flickered, and blue sparks still fizzed over the tracks. Rowan picked her way over the rubble, avoiding the crackling wires. What had happened here? Some kind of cave-in? Perhaps caused by the Alexandrian fire? Her boots crunched on dirt as she walked around the boulder. She shuddered as the tunnel gaped like a mouth about to swallow her up.

Dryads *needed* sunlight. As a tree nymph, she could sense the life above the ground – the tentative trickles of water and the thin roots of flowers. If she had more strength, she could possibly have brought up a few blooms, just to have something pretty to look at. She closed her eyes and felt around for her magic. She'd worked hard at the Academy to build up her resources – meditating daily under the Realm Tree, taking shots of willow bark every morning – but she was still a novice, and not even a very good one.

Sighing, she opened her eyes. She should never have been given this assignment. She'd been looking after the portal for just one day and the world was *literally* going to end. Hazel would probably have found Daedalus by now. *She* should be the one here, not Rowan. Not a *trainee.*

Rowan felt a tear slide down her nose as she strode toward the cracked remains of the tracks that Peregrine had rushed down. Poor, brave Peregrine, who was now probably lost, or dead, or both.

As the tear dripped from her nose and onto her scarf, Rowan looked down the tunnel. She *could* stomp around blindly, or she could be smart. Sniffing, she pulled Nim's CosGogs from her belt and adjusted them for thermal imaging (blinking once, slowly). There were some bright orange and blue blobs in the distance to her left, but they could be anything. Maybe a cave-widow nest or a cluster of lampfire bats? No, she was looking for a singular signature.

There! A small, amorphous mass was out to her right, about

two kilometres away. She looked at the time displayed at the top of the CosGogs. 'Floobarght,' she muttered as she bounced up and down a few times.

She started to jog across the rubble, the tracks crackling around her. Despite her distaste for both physical activity and peril, Rowan now found herself moving *towards* danger – at speed – for what felt like the fiftieth time that day. When she got back to the Cosmic Realm she would have to take a long, hard look at her priorities.

She checked the CosGogs again, to see how far away she was from the orange-blob-that-was-most-likely-Peregrine. Seven hundred metres, six hundred metres. The dull thuds made by her regulation Librarian boots echoed around the tunnel.

Rowan gritted her teeth and kept her gaze on the blue lights that lined the sides of the tunnel. She had literally no idea what she was running towards. Subterranean monsters? Possible. Apocalypse? Likely. A demotion – when and *if* she returned to the Cosmic Realm? Almost certainly.

A geyser of steam shot up from the ground in front of her. 'Aargh!' she squawked as she leapt sideways. What was she *doing*? No one was supposed to be in these tunnels, not even when the UUG was in legal operation. Not without explicit permission, and *definitely* not without a protective hazard suit.

The heat from the Earth's core made the air fuzzy. Rowan's jumpsuit stuck to her back, her throat felt papery, and she could feel her face going green with exertion. 'Where *are* you, Peregrine?' Surely she should be able to see her by now?

Four hundred metres, three hundred. How far could she have got, really?

'Peregrine!' Rowan called into the murk. The blue strip lights of the tunnel were flickering. The power was clearly weakening. 'Peregrine?' She scrambled forward. The lights flickered off. Then on. Then off.

Then stayed off.

Rowan's foot hit something. 'OW!' She switched off the thermal-imaging on the CosGogs and felt around the brim of her Librarian's hat until she found the high-beam function. She flicked it on and a strip of blue-white LEDs shone from the brim like a laser.

'What in Pan's sacred pipes *is* this?' The tunnel wall was covered in writing – every inch of it. Rowan recognised a few lines by poets she had studied at school: Epistolia the Erudite, Ruskin the Rhymer, Portia the Playful and . . . no! Was that an extract by Thucydia? All her scrolls were thought to have been lost!

Without taking her eyes away from the walls, Rowan tapped the dragonfly on her coat lapel. The CosBug buzzed into life and whirred in front of her face.

Rowan pointed at the wall. 'Record this,' she whispered.

FlutterBug flapped its wings once and whirred its way to the top left of the wall. A blue sheet of light beamed out as it recorded each section in turn.

Scratch, scratch. Scratch.

The sound was coming from a little further down the tunnel.

Scratch, scratch, scraaaatch.

'What was it again?' a voice muttered in the darkness. This was followed by a banging. 'Was it "as red as roses" or "as red as gorgon's blood"? I can *never* remember that line!'

Rowan felt as if her limbs had been dipped in a bucket of Styx water.

The gruff voice echoed through the tunnel. 'Probably gorgon's blood. Sounds . . . bloodier.' There was more scratching, an odd clip-clopping sound and then, silence.

Rowan took a deep breath, then swung her hat-beam to the right. There, a figure was bent low, facing the tunnel wall with a stick of charcoal in his hand and a lampfire bat perched on his shoulder.

As soon as the beam hit them, the lampfire bat turned its head, and screamed.

30

PEREGRINE

**Location: Maintenance Entrance, Alexandria Station,
Under Under Ground, the Under Realm**

'Aargh!' Peregrine's foot caught on one of the many rocks that littered the path. She bit her lip and hobbled forward, using the tunnel wall to steady herself. The *Ice It Now* was wearing off and her ankle throbbed with a pulsing, painful heat.

How far away *was* this library? She wished she could have asked Nim that.

She sniffed loudly. 'I wish I was home,' she whispered. It felt like a selfish confession. She couldn't go home. Daedalus was here, somewhere, and he needed help. A sob bubbled in her throat. Her mum would know she was missing by now and she would be looking for her, like Peregrine was looking for Daedalus. The thought of her mum coming home to an empty shop, with smashed windows and no daughter, sent another sob shuddering through her. As she cried she stopped walking, her body threatening to buckle under her.

You can do this. Peregrine imagined her mum's voice, calm and stern, like when they went on one of their long hikes. *One foot in front of the other, pumpkin.*

Wiping her eyes, Peregrine inhaled sharply. She slapped her palm against the tunnel wall and pulled herself forward. She might not be a hero, but she could pretend to be one – like the ones she'd read about – just for a little while longer, just until she found Daedalus. Daedalus would know what to do. All Peregrine had to do was find him.

She hobbled around the next corner and saw a dull, grey metal door set into the tunnel wall. Peregrine blinked. It looked completely out of place in the flickering moss-lit gloom of the cave tunnel. Excitement fizzed in her chest. Momentarily forgetting her pain, she skidded towards it.

On the dull, grey door, in even duller, greyer print was written:

OFFICIAL UNDER REALM STAFF ONLY
MAINTENANCE ENTRANCE

'The library,' she whispered. 'This *must* lead to the surface.'

She pushed the door. It didn't budge.

'Of course it's locked!' She slammed her fist against the door. She didn't know what she'd been expecting; they'd had such an *easy* ride up until this point. Everything was either locked, or broken, or dangerous, or *treacherous* . . .

She flicked her gaze to the timestamp on her CosGogs – only an hour and a half until the Thunderbolt reached Alexandria. Just over an hour, to reach Daedalus and get him out of there. Well, there was no point in rationing food; one way or another, this would be over by supper, and anyway, perilous rescue missions used up a lot of energy.

She shrugged off her rucksack and pulled out her raincoat to sit on. She peered into her bag. She'd already munched her way through two more of the seaweed scones that Nim had given them, but she was sure there was another. Bernadette's leaves shook a little, and then drooped with a plaintive sigh.

'OK, but just for a minute.' Peregrine slid the plant out of the safety of her bag and, careful to check for any flammable moss, placed her on the ground. Bernadette squeaked in delight. 'But we *have* to keep moving.' Peregrine tipped some water into Bernadette's soil and leaned back against the door, humming her lullaby softly: *'Light and bright and airy thing . . .'*

She yawned, then tapped her cheeks. No! There was no time for that. She shook her head to keep herself awake as she rummaged around inside her rucksack. She pushed aside *The History of Carnivorous Fungi* and her school pencil case. Now, where had she put that last scone?

A loud snort made her jerk her head up. Was it the mist monster? A burst of adrenaline shot through Peregrine's veins and, with her mum's training sessions kicking in, her limbs moved automatically. She grabbed her rucksack, then tucked and rolled behind a boulder just a metre up the path. Turning from her roll to land in a perfect aikido crouch, she looked back towards the door to see – Bernadette!

No! Peregrine's heart skipped as she saw the plant shaking where she had left her. How could she have been so *stupid*? She had *promised* to look after her! Peregrine darted her hand out, but another snort, louder this time, made her snatch it back. There was no time. She shrank back into the shadows, her eyes ping-ponging between Bernadette and the hulking figures who were striding towards them.

'You *know* the rules,' Earl said. 'Not until we get back to the portal.'

'But we're in the *Under Realm*.' Stan was scratching at his stiff shirt collar. 'No nosy little Terrans here. Plus, we've been wearing the glamours for almost a whole day. It *itches*, Earl.' He whined. 'I'm getting a rash – see?'

'Why are you always trying to show me your rashes?' Earl shoved him away in disgust. 'We're almost there. Look, there's the door.'

'Nasty Cosmic Magic,' Stan muttered, still pulling at his collar.

'Ugh!' Earl came to an abrupt halt. 'Fine!'

'Really?' Stan asked, gleefully. He was practically bouncing.

'Another second of your whining and I'll want to tear my *own* skin off.' Earl gestured again with his hand. 'Give me your GlamPass – go on.'

'Oh, thank you!' Smiling a thin, predatory smile, Stan pressed a button on the ID card around his neck and pulled the lanyard off in a flourish. Before the GlamPass even hit Earl's palm, the transformation had begun. First the shoes: the shiny, black leather brogues faded, glitching in and out, until they were replaced with long scaly webbed feet with sharp talons. Next, the suit. The smartly cut tailoring fell away to reveal what looked like a brown boiler suit with a hole slashed in it for Stan's dinosaur-sized lizard tail, which swished along the ground.

Peregrine's tongue felt heavy in her mouth. There was a golden apple tree embroidered on the back of the suit. It was the same one that was sewn on the back of her own jumpsuit, except Stan's had the words *Sewage Detail* written underneath it.

The dark sunglasses were the last to go. Stan blinked, and two sets of eyelids wetted his pupils, like Peregrine had once seen on a caiman on a nature documentary she'd watched with her mum. Peregrine could hear the presenter's calm, precise tones: *Due to their ferocious and deeply aggressive nature, caiman have very few natural predators . . .*

Spittle fell from Stan's reptilian mouth as he grinned a smooth, sharp-toothed grin. A forked tongue flicked from his mouth as he licked his incisors. 'That'sss better,' he hissed.

Peregrine gulped. So *this* was what BogBrethren really looked like! She had been scared of Stan as a human, but seeing him as a giant lizard sent chills right down her spine and into her toes.

Earl appraised his colleague, and then – clearly deciding it was the right choice – took his own lanyard off and tucked it inside his suit jacket. His skin became a sickly grey, as if it had never seen the sun, and then lizard scales began to bubble up underneath. His nose flattened, his ears pinned to the sides of his head and a green crest grew where his hair had been. He was also wearing an Olympic jumpsuit, but his had a badge with the word *Supervisor* pinned to the front.

Earl straightened it. The only thing that stayed the same in his reptilian transformation was his briefcase.

'Enough delays. She wants us back at the portal.' Earl picked at one of his terrifyingly sharp front teeth. 'It's almost time –'

Stan flicked his tongue out again and his slit nostrils flared. 'I sssmell sssomething.' He stepped forward, his tongue darting in and out at lightning speed.

Peregrine flattened herself even further towards the wall. If it had been possible to suck her eyeballs further into their sockets, she would have done it.

Stan dropped down onto his belly and slithered forward. The movement was so terrifyingly snake-like that Peregrine had to swallow a scream. She tried to remember what her mum had taught her about the martial art masters. Channelling everything she'd learned, Peregrine made her breathing shallow and whisper-quiet and steadied her heartbeat. She also balled her hands into fists, gripping her thumbs with her fingers, just in case she had to quickly thump Stan on his flat scaly nose.

He was only a few metres away when he stopped. 'Here!' He stood back up on his hind legs and swooped down on Peregrine's raincoat, plucking it from the ground. 'Trophy!' A smile spread across his reptilian face. Then he did something that Peregrine really didn't expect. Neither, apparently, did Earl.

'WHAT are you doing?' Earl said loudly.

Stan was trying to force his arms through the jacket sleeves.

'It won't fit, Stan.' Earl sighed.

'It'sss jussst a little tight . . .'

'Give it to me.' Earl stepped forward, holding out a scaly hand.

'No! It'sss mine!' Stan was clearly trapped inside the sleeves of the jacket now. 'I want a trophy! The harpiesss have troph—'

Earl tugged the jacket off Stan's arms and shook it out.

Stan hissed in annoyance. He spun around to grab it back, but Earl pulled it away.

'Thisss belongs to the Terran girl.' Earl stuck out his forked tongue and licked the jacket. 'Yesss.' He paused. 'I'm sure of it.'

Peregrine pushed herself further into the wall. That creature had just *licked* her jacket. That was SO gross.

'The girl is obviously ssstill in the tunnels somewhere.' Earl's beady eyes swivelled to the tunnel where Peregrine had just come from. 'We should go.' He threw the jacket back at Stan, who caught it and clutched it protectively to his chest.

'Hmm.' Forked tongue between his teeth, Stan patted the pocket and pulled out the last of Nim's scones. He unwrapped the CosFilm and bit into it. 'Mmm.'

Peregrine's eyes narrowed.

With the scone held in his mouth, Stan draped Peregrine's jacket around his neck like a scarf. The canary yellow clashed spectacularly with his grey-green skin. He took another bite of Peregrine's snack. 'Pretty good, thisss, Earl. Want sssome?' he said, crumbs flying everywhere. 'Ooh!' He stopped eating. His eyes locked on the ground.

Bernadette. He had seen Bernadette.

'A pretty plant!' Stan bent down.

'Leave it!' Earl snapped.

'But –'

'Don't be greedy!' Earl growled.

Peregrine's heart caught in her throat as Stan stepped reluctantly away from Bernadette. With a sigh – that sounded much more like a hiss – Earl walked towards the *Official Under Realm Staff Only* door and slid a key card into the lock. The outside of the door lit up in green and beeped once.

Thoughts buzzed around Peregrine's head as she tried to concentrate on what was happening. Despite her carelessness, they had not taken Bernadette, but as soon as Stan and Earl were through that door, that was it. That was her only way to the library, and who knows how long it would take her to get through? Minutes? Hours? Time was ticking down fast!

Earl had already slid through the door and was holding it open with his scaly webbed foot. 'She wants us back in the library. NOW.'

If she could follow them somehow . . . Peregrine chewed her lip. There was no way she could run for the door, they would see her for sure, but . . . She looked down at her jumpsuit, and GrumBug glittered back at her.

She tickled the bug and brought it up to her face. 'Follow them, GrumBug,' Peregrine whispered, her lips millimetres from the bug. '*Go!*'

The CosBug hovered off her hand for a moment, then set off towards the door.

Stan shoved the last of the scone in his mouth, flopped down onto his belly and slithered speedily towards the door. 'Sssorry, Earl.' He stood up too fast and belched.

Earl coughed and flicked crumbs from the front of his boiler suit back into Stan's face. Glaring, he quickly removed his foot from the door so Stan had to scramble to get through.

The door was sliding shut. Peregrine held her breath. GrumBug was almost there! It put on a turbo boost, its little wings hardly visible as they whirred frantically. Peregrine saw the tip of Stan's scaly tail disappear, she heard GrumBug buzz and . . .

'Oh no!'

The door snapped shut, trapping GrumBug in the gap with a thick sickening crunch and a drawn-out hiss.

31

ROWAN

**Location: Abandoned Tracks, the Scorpio Line,
Under Under Ground, the Under Realm**

'Aargh!' The figure screamed and spun towards Rowan. 'Turn that light off!'

'Ah, sorry.' Rowan clicked off the beam on her hat. The man in the tunnel had a long, matted beard and an unkempt mop of curly hair. He was wearing a filthy floral Hawaiian shirt. He was also, Rowan noticed, a centaur.

From the floral shirt down, he had the body of a dull grey horse, with tufty, tangled fur around his hooves. Rowan had seen centaurs before, of course – hoofers were a fairly common occurrence on the Mountain – but there was something very different about this one. For a start, he looked as if he hadn't washed in about a decade, which was particularly shocking as centaurs were known for their excellent hygiene and impeccable fashion sense. They were quite snobby about it, actually.

The centaur's eyes narrowed. Rowan was clearly not a welcome visitor.

'Hello!' she said, with perhaps too much enthusiasm. Then, without meaning to, she screwed up her nose. There was a smell. And that smell was horse dung.

A fly buzzed across her eyeline and she gently batted it away. 'May I ask who I am speaking to?' The fly buzzed back. 'And what you are doing in the Under Realm? I don't know if you heard, but it's actually a restricted area . . .'

The fly continued to *buzz, buzz, buzz* around Rowan until *bzzzzzzzzz*. FlutterBug sent out a tiny red laser. The fly landed on the ground with a crisp *fizz*, a tiny tendril of black smoke swirling above it.

The centaur swished his tail. 'Who's asking?' He glared at her. 'Are you from Olympus?' He clip-clopped so close to her she could see the whites of his eyes, shining pale and ghostly in the gloom. 'Did *they* send you?' He leaned so far forward that their noses were almost touching.

'No, no, absolutely not.' She said this through gritted teeth, trying not to inhale the centaur's pungent odour. It was true. Olympus Inc. had not technically sent her *here* – not exactly.

'Good,' he said, leaning away from her.

Rowan coughed, casually placing her hand over the golden apple pin on her lapel.

The centaur folded his arms over his chest and glared at her. 'Well then, who *are* you?'

She was about to counter by saying that she had in fact asked *him* that first, but time was ticking down, and exchanges of that nature often went on for a while. She had – she checked her CosGogs – around an hour and a half before the Thunderbolt arrived, and instead of *Peregrine's* signature, she had apparently been following that of a crazed subterranean-dwelling centaur. She needed help.

Rowan knotted her eyebrows together as she watched the centaur pick at his ear hair. Was *this* help?

She tried to remember what *The Librarian's Handbook* said about diplomacy. *Create a connection by sharing small details about yourself, but don't reveal too much – you never know what your opponent might use against you.*

'OK.' She took a deep, calming breath, and promptly gagged at the smell. 'I am Rowan Strong,' she said slowly, her hands out in front of her as if calming a bucking, biting horse. 'I *am* an Official Olympic Librarian, from CSI, the Oxford Desk.'

'Ha!' The centaur flicked some earwax in her direction. 'I knew it!'

'A *trainee* Librarian,' Rowan added, dodging the earwax and trying to speak without inhaling. 'This is actually my first day.'

'Nice shiny hat you have there.' The centaur nodded towards her Librarian's hat. 'I have one of those.'

Rowan touched the brim of her hat. It had been presented to her by Professor Demeter herself. It made her feel warm, valued, respected.

'I use it to shovel my dung,' the centaur said blandly.

Rowan pulled her hat off her head and held it protectively to her chest, as if at any moment the centaur might rip it from her and defecate into it.

'Now go away. I don't want any of your Olympus business

here. I need to get back to my . . . books.' He flicked his tail and clip-clopped back down the tunnel.

'No, wait!' Rowan took a gulp of the stale subterranean air. After all this adventure and rule-breaking, what had she accomplished? Nothing but a sweaty uniform and aching quad muscles. No way in Hades was she going to leave it here. She trotted after him. 'Hey! I need –' she sniffled – 'your *help* . . .'

The words died on her lips. The centaur had disappeared through a door in the tunnel, but around that door was painted a vast mural. A ten-metre-high figure of Zeus had been scrawled onto the wall in harsh lines of charcoal, crayon and what looked like felt-tip pen. It was Zeus all right – he was unmistakable with his lightning bolts clutched in his fists – but his face, usually so serene, was fixed in a terrifying wide-eyed mask of malice. He was standing like Colossus over the city of Alexandria, and he was hurling bolts at the library.

Everything was on fire.

Rowan felt hot, and then cold. Zeus glowered down at her.

She shook her head and looked again. This *couldn't* be real.

Zeus had retired centuries ago, leaving the everyday running of Olympus Inc. to Hera. But he was still occasionally seen at official functions, like when Rowan had seen him give her sister Elm her Enchanted Forest Guide Award. She remembered him – a bumbling, rosy-cheeked man with white curly hair. Last thing she'd heard, he'd been running a goat farm on the foothills of Olympus. He made cheese. She looked back at the mad-eyed figure towering over the demolished city. 'But . . . he makes cheese,' she said, out loud this time.

Having completed its scan of the wall, FlutterBug whirred

down and reattached itself to Rowan's jumpsuit just before she ran through the door.

'Hey!' She skidded to a stop as she almost ran into the centaur's chest. He folded his arms, and both he and the lampfire bat glared at her menacingly.

'I *told* you to go,' the centaur growled.

'Er, y-y-yes,' Rowan stuttered. Then a thought struck her. 'You said you have a Librarian's hat!'

'The one that I –' He mimed squatting.

'Yes,' Rowan said quickly, interrupting the mime.

He whinnied. 'What of it?'

This centaur had a Librarian's hat, that must mean . . . 'You're Tyron!' The puzzle piece fell into place with a satisfying snap. 'The lost Librarian of Alexandria!'

'What? No.' The centaur-who-was-most-definitely-Tyron-the-lost-Librarian-of-Alexandria nibbled greedily at his filthy, overgrown fingernails. 'Never heard of him.' He spat a globule of fingernail dirt onto the floor.

'You ARE!' Rowan stamped her foot. 'The old Librarian – it's you!'

'OLD?' The piece of charcoal landed on the floor with a dull thud. 'Who are you calling *old*?'

The lampfire bat turned its head three hundred and sixty degrees and let out an ear-piercing screech.

'I was a spry young thing when I got my library post, not even seven hundred years!' The centaur huffed.

Rowan's sensitive ears were still ringing. She rubbed them. 'But that was over *two thousand* years ago.'

'Not even seven hundred years . . .' the centaur continued,

ignoring her. 'I was so proud! My very own library post!'

Rowan remembered the pride she'd felt when Professor Demeter had handed Rowan her own set of portal keys, less than twenty-four hours ago.

'And then that . . . *maniac* demolished it.' Tyron mimed throwing a lightning bolt, then waved his hands around to mimic things exploding. The lampfire bat screamed again, for effect.

Rowan winced, and her hands flew to her ears as Tyron threw his arms open. 'Everything. Gone.'

She remembered the words on the wall. The centaur had scrawled pieces from the ancient scrolls, the ones that had been destroyed in the Great Fire, to try to *preserve* them. Something tightened in Rowan's chest. 'It was *Zeus* that destroyed Alexandria? Destroyed your library?' She dropped her hands. 'It wasn't just a fire?'

Everything was silent but for the buzzing of a hundred flies and an impatient clicking sound coming from FlutterBug.

Tyron nodded. 'That was no ordinary fire. Olympus knew, of course. They tried to lure me away from my post, but I knew something was up. I would *not* move.' Tyron shook his head with a little whinny. 'Next thing I know, *BOOM!* Zeus had hit the library. He was aiming for the portal, I'm sure. Book-burning charlatan!' Tyron shook his fist at the ceiling, as if Zeus, Lord of the Heavens, could somehow hear him. Maybe he could; Cosmics were funny like that. 'They sent a retrieval squad after me, so they could memory-wipe me. ME! The cheek of it! But I ran and hid here.' He indicated the cave. 'I knew they'd try to cover it up, the villains!'

'Did they destroy the portal?'

Tyron snorted. 'It's buried under rock and rubble, and under the new library the Terrans built. It would be almost impossible to uncover now. Believe me, I've tried.'

'And you've been hiding down here all this time?'

Tyron's shoulders slumped – the weight of the disaster clearly still there. He looked down at his tattered red and yellow floral shirt and nodded.

Rowan paused. They were going to destroy the Library of Alexandria again, and now *she* was the one who knew too much. She knew about the Thunderbolt, about Discord . . . Were they going to memory-wipe *her*? She'd heard that you were never the same after that. She took a deep breath. 'Do you know why they did it?'

Tyron shrugged. 'I don't get much reception down here.' He said this simply, as if it were obvious, like the fact that mermaids make good lifeguards.

'Ah yes, of course. Well, we – that is, my, er, *friend* Peregrine and I – met a nyad called Nim –'

'*You* know Nim?' Tyron lifted an eyebrow. He looked sceptical.

'Yes, sort of. Anyway, *she* told us that Zeus used the Alexandrian portal to banish Discord to the Fourth Realm –'

Tyron interrupted. 'So THAT is how they got rid of her. Through MY portal,' he growled. 'And then they destroyed the evidence.' Tyron's thin lips were set in a grim line. 'Destroyed my library. My *books*!'

'Exactly.' Rowan nodded and began to mirror Tyron's hand gestures of things exploding.

'You said –' Tyron coughed, and Rowan froze, mid-mime of a

celebratory lap around the library – 'that you needed my help?'

Rowan straightened her uniform. 'Yes, er, someone has found out about the portal. We – that is, my friend and I – think they are trying to open it up again, digging it up to bring Discord back.' She lowered her voice. 'Back from the *Fourth Realm*.'

Tyron's already ashen, sun-starved face turned a grimmer shade of grey. 'Bring her BACK?' His hooves pawed the dusty earth. 'This is madness!'

Rowan gulped. 'Yes, Olympus seems to think so too. They are sending in another Thunderbolt to try to stop them –'

Tyron's cheeks flamed. 'To the library?'

Rowan nodded.

'MY library?' Tyron let out a high-pitched whinny and clopped towards a chest in the corner. 'Not on my watch. Not again!' He pulled out a battered CSI jacket and turned around to face her. This involved a complex kind of twelve-point manoevre – he was a fully grown centaur, after all, and the cave was only so big. He held up the jacket – instead of the Realm Tree, it had a lightning bolt embroidered on the back. It had a line painted through it. Of course, it was *Tyron* who had scrawled that graffiti they'd seen on the UUG.

'So you'll help me?' Rowan asked tentatively.

'I'll help you.' He squeezed his arms into the jacket and tried to do the buttons up over his floral shirt.

A wave of relief washed over Rowan, quickly followed by one of panic as a gust of wind shot towards her and lifted her hat off her head. 'AARGH!' She flailed to catch it.

Tyron sighed. 'Will you *please* STOP screaming, Agent. You are scaring the weather.'

'Sorry.' Rowan wrestled her hat back onto her head. 'So –' she eyed the air above her warily – 'how do we get to the portal?'

Tyron gave up trying to close the buttons on his jacket and picked up the charcoal from the ground. He scratched a rough blueprint-style diagram onto the cave wall. 'The library –' he drew a box with an 'X' on it – 'and therefore the portal, is almost directly above us.' He sketched a detailed figure of himself – looking taller and broader-chested – standing next to a much shorter stick person.

'Hey!' Rowan yelled.

The wind moaned.

'*Hey!*' she said more quietly, placing a hand on her hat as she squinted at the charcoal map. All the CosTech in the known universe, and this was how they were going to save the world: drawing on cave walls with burnt sticks. *Fan-flooing-tastic.*

Tyron drew a line from the figures to the portal and labelled it 'UUG'. Tyron paused. 'Looks simple, doesn't it?'

Rowan exhaled. A straight line. Finally, something easy.

Tyron tapped the wall, turned, and then, wiggling his horse-behind, used his tail to erase the straight line. 'Well, it's NOT simple.' He turned back to the wall. 'Thanks to *your* Olympus, there are no *official* surface exits. No way to get up *there*.' He indicated upwards.

Rowan winced.

'We'll have to climb.' Tyron circled a point on the map. 'This hatch should take us out directly under the new Terran library.'

'Er.' Rowan eyed up the centaur's very old Olympus Inc. jacket and very horsey body. '*Can* you climb?'

'I am incredibly athletic!' Tyron huffed, obviously offended.

Rowan glanced at her CosPad. Tyron knew the layout of the old library: she needed him to find the portal, and then find Peregrine, and then there was Discord . . . Feeling nausea rise, Rowan rummaged around in her pockets for the paper panic bag Nim had given her. Her fingers brushed against something small, smooth and rectangular.

'I've got an idea.' She brought out the GlamPass.

Tyron took it from her. 'Sharon from –' he brought the GlamPass closer to his face – 'mark-et-ing.' He flipped it around, then bit it into it. 'Some kind of glamour?'

Rowan nodded.

'Nifty,' he said. 'Glamours in my day were helmets. Very bulky, heavy things. The metal made them sweaty too.' And with that observation, he looped the GlamPass over his head.

The change was immediate. First his shaggy hair curled itself into tight ringlets on top of his head, then his back legs seemed to fold in on themselves like a concertina.

'Whoooooa.' Tyron wobbled. Understandably. He wasn't used to being a biped.

Rowan darted forward to help steady him. As she grabbed his hand, his wrinkled, swarthy palm became more petite and his fingernails – chewed and jagged – morphed so they were now smooth and painted in pastel-pink nail varnish.

'Rowan?' His voice had become lilting and melodic. 'How . . . how do I look?'

Tyron stood awkwardly in front of her. He was now quite short, with a little extra timber around the middle, and was wearing a neat blue polka-dot blouse and pencil skirt.

'You look . . . wonderful.' Rowan smiled broadly.

'Excellent,' Tyron said, then promptly fell over sideways.

'Maybe we should lose the stilettos?' she offered kindly. This was clearly very difficult for Tyron, and he was doing very well. She helped him up.

He nodded in relief. He prised the shoes off, then, holding them in both hands, began slashing the heels through the air. 'These are fantastic! Agent, do you have some of these too? Maybe we could use them for some eye-gouging?' He hurled one, as if it was a throwing knife. It thudded against the cave wall. 'You know, in case we meet any Olympus scum?'

Rowan looked down at the lemon-yellow stiletto on the cave floor. 'Perhaps we should try to avoid any actual conflict?' She picked up the shoe carefully and handed it back.

'I suppose I *am* a little rusty.' Tyron shrugged, put both shoes in his handbag and clicked it shut.

Rowan gulped. 'So, we're ready?'

Tyron adjusted his hairband and ripped a slit into his pencil skirt. 'Ready,' he said grimly.

The lampfire bat screamed again. Twice.

Tyron stuck the charcoal behind his ear and crossed his arms over his chest. 'Oh, and Agent Strong?'

'Yes?' Rowan looked the centaur square in the eyes.

'You can tell no one that you saw me here. I help you and then I disappear again. Are we clear?'

Rowan nodded. 'As clear as Aphrodite's pores after a fairy facial.' She put her hand out.

'Well then –' Tyron shook her outstretched hand – 'you can't get much clearer than that.'

32

PEREGRINE

Location: Maintenance Entrance, Alexandria Station, Under Under Ground, the Under Realm

Peregrine dashed over to the grey door. GrumBug's left wing had been caught as the door had closed, and was now stuck there. The bug hummed meekly.

'Oh, GrumBug!' Peregrine grabbed a rock and tried to prise the door open with her fingers. Her face grew hot with the exertion, but finally the gap was wide enough to shove the rock in just above the CosBug.

GrumBug's one good wing flapped, and it managed to fly two feet towards Peregrine before it flopped on the dirt, broken and exhausted.

Peregrine picked the little bug up tenderly and peered more closely at it. The mechanism connecting GrumBug's wing to its body had been completely crushed. She turned it over onto its back so she could examine the joint. GrumBug's fine copper legs wriggled in the air plaintively.

'I don't have anything to fix you with,' she whispered. 'I'm so sorry.' What could she do? She placed a finger on its back in an attempt at comfort. GrumBug's wings flickered once in response.

Peregrine sniffed as she carried GrumBug over to Bernadette and placed it gently on the dusty ground. She shrugged off her backpack and picked up Bernadette, giving them a little squeeze. The plant squeaked. 'I'm sorry to you too. I never meant to leave you.'

She had come so close to losing them, Daedalus's precious plant. Peregrine scrolled through the list of Daedalus's precise instructions as he'd handed Bernadette to her: water frequently, keep away from fire, and sing the lullaby twice a day.

As Peregrine placed Bernadette back safely in the bag, she began to sing.

'*Light and bright and airy thing.*' She yawned, but the song made her feel stronger. '*Rarer than a fairy's wing . . .*' She was about to zip the rucksack up when she noticed tendrils sprouting from Bernadette's stem. These iridescent green shoots wound over Peregrine's hand and weaved towards GrumBug. Not knowing what else to do, Peregrine kept singing. '*Bring your strength to grow your leaves.*'

She watched in awe as the tendrils twisted around GrumBug's wing. They wound around and around to form a kind of bandage until finally, with a gentle tug, the tendrils shrank back.

'*Through you, nature's power weaves.*'

Bernadette squeaked again. It was quite a smug squeak.

'Yes, I *am* impressed!' Peregrine agreed in admiration. 'Well done, Bernie!' She tickled Bernadette's leaves. 'You are an *incredible* plant,' she said as she zipped up the bag. 'Now go to sleep.'

She picked up GrumBug to examine Bernadette's handiwork. The wing was certainly secure, but whether or not GrumBug could fly on it was another matter. 'Best stay there for now,' she whispered as she slipped the CosBug into her top pocket. It chirped once, then was still. Placing her hand over her pocket, she could feel the bug's tiny heartbeat-like vibration thumping over hers. 'Daedalus will know what to do,' she whispered. 'He *always* knows what to do.' Daedalus would be able to fix GrumBug; he would be able to fix everything. All she had to do was find him.

Standing up, Peregrine pulled the CosGogs back down over her eyes. She looked at the digital clock and grimaced. The Thunderbolt would be here in just over an hour. She could feel her own heartbeat quickening, thudding against the weight of GrumBug in her pocket. She needed to calm down. Her mum's voice rang in her ears: *Focus on what you know.*

Her heartbeat slowed a fraction. At least she knew the way to the library now. Peregrine looked at the crack in the door that the rock was still holding open. She patted her pocket once more, grabbed her rucksack and put her hands on the edge of the door. 'Let's do this.'

She pressed her good foot into the ground and gripped with her fingers. Inch by sweaty, difficult inch she prised the gap wider – first with her hands and then with her elbows.

Finally, she managed to get her hips in between the gap.

She pushed her feet against the side and heaved.

'Uugh!' With one last blinding effort she tumbled through into . . . *another* tunnel. Peregrine groaned. *This* tunnel was constructed of sand-coloured rock – which did make a nice change from grey – and rather than the orange moss-lit glow of the UUG, there were torches making the light flicker and the shadows long and foreboding. Pushing her bruised palms against the wall, Peregrine stood up.

She adjusted a dial on the CosGogs and blinked once, very slowly.

'That can't be right.' Her face tightened in concentration. There was a huge blue patch blocking her vision. Maybe she'd got the settings wrong? She blinked twice to go back to the normal lens. Maybe . . .

GrumBug buzzed frantically.

'Settle down, or you'll –' But before she could say 'hurt yourself', everything went an ominous, inky black.

'Hey!' she yelled. Someone had pulled a bag over her head. It smelled musty but also sweet, like lavender and hot chocolate before bedtime and . . . She could feel her brain uncoiling from its alert, watchful state into soft sleepiness.

'HEY!' she yelled, louder this time, but her voice was already slurring. She punched out with her arms and kicked with her legs, but her limbs felt heavy, as if they were wrapped in damp towels. Her eyelids began to close. 'No!' Her voice was meek and was getting quieter, like someone was turning down the volume on her words. 'No . . .'

Stan's voice hissed in her ear. 'I *knew* I sssmelled sssomething!'

33

CAL

Location: Behind a Plant Pot, Level Fourteen,
Olympus Inc., the Mountain
CosDate: 300.23.241

Cal had been hiding behind the daisies for about half an hour now. Or at least he *thought* it had been half an hour; he couldn't be sure exactly, as he'd eaten all of his CosTech in an attempt to stop his signal being traced and also so he wouldn't eat the daisies, which were currently his only cover.

Clack. Clack. Clack.

Anxiety erupted like fireworks inside Cal's chest. Which was a curious sensation, as fireworks are incredibly frightening to fauns. If this was Hansel he would have to make a run for it, and fast. He leaned forward, and almost choked on a stray circuit wire.

Grand Architect Hekate was striding gracefully down the

hallway, wearing a tailored purple silk lab coat with a high collar and boots made from polished chimera hide.

Cal winced. It was considered incredibly bad taste to wear any kind of animal skin on Olympus, especially with so many hoofers about. He peered closer. Questionable fashion choices aside, what was she doing *here*? HekTek Laboratories were on Level Seventeen. Was she visiting someone?

The nymph stalked over to the door Captain Pine and Admiral Prim had gone through earlier and placed a hand on the keypad.

Cal's horns tingled. Fauns' horns are particularly sensitive to Cosmic energy. Acting a little like antennae, they prickle when magic is around. Cal scratched his ear. Hekate was *definitely* using magic to open the door, but why?

'ACCESS GRANTED,' a computerised voice chirped pleasantly.

Glancing behind her, Hekate pushed the door open. It swung wide and then closed, but not all the way. Maybe the magic had muddled the locking system.

Cal tuned his ears into the Command Hub, which he could just see into from his hidden vantage point.

'Aww, how sweet,' Hekate drawled. 'Three *whole* Thunderbolts, how *very* frightening.' She giggled. 'I am practically *quaking* in my boots.'

She was clearly mad, Cal thought. What had Hansel said? That that amount of firepower could flatten half a *continent*?

Hekate hummed a little, then another voice rang out. Cal's ears pricked.

'We've been trying to call.' The words cut the air like razors.

'Communications have been hit and miss with the power outages. I'm having to use –' she paused, as if the very idea was distasteful – 'the Council's Command Hub.' She wrinkled her nose. 'The last dribbles of power are being diverted here for the Thunderbolt launch.'

'The what?' the voice asked.

'Never mind about that.' She waved her hand in the air. 'Do you have the girl?'

'We have her.'

Pear-grinn! They must mean Pear-grinn!

'Oh, splendid!' Hekate clapped her hands together. 'Does she happen to have a . . . plant with her?'

'I TOLD you we should have brought the plant.' Another, deeper, voice cut in.

'We've got it,' the first voice snapped. 'It's in the Terran's bag.'

A clang echoed down the hallway. 'The security breach came from this quadrant! Check all the rooms!' Cal recognised Captain Pine's voice calling to the team. 'And if anyone sees my assistant, Cal, tell him I want a Cospuccino, stat!'

'I shall meet you at the library. It is time. *Eris rises.*' Hekate pressed a button to end the communication.

Cal crouched even lower behind the plant as Hekate looked both ways out of the door, then strode back the way she'd come, the heels of her boots clacking on the marble floor.

Cal's brain whirred. Grand Architect Hekate was somehow involved in all this – in Daedalus's kidnapping, in the portals shutting down, the whole lot!

A clatter made Cal spin around. At the end of the corridor

he could see two junior OPS agents carrying a golden battering ram between them. The ram's head had an intense, vengeful expression. It reminded Cal a lot of his Uncle Ignatio.

Quickly Cal clopped over to the Command Hub and pulled the door firmly shut behind him. It clicked, just in time. The security team raced past.

Breathing heavily, and with his back against the door, Cal sank slowly to the floor. This was *not* what he had signed up for. He was out of his depth. Which was not very hard, as not only are fauns limited vertically, but they are also terrible swimmers.

From his position on the floor, Cal looked around. There were dozens of holo-screens hovering above the consoles, each casting a ghostly blue glow into the otherwise dark room. One showed lines of disappointed tourists whose Terran holidays had been scuppered by the portal disaster, one showed a bored trapped Librarian playing on his phone, and another had live footage of an interview with Thoth Thompson. A transcript ticker-taped underneath the screen. Cal gulped. He hoped Sibyll hadn't seen that.

Cal propped his elbows on his knees and leaned his horns on his hands. Had he just heard Olympus Inc.'s Grand Architect admit to *kidnapping*? He groaned. At least he was safe in the Command Hub for now, thank Pan for small mercies.

'Hello?'

'Baaaaaa!' Cal bleated, snapping his head up. 'Who? What? Where are you?'

'Over here, Cal!' Thoth Thompson had disappeared and had been replaced by a flickering image of a weathered, smiling face.

'Daedalus!' Cal rushed towards the fuzzing screen. The old

Grand Architect, usually so full of life, looked pale and tired.

'Callimachus. Good to see you, old boy. Haven't seen you since they invented decent Terran underwear! It is remarkable what elastic can do – remarkable!' Daedalus nodded enthusiastically. 'If we ever get out of this mess, remind me to send you some.'

'Daedalus, where *are* you? We've been looking everywhere!'

'Ah, well, that's the thing. I am currently being held in a "magical vortex".' He air-quoted. 'I'm using some pretty complex conjuring to communicate right now, and I'm a bit out of practice, if I'm honest.' He scratched the back of his head and the image flickered again. 'I've been bouncing across holo-screens trying to find a friendly face.' He grinned at Cal. 'I thought I might find Sibyll, but I am *very* glad to have got you!'

Cal nodded. He understood. Sibyll was many things, but 'friendly' was *not* one of them.

'It has taken longer than I thought.' Daedalus lowered his voice. 'And I got a bit of a shock on Level Fifteen, let me tell you.' His eyes widened.

'What –' Cal began.

Daedalus interrupted. 'Best that I don't *actually* tell you, old boy.' He shook his head. 'Anyway, the signal has been quite tricky to triangulate. Are you experiencing power shortages?'

Cal nodded. 'They've diverted most of the power here, to the Command Hub, because of the Thunderbolts,' he explained.

'Thunderbolts?' Daedalus sighed a long, tired sigh and his image flickered. 'Well, it's nice to see that Olympus isn't above repeating the same mistakes.' All talk of underpants forgotten, he suddenly became serious. 'Now, listen to me carefully, Cal. We don't have much time.'

34

ROWAN

Location: Sheer Cliff Face, Somewhere Under Egypt, the Under Realm

What had Rowan thought being a Librarian would be like? Perhaps some realm-lag headaches? Telling off arrogant sprites trying to queue-jump at the portal? The occasional free ticket to the latest tragedy at the Cosmoplex?

'I think I might be sick,' she confessed as she clipped another quickdraw onto the rock face.

'*Please* don't be sick,' Tyron called from beneath her. 'Or if you *are* sick, maybe do it into your hat?'

Whatever Rowan had thought being a Librarian would be like, this was *not* it.

They had been climbing for twenty minutes now. Her forearms ached, her fingers had rope burn, and she was thirstier than a sap-sucking sea slug. The weather was also getting antsy.

It danced around them on the wall until a gust of hot dry air blew Rowan's scarf into her mouth and over her eyes.

'Aarft!' The sudden blindness made her wobble and her foot slip from its foothold. She grabbed hold of the wall and dug her fingernails painfully into the surface. Breathing hard, she heard a fragment of rock bounce off the side of the cliff.

PLOP! It dropped into the pool of lava that bubbled beneath them. Rowan sucked air in through her nose and squeezed her eyes shut.

'Eyes on the wall, Agent!' Tyron snapped. 'That rock almost hit my perm!'

The weather blew an apologetic gust of wind in Rowan's ear. 'Bleergh!' She spat scarf out of her mouth and shook her head so her hat beam cast its light wildly from side to side. She pulled on the rope and brought up another hand to feel for the jagged stone. Apparently, *this* was the kind of law-shirking madness that you got yourself into when you decided to have 'friends'.

'How much longer?' she shouted as she slid her foot up the rock to feel for the next foothold.

'How long is a cockatrice's digestive tract?' Tyron called back.
'I *meant* –'
'Endless, *potentially*, but often very short. Patience, Agent.'

Rowan scowled at the rock face. To reach here they had already army-crawled through bat-infested tunnels, scrambled along boulders and teetered along a bridge over an abyss (not the Abyss of Eternal Despair, though; Tyron had made that very clear). She *was* patient, but she was also now covered in bat poo. Surely they were almost at the surface?

Time was running out, and who knew how far Peregrine was ahead of them?

At last, she clambered up the last few handholds and, hauling herself onto the final ledge, lay flat on her back, staring upwards. There were the steps that Tyron had promised, carved into the rock. She could also just make out a wooden hatch at the top of the steps. She had never been so relieved to see the Terran Realm.

Getting her breath back, she rolled onto her front and risked a look down. Bad idea. The floor, which was actually lava, and which had seemed so far away, rushed towards her at such a speed that she collapsed back on the ledge, panting. Very, *very* bad idea.

The weather was playing with Rowan's hair, lifting up her curls and then letting them fall down. Up then down, up then down.

'Stop that!' Rowan waved her hands over her head.

'Ooft.' Tyron's hands appeared over the edge. Rowan went to help him. 'No, no, I can do this by myself,' he said as he got one knee onto the ledge.

In what was probably an attempt to be helpful, the weather swirled into a gust of wind under Tyron's backside and pushed.

'I am FINE!' he snarled. The weather whistled in response, then pushed again. 'Really!' Tyron huffed. Finally with both feet over the ledge, he stood up and tossed his curly hair back and forth, as if it was, well, a mane. 'You bipeds.' He looked at his chipped manicure, then turned his hands over to peer at the blisters on his palms. 'Seriously, you call this evolution? Ridiculous!'

The weather had retreated to somewhere above Rowan's

head, where an irritated FlutterBug was clicking at it. Before the weather could try to help *her*, Rowan sat up and peered into the surrounding gloom. 'Why do you live here again?' She waved her arms around to indicate the darkness. The beautiful orange moss-light of the lower levels was gone, and above them was just rock, damp and probably more bats.

'Lots of reasons . . .' Tyron looked away and began to pull up the rope. 'For one, no one tells me what to do. *Usually.*'

Rowan decided to ignore that last comment. 'You wouldn't rather be in the Cosmic Realm? On Olympus with all the other centaurs? I'm sure Inspector Sibyll could arrange something, maybe even get you an interview for a teaching post at the Academy –'

Tyron looped the rope noisily around his forearm. 'Nope.'

Rowan narrowed her eyes. 'You'd rather live in a *cave* than on Olympus?' She didn't buy it. 'Centaur droppings!'

'I beg your pardon?' Tyron looked genuinely shocked.

The weather blew a long, low whistle and Rowan mumbled an apology.

'Please stop this nonsense, Agent.' Tyron looked as if he might say something else, but instead dropped his gaze, and the rope, to the floor. An awkward silence poured over the conversation like wet cement.

Hesitating for just a moment, Rowan unclipped her Academy pin. The golden apple glinted like a winking eye in the murky light. Before she could think about it too much, she grabbed Tyron's wrist and pressed it into his palm.

'Why are you giving me *this*?' Tyron turned it over then looked at her. His eyes – the only things that a GlamPass couldn't change – were a dark brown with scraps of green, like algae floating on the surface of a pond.

Rowan shrugged. 'If the portals ever open again, show the Librarian on duty that –' she pointed towards the pin – 'and they should let you through.'

Tyron whinnied and tried to put the pin back in her hand.

Rowan put her hands up. 'Just for a visit,' she said quickly.

'Not likely,' the centaur huffed.

Rowan rolled her eyes. 'Whatever.' She turned to climb the carved steps that led upwards towards the light, towards the Terran Realm. A gentle breeze lifted her hair and Rowan turned to see Tyron just behind her, the shiny apple pinned to his blouse.

'Stay here,' he muttered, presumably to the weather. 'I'll be back before you can say "Olympus scum".'

Rowan sighed, and the weather, which couldn't really *say* anything, whistled.

When they finally reached the simple wooden hatch, Rowan hesitated. She pressed her hand against the wooden planks, inhaled and closed her eyes. Time to take stock of the situation. One, she had enlisted the help of a lost fugitive. Two, the place that she and said fugitive were going into was about to be blown up. And three, all of the above were in direct opposition to orders she'd received from Olympus, from Captain Hansel Pine *himself*, no less. Rowan exhaled. Well, as long as that was clear, there was no going back now.

'Problem, Agent?' Tyron whispered.

'Oh no, no problem,' Rowan lied as she pushed up the wooden hatch and poked her hat out. No problem at all.

What she saw was a room filled with camel-coloured cardboard boxes. She breathed in slowly through her ultra-sensitive nymph nose. She could detect around seventeen species of dust mite, eighty-three kinds of paper, a controlled moisture level and old coffee grounds. A warm, fuzzy feeling welled up inside her. She would know those smells anywhere. This was a *library*.

She switched her hat-light off. She didn't need it. The glaring electric strip lighting was burning her eyes after the tunnel's gloom.

'What do you see?' Tyron whispered. 'Are we in time? Has Olympus decimated knowledge once more with its mighty fist, leaving nothing but splinters, ashes and despair?'

'Well . . .' Rowan pulled her CosGogs up. 'The basement is still here . . .'

'Oh, phew!' Tyron tapped Rowan's boot. 'In that case, hurry *up*, Agent!'

'OK, OK!' She blinked once, switching to the CosGogs thermal-imaging function. 'No hostiles detected.' She grabbed hold of the sides of the hatch and belly-flopped onto the library floor. Sliding to a sitting position, she took *The Librarian's Handbook* from her jumpsuit pocket. She flicked to 'Standard Library Layouts'. Of course there was no mention of Alexandria.

Tyron hauled himself through the hatch, then walked over to a stack of boxes and placed a hand on it reverentially.

'What is it?' Rowan looked up from *The Handbook*.

'It's just . . . it's just good to be back here again. That's all.' His voice cracked with emotion. 'Let me see, now.' He strode four paces one way and three the other. He licked a finger and traced a circle in the air.

'Do you know where you're going?' Rowan asked tentatively. She didn't want to undermine the centaur. This was *Tyron* – the famous Librarian, the *first* Librarian! But this was also the centaur that she had met wearing a filthy Hawaiian shirt, talking to a bat and scribbling forgotten sonnets onto a cave wall. They didn't have time enough to walk around in circles. Not with the Thunderbolt just twenty minutes away.

'It says here –' she read out from *The Handbook* – 'that the portals were traditionally housed in the south-westerly wings.'

'Uh-huh.' Tyron nodded. 'It's all changed, *obviously*, but I know my library.' He stamped the floor, then walked over to a wall and pressed his ear against it. 'Yes, the portal is this way.' He pointed over Rowan's shoulder.

'You're sure?' she asked.

'As sure as a queue at the Bacchus Bar on a Friday!'

Rowan nodded. 'OK then.' Hoping that the famous Cosmic watering hole was at least as popular in Tyron's time as it was in hers, she snapped *The Handbook* shut and put it back in her pocket.

'There is no way Olympus would have let a library be built over the portal without having a hand in the planning.' He lowered his voice. 'They have agents *everywhere*.'

Rowan looked at him blankly. 'I know.' She pointed to her hat. 'I'm one of them. And so were *you* once, remember?'

'This way!' Tyron walked past her.

Rowan sighed and stood up. Even as a biped, Tyron walked surprisingly fast.

35

PEREGRINE

Location: Archive Room Four, the Basement, Bibliotheca Alexandrina, Alexandria, Egypt

A sound like the beating of a hummingbird's wing throbbed in Peregrine's ears.

Hummmmm. Hum. Hummmmm.

'Ooft!' Stan grunted as he shifted Peregrine to his other shoulder. 'Next time YOU are carrying the hostage.'

'Stop complaining!' Earl snapped. 'She's sedated, isn't she?'

No, actually. Peregrine was not sedated. She was awake. And she was very, *very* angry.

Her muscles twitched. She wanted to scream, roll off Stan's shoulder and let out some serious Penelope-Quinn-inspired fury on these lizard men. There were, however, a number of factors that stopped her from doing this. One, she had no idea where she was. Two, she had no idea where she was going. And three, there was Mum's very strict policy on unnecessary violence born from anger. Although Peregrine was 98 per cent sure that she would have made an exception in this particular case.

'That bag we put over her head was drenched in HypnoTek. She'll be out for hours yet.' Earl laughed coldly. 'Fragile Terran female.'

HypnoTek? Clearly some kind of Cosmic sedative, but what did he say? Hours? How long had she been passed out for? The Thunderbolt could be here any minute!

Trying not to move her nostrils, Peregrine took in a thin, measured breath. The air was different. It was musty and a little damp, but clearer somehow. They must be back in the Terran Realm.

There was a knock, the creak of a door opening and some shuffling. 'She'sss not here yet,' Stan muttered.

'She WILL be here!' Earl's voice shook slightly.

Who was *she*? Perhaps the voice that had chased her in the tunnels? Earl sounded afraid, and anything that made a six-foot lizard man quake must be something very fearsome indeed. Even the memory of that voice sent a chill shuddering down Peregrine's spine: *Chaos is creeping out of her pit . . .*

She tried to calm the pounding in her chest, just in case Stan could feel her heart thudding against his shoulder.

'What do we do with the girl in the meantime?' Stan swapped Peregrine onto his other shoulder. She kept her limbs loose so she bounced up and down like a ragdoll.

'Throw her in with the old man, I guess.' Earl sounded distracted.

Old man? Did they mean Daedalus? They must be in the

library then. Peregrine opened her eyes the tiniest fraction and peered through her lashes. Everything was cast in a strange green pulsing light.

From her vantage point over Stan's shoulder, she could see his lizard tail swishing back and forth beneath her. She watched it for a second but the movement mixed with the pulsing light made her feel queasy.

She slid her gaze to the left. She was in a large storage room with books and beige boxes everywhere – they must be the source of the musty smell. The boxes were piled precariously high against the wall, as if they had once been organised but had been pushed out of the way to make room for something.

She slid her gaze to the right.

Oh. To make room for something like *that*.

Peregrine's stomach lurched like she was back in the AquaPod. So *this* was what a portal looked like.

On the right side of the room was an enormous crack in the floor, like a split in the ice of a frozen lake. From there, vines pulsing with that same green light spilled out onto the library floor, interwoven with wires crackling with purple electricity. Some of the thicker vines had been pulled out and wrapped around a metallic oval framework that was attached to the wall, and some had been connected to computer screens.

Realisation flooded through Peregrine. The portals were *plants*. No wonder Daedalus had been so concerned about Bernadette – Bernadette was a portal! Another wave, this one of shame, crashed through her. Why hadn't she realised that sooner? And how had Rowan – who apparently knew *everything* – not known what Bernadette truly was?

She took another shallow breath. The portal's surface looked a bit like a mirror, with its shining metal frame and green light rippling over its surface. If she managed to free herself now, could she get to the portal? Destroy the gateway before it was too late – before Discord came through? She looked again at the iridescent surface and the delicate, light-filled tendrils of the plant. It was so beautiful! How could she even *think* of destroying something so precious? So . . . alive?

She was distracted by movement on the screens. It looked like CCTV footage from security cameras. There were half a dozen screens showing different rooms: some showed people sitting at desks and reading, one showed the library entrance, and one showed the busy street outside with food vendors, locals and tourists going about their day, not knowing the chaos that was unfolding beneath their feet.

'*The first and last* . . .' The whistled notes fluttered to Peregrine's ears. Emotion welled up in her chest and tears pressed behind her eyes, threatening to spill out. Daedalus!

'Look what we have for you!' Earl crowed. 'Your *apprentice*.' He snorted and Stan rolled Peregrine off his shoulder, depositing her on the ground with a thud.

'What do you think, Grand Architect?' Stan snorted. 'Is this part of your *grand* plan?' He prodded Peregrine with his foot.

'*Former* Grand Architect,' Daedalus corrected him. 'And no, not quite.' There was a pause. Peregrine could hear Daedalus taking a very deep breath. 'But it is very good to see her, I must admit. Oh, and all limbs intact! That is excellent! I gather you have had quite an adventure?' His voice sounded croaky and thin, but he was alive. He was *alive*.

The corner of Peregrine's mouth twitched.

'She can't *hear* you, old man.' Earl sounded bored. 'We gave her a double dose of HypnoTek. Terran skin soaks that stuff up.'

From her vantage point, lying with her cheek to the ground, Peregrine couldn't see Daedalus. But she *could* see Earl, and he was placing her rucksack in the corner of the room, close to the portal. Bernadette must still be in there.

Daedalus coughed. 'Even so. I am curious – how did two such upstanding members of the BogBrethren end up in this mess? Do you *really* want Discord to return? You remember all the devastation and suffering she caused.'

Stan hissed at the mention of Discord's name, and lowered his voice to a sinister whisper. 'She will burn the edgesss of the realmss.'

A chill crackled down Peregrine's spine.

'When she triumphs, there will be no high and mighty Cosmics ruling from the Mountain while we *lower immortals* ssslosh about in filth.' Earl spat the last word. 'With no one guarding the portals, we'll be able to go wherever we want, when we want.'

'Filth?' Daedalus sounded curious.

'Sewage Detail,' Earl snapped. 'It was punishment. For a *paltry* crime –'

'We stole Heliosss's chariot,' Stan said excitedly. 'It was shiny.'

'I don't doubt,' Daedalus mused. 'How fast did it go?'

'Want to see a holo-pic?' Stan was patting his pockets. 'That thing can go zero to forty Coseks in 2.4 ssseconds –'

'Enough!' Earl roared, and Stan froze mid-pat.

Peregrine closed her eyes again.

'Hmm.' She heard Stan hiss near her face. 'I think I want another trophy,' he mused. 'Do you think the bosss would mind if I took an ear? She doesssn't need *two*.' She heard him patting his jacket again, this time probably looking for an ear-removing tool.

'Time to get moving, don't you think?' Peregrine heard Daedalus whisper. *'Tempus fugit.'*

Was he talking to her?

'What?' Earl snapped. 'What did you say?'

'Tempus fugit,' Daedalus said again, this time louder. 'It's Latin. It means TIME FLIES.'

Peregrine scrambled upwards and spun her head. Her vision was still blurry at the edges, so she had to look twice to make sure that Daedalus was indeed floating off the library floor. He was, and he was wrapped in the same ropes of purple mist that she'd seen at the shop. He was spinning slowly.

'In you a precious gift we find.' Daedalus nodded and looked pointedly towards the rucksack in the corner.

'How . . . ?' Earl's eyes widened. Then he shook his head, as if remembering his own rule: shoot first, ask questions later. 'Stan! Get her!' Earl sprinted towards Peregrine, but she had already rolled sideways – a classic somersault, nothing fancy – and skidded towards her rucksack.

Before she could turn, Stan grabbed her foot. A jolt of pain shot through her ankle. She kicked out, flailing her legs like a mermaid's tail, hoping to shake him off, but his grip was vice-tight.

'Gotcha!' he sneered, his puffy reptilian eyes narrowing.

Peregrine smiled grimly, grabbed his forearm and – using it to yank herself forward – bit down on Stan's hand. Hard.

'Well done, dear!' Daedalus whooped at the same time as Stan yowled in pain. He snatched his hand back and clutched it to his chest. 'She BIT me!' he wailed.

'SO?' Earl screeched. 'She's a child, not a *Rottweiler*. Get her!'

Peregrine grabbed her rucksack and jumped over Stan's tail. Before Earl could spin around, she had made it to the portal. The humming sound throbbed in her ears.

She pulled the rucksack onto her back and, breathing hard, grabbed the nearest of the wires that were wrapped around the vines and held it in both hands. 'Let Daedalus go, or I *will* destroy this.' A purple crackle burned her fingers, but she did not let go.

Daedalus sucked in his breath.

Earl took his laser blaster from inside his jacket. 'No need to do anything *rash*, kid.'

'Rash?' Stan looked at his arms, panicked. 'Where?'

Peregrine gave the wires a yank. They fizzed under her fingers. 'LET HIM GO!'

Earl slunk onto his belly and slithered over to the right. 'Give up, kid.'

'How many wires do you think I need to break to stop the power getting to this portal?' Peregrine yanked another lead out. 'One?'

'Peregrine . . .' It was Daedalus, his voice loaded with warning.

'Two? Or –'

The humming sound was louder now, and getting louder still. Stan and Earl stepped back, apparently too frightened to get any closer to the portal.

'Peregrine, watch –' There was a low crackle and a finger of mist wrapped itself over Daedalus's mouth before he could finish his sentence.

Peregrine spun around and was immediately thrown backwards by a wall of purple light. 'Aargh!' Something in her ankle popped. The pain was instant and enormous.

Sip. Sip.

Holding back a sob, Peregrine looked up.

A woman dressed in a purple silk lab coat was standing in front of the portal, holding a porcelain teacup and saucer. She dipped the cup in Peregrine's direction. 'Daedalus's *other* apprentice, I presume?'

36

PEREGRINE

Location: Archive Room Four, the Basement, Bibliotheca Alexandrina, Alexandria, Egypt

Other apprentice? Emotions exploded within Peregrine like multicoloured fireworks. Pink, anger. Red, pain. Green, was that . . . jealousy?

The woman cocked her head to the side and peered at Peregrine, who was still lying crumpled on the ground. 'What are you *doing* here, Peregrine?' She sighed, her raven-black fringe slicing through the air as she shook her head. 'This is not your story.'

That *voice*. It was her, she was sure of it.

'You!' Peregrine scooted back on her bum. 'You're the one that sent the mist after me!'

A dead-eyed smile stretched across the woman's beautiful face. 'Hekate. Heh-Car-Tea.' The woman tipped the teacup towards Peregrine in greeting. 'Fourteenth Grand Architect of the Cosmic Realm. Nice to meet you.'

'No.' Peregrine clenched her fists. 'It isn't.'

Hekate shrugged. 'Hmm.' Her cherry-coloured lips twitched upwards at the corners. 'Given the circumstances, I suppose not.' She raised her eyebrows. 'I am *impressed* by you though, Peregrine. I never thought you'd actually make it here.' She took a sip of tea.

Peregrine scrambled to her feet and leaned her back against the wall, wincing at the pain. Her ankle must be fractured. She glanced behind her to Stan and Earl, who were still patrolling the perimeter. 'How did you even get here? The portals are shut!' Peregrine glared at Hekate accusingly.

Hekate's fancy lab coat rippled as she laughed. 'Who do you think shut them, darling?' She shrugged. 'I had to. I needed all of that delicious power to help fuel my little project here.' The portal behind her crackled in response. 'Plus, it stopped those pesky CSI agents messing with my plans. Well, most of them anyway.'

Rowan. She was talking about Rowan.

'Not all of us *need* portals to travel between realms, but they are a tad more reliable.' Hekate sighed and put her lipstick-smeared teacup down on top of a pile of boxes. 'Which brings me to my point.' She slid her glasses onto the top of her head and pulled a pin from her bun. 'You have something I need.' She let the pin sit casually in her hand like a long cigarette. '*Portalis majoris*. That little plant you've been carrying around with you. I'd *so* like to see it.' She said this lightly, but her eyes glinted with malice.

Peregrine's gaze flicked from Hekate's eyes to her thin smile, and finally to the deadly-looking pin. It glinted gold in the crackling light, and a thin wisp of acid-green smoke spiralled from its sharp point.

Hekate saw where she was looking and smiled. 'You're smart to be worried, Peregrine. One scratch from this will petrify your nervous system.' She flashed her pristine teeth, which glowed yellow in the pulsing green light. 'My own invention – a forty–sixty ratio of man-of-war and rattlesnake venom, with just a dash of porcupine and a sprinkling of nightshade.' Her eyes glittered. '*Eventually* deadly, but gloriously painful first. What do you kids say nowadays? FYI.'

Peregrine felt GrumBug buzz angrily against her chest, trying to get out. 'Hush.' She put her hand over her pocket, attempting to calm the frantic CosBug. 'It's OK.'

The bug was not listening. It had clearly sensed danger, and with a desperate burst of energy it shot out from between her fingers and whirred lopsidedly towards Hekate, buzzing with anger.

Peregrine saw a blurred arc of gold, and then GrumBug was on the floor, twitching. 'No!' she screamed. 'GrumBug!' Peregrine reached forward.

'Ah, ah, ah,' Hekate taunted. She shook her head, her fringe swishing as she pointed the same pin at Peregrine.

Peregrine watched, frozen in horror, as Hekate lifted her boot and stamped it down, crushing the twitching CosBug beneath her heel.

A sob bubbled in Peregrine's throat, a sob that erupted into a roar. 'You . . . you monster!'

'Oh, please.' Hekate used the pointed toe of her purple leather boot to kick the CosBug's crumpled body aside. 'I recognise a scrap of Nimhue's tat when I see one. Hardly worth the CosDust it's forged with.'

Tears streamed down Peregrine's cheeks.

'Don't cry, dear,' Hekate said flatly. 'There really is very little point.'

Peregrine scrubbed at her eyes – the tears were getting in the way of her vision – then turned her gaze from Hekate to stare at the portal gateway. The rippling, iridescent surface was becoming more and more opaque by the second.

There was also something moving behind it.

'Er, boss?' Stan had his head bowed. Peregrine had almost forgotten that he and Earl were there.

'What?' Hekate didn't take her eyes from Peregrine, but shifted her head to the side with a sickening crack.

'You might want to look at this.' Stan tapped one of the computer screens.

Peregrine gasped. Rowan and another woman were creeping through another library room lined with boxes. Peregrine's heart leapt to see the dryad. She'd followed her, even though it meant going against direct orders. But now she was here, just minutes before the Thunderbolt was due. Peregrine's leaping heart plummeted down, down, down.

'We have visssitorsss,' Earl hissed.

'How wonderful!' Hekate swung her hairpin towards the screen. She clearly didn't need it as an actual *pin*; not a hair moved out of place from her super-tight bun. 'I have this under control, gentlemen. I think you had better go deal with our guests.'

'Ha, guests.' Stan chuckled pointlessly.

Peregrine watched them take their laser blasters and slink towards the door. Before reaching it, Earl turned, bowed, then tripped over Stan's tail.

She had to warn Rowan! Peregrine's gaze darted around the room: to the portal, to Daedalus, then back to the screen.

'*THUNDERBOLT LAUNCHED,*' a perky computer voice chirped.

'Goodness me, is that the time?' Hekate tucked the pin behind her ear and plucked a shiny purple CosPad from inside her lab coat. 'This wasn't in the initial plan, of course.' She clicked a button. 'Olympus wasn't supposed to know about the portal until it was too late, but –' she put the CosPad in her coat pocket – 'preparation is everything.'

There was a metallic clang, and the whole room was temporarily flooded with purple light.

'What ... what's happening?' Peregrine's gaze darted around the room.

'I made some modifications to the library, just in case. Titanium shielding, with a little magical reinforcement.' Hekate clapped her hands, apparently delighted at her own cleverness. 'We don't want pesky Olympus getting in the way of our welcome party now, do we? Don't worry, we're quite safe. I couldn't risk the portal being buried a *second* time.' She nodded towards the computer screen, where Rowan was edging forward along a corridor.

Moving closer to her teeth. Peregrine pushed her nails into her palms.

'I can't say the same for your friends, though,' Hekate purred.

Peregrine's insides burned. Her brain whirred as she tried to think what to do. Hekate must have some kind of control over the Thunderbolt – maybe Peregrine could get hold of her CosPad?

'The Thunderbolt will destroy the library!' Peregrine took a step forward towards her. 'Y-you could stop it!'

'Probably. But why?' Hekate looked genuinely confused. 'Better that Olympus *think* that they've stopped us, surely? That way it will be a surprise when my mistress returns to destroy the Mountain. Don't you just LOVE surprises?'

Peregrine did usually love surprises, just not evil ones. 'Your mistress – you mean Discord?'

'Don't you *dare* speak her name!' Hekate's eyes flashed. 'She is an Old One.' Her voice rose. '*She* was first. Before the *realms*, before the worlds were split, this was ALL hers. Everything was built on her domain. On the void.' She coughed, and smoothed down the lapels of her lab coat.

'Hmm.' Hekate pulled the pin from behind her ear and spun it around her fingers. She was peering at Peregrine as if she was a cat and Peregrine was a small bird and she was wondering whether to play with her or simply just bite her head off. Hekate stretched her fingers so the joints clicked.

A crackle from the portal made them turn. The portal's surface was almost solid now. The shadow that Peregrine had seen lurking behind the ripples was closer, its form more tangible. For one terrifying moment, she thought she saw a pair of glittering eyes. Peregrine's heart beat so fast it threatened to burst through her chest. She ripped her gaze from the surface to look back at Hekate, who was clutching a red ruby-like crystal to her chest.

'*Eris rises!* She is here!' A look of something like peace passed across Hekate's face. She snapped her head towards Peregrine. 'Now, little apprentice, where were we? Oh yes, you were going to give me that plant.'

37

ROWAN

Location: The Basement, Bibliotheca Alexandrina, Alexandria, Egypt

Tyron marched purposefully towards the end of the corridor and then, without pausing, turned sharply right and then left. Rowan jogged to catch up with him.

'So what's the plan, Agent?' Tyron said, swinging his arms for extra speed.

'Plan?' She was already out of breath.

'Yes, your *plan of action*,' Tyron repeated.

'Ah, well . . .' Of course she *had* a plan. Rowan did a quick time check. Seven minutes. They'd have to be rocket-fast, but they might just have enough time to find Peregrine and drag her back down into the Under Realm tunnel. Maybe.

'You of course remember the three checks for entering a hostile environment?' Tyron prompted.

Rowan nodded. As they wound through the maze of basement corridors, she counted on her fingers. 'Check One, is this really necessary?'

Tyron whinnied. 'A chaos goddess is going to break through from the Fourth Realm and bring with her unending devastation and death!'

'So . . . ?'

'So yes, Agent. I think we can tick that one off.' Tyron rolled his eyes.

She nodded. 'Yes, of course. OK, Check Two – use all available tools.'

Tyron tapped his chin. 'We *are* a little low on weaponry. Very odd that Nim didn't kit you out more. Very odd indeed. Maybe her Hero Support Services aren't what they once were?'

Rowan coughed. 'Yep, um, no weapons. Weird that. And Check Three . . .' She spoke a little faster. 'Expect the un—'

They turned the corner and were faced with two grinning BogBrethren. One had a supervisor tag, the other a cloth hat, and they both carried HekTek laser blasters.

'. . . expected.' Rowan gulped.

'*Sprite.*' The shorter, squatter of the lizard men licked his lips. She recognised the hat he was wearing. It was *Stan.* So the other, taller one must be Earl. They both had the Olympic insignia embroidered on their boiler suits.

Rowan glared. 'I told you, I'm *not* a –'

'We've got your little friend,' Earl hissed.

Her friend? Rowan gasped. They must mean Peregrine.

'Yeah, the one with the sharp teeth!' Stan flexed his webbed fingers. Rowan could see what looked like molar marks around his swollen left index digit.

'And you thought you could beat us? Beat *her*?' Earl shook his head. 'You're too late. She's almost here!'

Tyron edged closer to Rowan. 'Use *all* available tools,' he whispered. He then turned to the thugs and started to swing his handbag around in a circle, faster and faster, like it was a slingshot.

Rowan was edging backwards. 'Um, Tyron, they've got *laser blasters* . . .'

Tyron wasn't listening. 'AARGH!' Screaming, and still swinging his handbag, he ran past her like a harpy out of hell.

Before Stan could even lift his weapon, Tyron was inches from the lizard and whacking him full in the face with his handbag. After several moments of trying to fend off the angry centaur-in-human-form with his fists, a confused Stan stepped back. His confusion only lasted for a few seconds, however; then, roaring like a bear being buzzed at by a fly, Stan turned and thwacked Tyron with his lizard tail. Something snapped.

Rowan winced as Tyron doubled over, obviously winded. When he looked up, he was grinning. He had something in his hand.

In thwacking him with his tail, Stan had inadvertently snapped Tyron's GlamPass. The change was instantaneous. Perm, blouse and pencil skirt gone, Tyron shook out his shaggy mane and stomped his very heavy, very horsey hooves. He whinnied and reared up on his hind legs.

Stan backed away down the corridor. 'This is mad,' he muttered. 'Completely mad!'

'Think you can come waltzing into my library, do you?'

Tyron growled. 'Tell me – do you even have a library card? DO YOU?'

Earl turned towards Rowan. She backed away. With Tyron busy, she was helpless; a small, frightened mouse in front of a hungry lion. He slunk towards her, his laser blaster pointed at her head. 'Time's up, girlie.' He grinned, showing his back fangs. 'At least I get to shoot *one* of you.'

Rowan looked around frantically for something to use. *She* didn't have a handbag! Or hooves! Why had she said no to Nim's weapons? All she had was her hat. She reached up and touched the brim.

All she had was her HAT.

She clicked the button and a three-hundred CosWatt high-beam blazed from the rim, straight into Earl's face.

'Argh!' He staggered back two steps and threw his arm over his eyes. At the same time, he fired his laser blaster. A purple ray of deadly unaimed laser light shot out and seared a smouldering arc in the ceiling. Another hit a stack of cardboard boxes and set them instantly ablaze.

Rowan watched in horror as another box caught fire. She put her hands to her cheeks, which she could tell were going green from the heat. Dryads had a deep-seated fear of fire; it was the tree in them. 'Tyron, the library!' she wailed. 'We'll be trapped!'

Red-hot flames climbed hungrily towards the ceiling. The first pile of boxes crashed onto another and soon a whole wave of them had caught alight, sending thick dark smoke billowing along the corridor.

Rowan saw the whites of Tyron's eyes as he turned from

a battered-looking Stan and looked towards the flames. 'My library!' he cried.

Earl had recovered from his temporary blinding and was now about as angry as a wasp trapped in a curtain. 'That's it!' He pointed the laser blaster at Rowan. 'Time's *really* up!'

Rowan squeezed her eyes shut and prayed.

38

PEREGRINE

**Location: Portal One, Archive Room Four, the Basement,
Bibliotheca Alexandrina, Alexandria, Egypt**

'THUNDERBOLT DETONATION: T-MINUS TWO MINUTES,' a peppy computer voice sang out.

Peregrine's gaze flicked to the screen. She watched in horror as Stan spun, using his tail to hurl the woman backwards. Earl raised his blaster at Rowan.

A swell of molten rage surged inside Peregrine. She shot towards Hekate like lava from an erupting volcano. 'Aargh!'

'No.' Hekate held up a hand, the other still waving her hairpin.

Peregrine froze. Literally. She tried to move her fingers . . . nothing. She tried to move her head. That didn't work either, but she found she *could* move her eyeballs. She glanced down at her feet. They had disappeared – or rather, a swirling whirlpool of mist had risen up to swallow them, shielding them from view. She tried to move them but her legs were well and truly stuck, held fast in what felt like hardened concrete.

'Well, this chat has been *lovely*.' Hekate extended the last word. 'But sadly I am under a teeny, tiny bit of time pressure.' She tapped the crystal at her throat and walked towards Peregrine, stepping delicately over the snaking vines that wound across the floor. 'There is a very small window in time where my mistress can come back through the portal.' She pinched her fingers together to indicate just how small this window was. 'And it is getting smaller.'

Peregrine tried to take a deep breath, but even her chest wouldn't move, so instead her breath puffed out in short, shallow bursts. She looked at Daedalus, still suspended in mist. If he had told her why he was checking the Oxford portal, would they still be here? Him trapped and her . . . stuck?

Hekate spun her hairpin once more in her hand, then speared her bun with it. 'Daedalus didn't think anybody else would know about it, of course.' She rolled her eyes, then reached out and grabbed Peregrine's chin. 'Or rather, *should* know about it.'

Peregrine felt the sting of sharp fingernails as Hekate turned her chin so she was forced to face her. 'You must *know*, Peregrine –' Hekate cocked her head to the side – 'how annoying it is to be constantly underestimated.' She released Peregrine's chin and sighed. 'Such hubris! Such arrogance! Of course *I* knew! *I* was taught by a goddess! A TRUE Cosmic! I know the *old* magic.' Her eyes glinted as she reached around Peregrine towards her rucksack. The red crystal swung from its thin chain and pressed painfully into Peregrine's shoulder.

Peregrine tried to move, to kick, to bite, to do *anything*, but all she could do was roll her eyes in alarm like a frightened cornered animal.

Hekate sneered. 'I had everything planned perfectly.' She tugged at the rucksack. 'The right year . . .' Tug. 'The right stars . . .' Tug. 'The right spells.' She pulled the rucksack off Peregrine's back and held it, victorious, in her hand. 'We waited *centuries*. But still the portal refused to open. "Why *is* that?" I thought. And then *you* kindly brought me my answer!' Hekate unzipped the bag and pulled out Bernadette. 'And here we are!'

Bernadette squeaked loudly.

'Oh, hush, hush!' Hekate crooned. She wrapped her fingers around the shaking plant. 'You, my dear –' she stroked the shaking leaves – 'are the key to an older, better world!'

Bernadette reached out towards Peregrine, but there was nothing she could do. Something very deep, and very dark, twanged in Peregrine's heart as she watched from her bonds of mist, helpless. She couldn't take it. 'Please –' she began.

'It is time.' Hekate smiled a thin, cold smile, then wrenched Bernadette out of their pot.

Peregrine wished more than anything that she could put her hands over her ears as Bernadette let out a heart-rending shriek. *No!*

Still smiling, and clutching Bernadette in one hand, Hekate held the turquoise terracotta pot in the other. She opened her long, delicate fingers and let it drop. Star-spangled ceramic shards flew across the floor, scattering dirt everywhere. Peregrine's breath became faster and even more ragged. If only she could *move*!

Fingers tight around Bernadette's stem, Hekate turned and marched towards the portal, crushing the pottery noisily beneath her leather boots.

Afraid of what she might see there, Peregrine looked towards the portal. The surface had crystallised and the shadow behind writhed and turned. Within the shadow, two coals that might have been eyes flashed a searing red. As Peregrine watched, the shadow retreated – and then *BAM*. The shadow threw itself against the surface. The humming of the portal became quiet and in its stead a new sound arose. It was a buzzing, as if a swarm of angry wasps were amassing.

'THUNDERBOLT DETONATION: *T-MINUS ONE MINUTE,*' the computer trilled.

Once again Peregrine wrenched her gaze away from the creature emerging from the portal and scanned the computer screens for signs of Rowan. She was there, now surrounded by fire. Was the library *burning*?

Run! Peregrine wanted to scream at the screen. *You need to run!*

'*T-MINUS THIRTY SECONDS.*'

What am I going to do? Peregrine turned to stare at her godfather, wrapped in mist. *Help, please.* She tried to push the words towards him with her mind. *What do I do?*

'*NINE. EIGHT.*'

Daedalus snapped his eyes open. Peregrine's rapid breathing stopped, caught in her chest.

'*FIVE. FOUR.*'

He smiled, his eyes crinkling.

'*THREE. TWO.*'

He nodded.

'ONE.'

The whole room shook. And just like that, Stan, Earl, Rowan, the people out on the street drinking their coffee – all the moving images – disappeared, and were replaced with the black-and-white buzz of static.

39

CAL

**Location: Council Control Hub, Level Fourteen,
Olympus Inc., the Mountain
CosDate: 300.23.241**

Panic.

That is what every fibre of Cal's half-goat body told him he should do. First, panic. Then, when panic had been suitably established, run. Or, if running felt too dynamic a response, hide somewhere and cower.

Cal took another long, deep breath and stared at the console. Unfortunately, none of those preferred actions were options right now. They had six minutes until the Thunderbolts landed in Alexandria, and panicking would take up at least four of those minutes. Maybe five.

How had *he* – scared, sweaty Callimachus – ended up in this situation?

Following Daedalus's instructions, Cal had so far successfully broken through the HekTek firewall and isolated the three Thunderbolts. Holo-pics of them hovered over the console, spinning slowly. Three of the deadliest weapons in all three realms, and they were heading straight for the library. One for Rowan, one for Daedalus and one for Pear-grinn.

Cal wiped his brow and wiggled his fingers over the console. The next step was to open the Thunderbolt control panel remotely. Cal gulped, and typed in a few lines of code.

'CONTROL PANEL ACCESSED.'

'Excellent, thank you,' he said to no one in particular.

'VOICE ACTIVATION NEEDED.'

'Flooharght!' He slapped his forehead.

'VOICE ACTIVATION NOT RECOGNISED.'

Cal bleated under his breath. Daedalus hadn't mentioned this. Voice activation? The red button pulsed on the console in front of him. This was the last step – he was *so* close. Maybe there was a voice recording from Hansel on his CosPad somewhere? Maybe a movie clip from CosTube? He might have the authority to authorise a deactivation.

BASH! Cal had just reached into his pocket when the door swung open.

Hansel had one arm slung over a laughing Admiral Prim's shoulder. In his other hand he held a bottle of St Elmo's Fire ale. When he saw Cal, he quickly hid the liquor behind his back. 'Scruffers!' he snarled. 'What are *you* doing here?'

Cal whirled around and threw his hands up in the air. 'Nothing –'

'What is going on?' Admiral Prim stepped forward, then saw

the holo-pics of the Thunderbolts. His mouth fell open. 'I don't believe it!' He took a further step towards the console. 'He's trying to deactivate the Thunderbolts!'

'Nothing . . . much,' Cal corrected, quietly.

'What? Scruffers? *Really?*' Hansel looked genuinely confused.

Admiral Prim pushed past Cal and began typing furiously into the computer. 'He's bypassed our security systems!'

'How?' Hansel put the ale down and rushed to the console. 'He's just a faun!' He turned towards Cal. 'Who helped you?'

Cal looked down at his hooves. Daedalus was counting on him; Rowan *needed* him. He couldn't fail them now.

'I don't know how far he got.' Admiral Prim was scanning the code on the screen. 'They still seem to be primed . . .'

'Who *helped* you?' Hansel repeated. 'Who is our security leak?'

'No one helped me,' Cal muttered.

Admiral Prim's gaze darted between Cal and the console. 'I will have you demoted, faun!' His face reddened. 'Three centuries in Sewage Detail! You will never work on the Mountain again!'

Hansel stepped towards Cal and sneered. 'You will go home in disgrace!'

Cal looked up from his hooves and stared at Hansel. What Hansel didn't know was that Cal's family would be more than happy for Cal to go home, in disgrace or otherwise. They actually weren't too pleased about him working on the Mountain in the first place.

No place for a faun, his mum had said. *No place at all!*

It had been Nanny Goat who had insisted that he follow

his dream to attend the Academy; Nanny who had packed him a lunch for his journey from the foothills; Nanny who had convinced Cal's mother to let him go. She'd even given him the dinars for the tram fare.

Cal stood up a little taller and straightened his cardigan. Nanny Goat would understand. He paused. What would *she* do in this situation?

A smile played on Cal's lips.

'I'd wipe that smile off your face if I were you, faun.' Hansel prodded Cal's chest. 'Because I am going to make your life *miserable*.'

'THUNDERBOLT DETONATION IN FOUR . . .'

'Enough!' The Admiral sighed. 'The missiles are on course. Whatever he was doing, he didn't finish.'

'IN THREE . . .'

What would Nanny do? Cal paused, then positioned his buttocks over the red voice-activation button. He turned to Admiral Prim. 'Oh, Admiral?'

'WHAT?' the Admiral yelled.

'VOICE ACTIVATION VERIFIED,' a computerised voice rang out.

'Bite me.' Cal spun and punched the button with his fist.

40

ROWAN

Location: The Basement, Bibliotheca Alexandrina, Alexandria, Egypt

A strange pulse of air, like a warm evening breeze fired out of a cannon, washed over Rowan. It made her ears crackle and her tongue fizz. This was *not* what she'd expected being shot with a laser blaster to feel like. She opened one eye.

Earl had a look of shock on his face. He pressed the trigger button of the laser blaster. Nothing. He pressed it again. Nothing.

Tyron was patting his torso, his apple pin still winking on his jacket. 'We're not dead?'

'Not yet!' Rowan ducked as another flaming cardboard box fell from the top of its pile. She moved slowly backwards until she was hat to shoulder with Tyron.

Befuddled by their faulty HekTek, Stan and Earl were also

edging backwards, but towards the corridor they had come from. Rowan squinted. She could just make out a pulsing green light behind them. That *must* be where Peregrine was.

'We need to follow them!' She tugged on Tyron's jacket sleeve. 'Come on!'

Earl gestured to Stan with his laser at a row of archive boxes leaning against the wall. It took a moment for Rowan to realise what they were doing.

'NO!' she yelled. But it was too late. Stan pushed over the boxes and stepped back, victorious. Acting as tinder to the roaring fire, the burning boxes created a wall of flame between Rowan and her route to help Peregrine and the portal.

Rowan shook her head in dismay. Smoke stung her eyes, but she kept them open to watch Earl's teeth glinting in the flickering light, before he turned and ran back down the corridor, followed grudgingly by Stan.

'This way is blocked too, Agent.' Tyron coughed, then neighed. 'Those scoundrels! They've left us here to be toasted!' He spun on his hooves. 'Come back and face me –' he shook his fist – 'lizard to horse!'

Rowan stopped listening and stared at the fire dancing in front of her. A bolt of dread shot through her dryad bones. Dryads do not make a habit of running towards flames, but this was an exception. Rowan gritted her teeth as she took a deep breath and crouched down. If going through a wall of fire was her only way to Peregrine, then through a wall of fire she would go.

She leapt towards the row of burning boxes.

Tyron grabbed hold of her shoulders, mid-leap. 'Don't be a

fool, Agent!' He pulled her back, away from the flames. 'You'll combust as fast as I can say –'

'Aargh!' Rowan screamed as she put her hand to her face. She had just felt something land on her cheek. Surely it was a burning spark, or a piece of red-hot ceiling tile crumbling down on her? She patted her cheek. Wait, it wasn't burning, it was . . . wet.

'Is that *rain?*' She looked up towards the basement ceiling and, as if in answer to her question, a bucketful of raindrops splattered on her face.

'*That* is weather!' cried Tyron, stomping his hooves excitedly.

'Oh!' Rowan turned just in time to see a gust of wind ripping through a pile of soggy, smoking boxes. The weather was racing to dump water on each area of the fire before pausing above Rowan and pouring another bucketful of water unceremoniously over her head.

Rowan looked down at her scorched uniform. 'Er –'

The weather was prodding her, as if scanning for missing limbs.

'Yes, yes, I'm OK.' She flapped her hands around herself.

Tyron trotted over. 'Now *that* was helpful!' He grinned.

In a matter of seconds, the weather had put out most of the flames and was now clearing the air with a swift cool breeze. Rowan gulped in the fresh air hungrily. The inside of her mouth still felt sandpaper-dry, but just as she was about to say something that might have been 'thank you', a piercing shriek made them both turn.

'To the portal!' Tyron bellowed as he charged down the corridor.

41

PEREGRINE

Peregrine stared at the fuzzing screens. She couldn't breathe, let alone talk. All of her rage was gone; she had nothing left. She felt flat, empty, hollowed out. What was the point? Rowan was gone, and Hekate had Bernadette. She hadn't been able to save them, any of them.

'Curious.' Hekate sounded distracted. 'No matter.'

A single tear trickled down Peregrine's cheek. She automatically went to brush it away. She didn't want Hekate to see her cry; she could at least keep her emotions safe. Her hand was halfway up to her face when she stopped and stared at her palm. She could *move*. The quake from the Thunderbolt must have distracted Hekate long enough for her to accidentally loosen the magic that was holding Peregrine!

Peregrine looked over to check whether Hekate had noticed. She needn't have worried. Hekate had hitched up her lab coat and was kneeling by the crack in the floor, completely absorbed in her task.

Nodding, as if she was agreeing with someone, Hekate pulled out some wires and wrapped them tightly around Bernadette's stem. The wires sparked and fizzed as green light poured through them and into the portal.

'Yes.' She breathed reverently. *'Eris rises.'*

There was a sound like the breaking of a car window, like the very air itself had been smashed. Peregrine stared as a thin crack appeared on the surface of the portal, about as wide and long as one of the hairs from her plaits. From the crack, a thick fog began to seep out.

'YES!' Hekate narrowed her eyes. 'We begin again!'

CRACK. Another fracture appeared across the portal surface. The red glowing eyes were closer now. Not animal, but human – or something like it – they swivelled manically around, taking in what they saw, searching for something. They stopped on Peregrine.

The air splintered once more as a high-pitched screech tore through the room. Thick dark mist erupted from the crack, like water from a geyser. The strands of mist began to twist and bind themselves together, forming pale, thin fingers.

Peregrine's mouth went dry. The fingers were trying to prise open the portal surface! Discord was almost here.

The wasp-like buzzing became louder, angrier, and even more grey fog slithered into the room, darting like the snakes of mist that had chased Peregrine through the tunnel.

They slid onto the floor, slithered up the piles of books and scurried along the walls.

Peregrine blinked, trying to peer through the murk. She could still see the glowing red eyes, sparking like lightning in the fog, but she couldn't see Hekate. She couldn't even see the portal.

'*More.*' A cold, hollow voice echoed through the room. '*I need more . . . power to break through.*'

'But the plant should be working.' Hekate's voice was strained, barely containing the panic that was tearing to get out. 'We've used *all* the old portal energy. W-why isn't the plant working?'

The snaky tendrils of smoke licked the ceiling, and then, as if reacting to an unspoken command, they rushed towards Peregrine – one hundred tiny grey hissing arrows. Peregrine flinched and sucked in a short, sharp breath through her nose. The smoky tendrils stopped just short of her body. They hovered there, wrapping her in a wall of grey.

'*The girl knows,*' the voice hissed. The mist swirled around Peregrine like an army of adders.

She shook her head. She didn't want to open her mouth in case the mist went down her throat.

The mist crackled again. '*Kill the Architect.*'

'No!' Peregrine yelled.

Wanting her to see what was about to happen, the mist created a window. Peregrine could now see Hekate and Daedalus – his eyes closed again, still trapped in those thick violet ropes of mist.

'Excellent.' Hekate grinned and pulled out her hairpin.

She held it in her hand, as if it were a scalpel, and stalked, eyes narrowed, towards Daedalus.

The mist wrapped itself around Peregrine's limbs, squeezing her like a python.

Hekate paused next to Daedalus. She held the pin high. 'Tell me, *Peregrine*,' she spat. 'Why isn't this plant activating? What do I need to do to open this portal?'

Before Peregrine could speak, Hekate's hand had sliced through the air and scratched Daedalus on the cheek. He convulsed as if he'd been electrocuted.

'*What* do I have to do to make it work?' Hekate tilted her head to the side. 'Hmm?'

'I don't –'

Hekate scratched Daedalus's other cheek. 'Well?'

He let out a low moan.

'It's a song!' Peregrine cried. She couldn't bear to hear that sound again, the sound of her godfather in pain.

'A song?' Hekate raised her eyebrows. 'Seriously?'

'Yes!' Peregrine nodded. Was Hekate waiting for an explanation? 'Daedalus is very interested in the propagation properties of lyrical melody. He actually wrote a paper on it for –'

'*Tempus fugit!*' the icy voice crackled through the mist.

Hekate raised her hairpin again.

'*Light and bright and airy thing,*' Peregrine began. '*Rarer than a fairy's wing . . .*' The tune was wistful, just as Daedalus sang it.

Bernadette's tendrils extended from her stem and wrapped themselves around the original portal vines that trailed along the floor.

'Bring your strength to grow your leaves.' With every green pulse, Bernadette's tendrils grew another few centimetres.

'Yes!' The cold voice rang with triumph. 'I WILL be free!'

Peregrine faltered as she saw an arm emerge through the crack in the portal's surface. The arm was bone-pale, glistening and wrapped in a cloak of mist.

Discord's fingers reached forward.

'It's working!' Hekate lowered the pin and, clutching the crystal at her throat, walked toward the portal, as if magnetised to this terrifying goddess.

'Through you, nature's power weaves.' Peregrine squeezed her eyes shut. *Remember, you were born for adventure, Peregrine Quinn.*

She remembered Daedalus, his fingers curled around his mug with the half-moon handle. *Remember, under no circumstances let Bernadette near fire, flame or electrical sparks.*

Let it . . . flicker?

Peregrine put her hands in her pockets, feeling for the magma moss. 'From stem to tip you glow and shine –' she sang louder – 'your roots the unknown magicks mine.' She wrapped her fingers around the moss and brought it out, hidden in her clenched fists. She raised her voice. 'The first and last of your wondrous kind . . .' She hoped this was the right thing to do. 'In you, a precious gift we find.'

She took a deep breath and began the new verse. 'Let it flicker, let it . . . die.' The words of the song propelled her forward as Peregrine pushed her way through the mist to the portal. She ducked to avoid Discord's grasping outstretched fingers.

One of the vines reached out and wrapped itself around her arm. Peregrine gasped, suddenly unsure, but the vine squeezed – not hard, but like a friend might squeeze your shoulder to let you know they were there. Tears pricked Peregrine's eyes, and she nodded.

'*For realms in earth, in sea and sky.*' Cautiously, she took hold of the portal vine in both hands and blew. Hard. Her hands heated up immediately, sparks glittering underneath her palms. A tingling sensation – more painful than the feeling of magic she had got used to – laced its way up her arms. Instantly the vine let go and she snatched her hands away, as flames erupted underneath them.

Hekate spun. 'What are you doing? Stop!'

Lines of red raced along the vine like lightning, and then, to Peregrine's surprise, the vine exploded in a shower of orange dust.

Another tendril reached forward and flicked a tear from Peregrine's cheek. She sniffed and kept on singing. '*This is a magic held by few.*' With clumps of moss still in her palms, she gripped the vine, inhaled and blew.

Just as before, flames crackled along the vine before it crumbled in her palms, leaving nothing but dust. Peregrine stepped back and looked up at the portal's surface. It was beginning to flicker and fade, and the arm that had been there just a moment before had disappeared.

Was Discord *retreating*? No. No, she wasn't. The smoke flashed red and – BAM. With a scream of fury, Discord threw herself against the portal's surface.

'Aargh!' Peregrine was knocked back by the shock. There was a hiss as more smoke escaped from the cracks, billowing into the room. Peregrine scrambled back and flattened herself against a pile of books, squeezing her eyes shut against the stinging smoke. This was too much for one person, one *mortal* person. What was she *thinking*?

Don't give up, darling. Just a little longer.

Breathing hard, Peregrine opened her eyes a fraction. The room was in chaos. Another vine reached out to her and Peregrine stretched out, letting the vine wrap itself around her arm. She stared at the glowing tendril. She *couldn't* give up, not now. The portal itself was fighting Discord, refusing to let her through, refusing to let itself be used. If the portal could do it, then she could too.

'*Prune it now, to grow anew.*' Taking another handful of moss, Peregrine leaned forward and blew. Flames once again erupted from the vine, and the orange dust scattered, sparkling into the air. Peregrine inhaled. It was working! The portal was shutting down.

Discord must have thought that too.

'*Kill her.*' The instruction echoed, cold and deadly, around the room. '*NOW.*'

Peregrine only had enough time to glance up and put her hands over her face before an arc of gold, wielded by Hekate, sliced through the air.

'Aargh!' Red-hot pain cut through her arm. She fell, and she would have smashed her skull on the side of the portal had a vine not caught her and lowered her to the ground. Blood seeped through her jumpsuit. Peregrine could see it dripping onto the floor beneath her. Her stomach lurched, and vomit rose in her throat.

Hekate was at the portal now, using her fingers to try to

prise open the cracks. 'Don't leave, mistress!' Hekate's voice splintered as her desperation poured out. 'I need more time!'

The portal vine squeezed Peregrine's shoulder and laid itself across her palms. *One more. Just one more.* She knew what she had to do. Peregrine held on to the vine, and blew. Red lines crackled and, as flames burst from its sides, the vine exploded into dust.

'Let it flicker, let it die.' Peregrine's voice was shaky. She had been right. Nim and Daedalus, they had *all* been right – the fire was destroying the portal.

THUMP. THUMP. The vines around the makeshift metal structure of the portal gateway were falling away, turning to dust as they hit the floor. One – *THUMP* – by one.

A thought suddenly seized Peregrine, a vivid, green thought: Bernadette! Had they been caught in the fire? Peregrine could feel the poison from the hairpin taking hold, but she pushed one palm, then the other, down on the floor to pull herself forward in a crawl. Where were they?

There! Through the haze she could just see Bernadette, safe but surrounded by a cloud of amber dust. Peregrine gave a painful sigh and slumped onto her stomach. She lifted her gaze to see that the portal's fading surface was flickering green, then purple, then green again.

'No!' Hekate screeched. 'You can't! You shouldn't be able to . . . you . . . can't!' She flung herself at the gateway, desperately grasping at her mistress's fingers, as if she could physically pull her through.

'For realms in earth, in sea and sky.' Peregrine's vision was becoming murky. The air was so thick with fog and dust it was

hard to breathe. Her whole body was twitching, and it felt like electricity was burning under her skin.

'*NO!*' The room rattled and shook as Discord threw herself again and again against the surface, while Hekate clung to the metal frame.

'*I WILL be free.*' Discord's pale claw-like hand was still clutching Hekate's.

THUMP. The last of the glowing vines slipped from the portal gateway and crumbled into dust. Peregrine stared. Had they done it? Had they . . . won? Was Discord . . . gone?

A high-pitched hiss, like the whistle from a boiling kettle, filled the room. This was followed by a mournful keening that was so painfully sad it made Peregrine clap her hands over her ears, desperately trying to dull the sound.

What happened next looked like a very slow explosion but in reverse, as the thick grey fog was sucked swiftly back towards the portal. There was a flash of red, then the portal light flickered, then faded, then was gone.

Where Hekate had been just a moment before, there was nothing but a puff of purple mist and a thin layer of orange ash on the library floor. Had *she* been pulled into the portal as well?

Peregrine blinked. Without its green and purple hue, the room looked almost like a regular room in a regular library, though maybe after a herd of angry buffalo had trampled through it, and then, as an afterthought, set it on fire. Books and paperwork were strewn across the floor, and the few remaining bookcases leaned drunkenly against each other.

She pulled herself towards the crack in the floor and peered through. Inside was the lifeless husk of a plant. She recognised it, dry, brittle and dead as it was. She reached out her hand and stroked the brown, broken and charred leaves.

'Portal One,' she whispered. This is where it had all begun, right here in this little bed of soil. The first portal between the Cosmic and Terran realms, planted in the first library. She wondered what the plant's name was – or what it had been.

The corners of her vision were darkening, but she could see Bernadette by the metal frame, tipped on their side, their roots exposed to the air. 'Bernadette!' Peregrine croaked. The plant looked so small and so weak; their leaves were curled over, and their stem was bent down, exhausted. They needed water!

Peregrine looked behind her for her rucksack. The poison pulled at her limbs. It was too far, she wouldn't make it. But Bernadette . . .

BANG! The door was thrown open and Peregrine saw silhouettes rushing towards her. The taller silhouette scooped up her rucksack. Peregrine attempted to push herself up, but she was too weak.

Was it Stan and Earl? The figures loomed over her and something cool was pressed into her hands. Her water bottle!

'We need to act fast,' a low, familiar voice whispered. *Daedalus?* He had escaped the mist!

The other silhouette lay down on her belly next to Peregrine.

'Rowan, dear,' Daedalus urged the figure. He sounded faint and far away. 'We need your help.'

Rowan? She's here? *Alive?*

There was a scraping as Rowan dug another hole in the cracked ground. Feeling her way with her hand, Peregrine tipped water into the earth. And when the plant's tendrils wrapped around her fingers, she placed Bernadette's roots firmly in the soil.

'Now, Rowan,' Daedalus urged gently.

Rowan put her hand over Peregrine's. A warm breeze washed over Peregrine, and she heard Bernadette squeak. Daedalus hiccupped, which he only did when he was truly happy, or surprised – or both.

'You did it, Peregrine,' she heard Rowan mutter. Something sparkled under her fingers, and she felt Bernadette's tendrils dig down into the earth. 'You did it.'

'I *told* you,' Peregrine breathed.

'You told me what?' Rowan asked softly.

'I told you we needed . . . lasers.'

And with the first three bars of a lullaby whistling in her ears, Peregrine closed her eyes and let darkness swallow her up.

42

CAL

Location: Council Command Hub, Level Fourteen, Olympus Inc., the Mountain
CosDate: 300.23.241

'What just happened?' Using the back of his hand, Admiral Prim swiped Cal off the console and onto the floor.

'Ouch,' Cal muttered, rubbing his behind. He considered getting up and standing his ground, but decided it was best to just stay down.

'What did you do, faun?' Hansel hissed.

'I don't believe it!' Admiral Prim slammed the console with his palm. 'He reprogrammed the Thunderbolt to an electronic pulse.'

'I-I don't understand –' Hansel stammered. This was the first time that Cal had ever seen Hansel actually lost for words.

'It means that all tech within the blast radius will have been deactivated, but the *explosive* detonation was rendered inactive,' Admiral Prim explained.

'No explosions?' Hansel asked plaintively.

Admiral Prim shook his head. 'No.'

Hansel turned on Cal, his face as red as a jungle crawler's backside. He reached out and, grabbing Cal by the scruff of the neck, hauled him up over his head. Then shook him. Twice.

'Please take your hands off my agent, gentlemen.' Sibyll's voice boomed out into the room.

Everyone turned to look at her. Sibyll was standing in the doorway with Simon the weather sprite hovering beside her, his wings beating angrily.

'Agent?' Cal echoed meekly. His hooves were a metre off the ground, clicking together like wind chimes. He looked down and gulped.

Sibyll glared at Cal. The look said very clearly that he should not be talking.

'But Discord, she –' Hansel began.

'NOW, please, Captain Pine.' Sibyll's neck flapped dangerously. Simon flew a little higher, his blue hands on his hips.

'You got lucky, faun.' Hansel shook Cal once more, then dropped him in an undignified heap.

'Ouch,' muttered Cal, again. If this continued, he would have to start wearing padded underwear. Maybe Daedalus could point him in the direction of a Terran supplier.

'The threat has been taken care of.' Sibyll beckoned Cal over. 'My operatives on the ground have secured the situation.'

'CSI has secured ... the ... situation?' Hansel slowed

down the words, as if trying to understand them by saying them out loud.

Simon flew down and started to push Cal out of the room.

'I get it, I'm going!' Cal muttered as he brushed the sprite off.

Admiral Prim expelled air angrily through his nose. 'Sibyll, you can't seriously let this faun go unpunished!' He pointed to Cal. 'He has performed a wanton, and mysteriously *effective*, act of sabotage on an OPS operation!' he blustered.

'Callimachus was working on my orders,' Sibyll said airily.

'*Your* orders?' Prim sounded sceptical.

Her orders? Cal turned to look up at Sibyll, but she had her gaze firmly glued on Admiral Prim.

'Yes. Someone has to keep an eye on you OPS cowboys.' She nodded to the holo-pics of the three Thunderbolts spinning over the console. 'I received an anonymous tip-off that you were initiating a detonation of unsanctioned weaponry.' She raised an eyebrow.

'Unsanctioned?' Admiral Prim stepped in front of the console, swiftly turning off the holo-pics. 'Preposterous! The Council agreed to –'

'ONE Thunderbolt.' Sibyll raised an index finger. 'Luckily for you, the incident has been dealt with. Nevertheless –' she stepped aside so Simon could prod Cal out of the room – 'I think the less the Council knows about this little episode, the better, don't you, Admiral?'

Admiral Prim narrowed his eyes, but nodded slowly.

Cal clip-clopped past Hansel, not daring to meet his molten expression.

'This isn't over, faun,' Hansel hissed as he walked past. 'Not even close.'

Sibyll opened the door a little wider. 'Have a Cosmic day, gentlemen!' She waved at the two red-faced nymphs, then, as soon as Cal was through, let the door slam shut behind them.

Without looking at Cal, she and the weather sprite strode off down the corridor. After taking a moment to stare at the closed door, Cal jogged after them.

'Nice work, Simon.' Sibyll nodded to the sprite, who was now hovering behind her, ticking something off his clipboard.

Nice work, *Simon*? Cal shook his head in disbelief. 'Inspector, what you said back there, about me being an agent –'

'We'll talk –' she said quietly – 'in my office.'

'But –'

'Walk faster, Callimachus!' She glanced behind her and sped up. 'Before those flittertwits change their tiny minds.'

43

PEREGRINE

Location: Ward Seven, Medical Facility, Level Eight, Olympus Inc., the Mountain
CosDate: 300.23.243

Peregrine woke up to find a thick, glowing golden rope curled at the end of her bed. She blinked and shifted a little. As she moved, a prickling sensation jittered down her limbs, all the way to the tips of her fingers. It didn't feel unpleasant, exactly, more itchy, like static electricity buzzing underneath her skin. As she sat up on her elbows, the rope also raised its arrow-shaped head to look at her. Oh, *not* a rope then.

Peregrine's jaw tightened. *Snake*. The snake tipped its head to the side in what to Peregrine seemed a very teacher-like fashion. It emanated a kind of restful buttercup-coloured glow. Peregrine put her hand to her cheek, and felt an unexpected smile stretch across her face.

Apparently satisfied, the snake nodded once, slipped off the bed and glided along the floor towards a brawny man in a white toga who was typing something into a CosPad. Another snake slid across the room to join the first and, meeting at the hem of the man's toga, they stood up on the end of their tails and wrapped themselves around each other to form a glowing, knotted staff. The man held his hand out for the snake-stick and, still looking at his CosPad, promptly walked out of the room, muttering to himself.

Peregrine blinked. This must be some kind of Cosmic hospital. She gasped. That meant that . . . she was in *the Cosmic Realm*! Finally! OK, this wasn't exactly how she had imagined experiencing it for the first time, but she was *here*, in the place she had been dreaming of for *years*!

Anxious to see more, Peregrine pushed herself up a little further. 'Ow,' she mumbled. Despite the warm, fuzzy feeling, her head ached with a low, consistent throb, just intense enough to remind her of the events of the day before. Or maybe the day before that – she had no idea how long she had actually been lying here in this bed. She remembered falling, and the golden flash, and somebody singing Bernadette's lullaby, then . . . darkness. Her smile faded and she squeezed her eyes shut, breathing slowly.

She *was* safe here, she was sure of it.

Snuffle snuffle, snoooo snuffle.

The snore made her open her eyes. There were half a dozen beds in front of her, all made neatly with crisp white bedding embroidered with tiny golden stars. All were empty, except one.

'Nim!' Peregrine yelled, then winced. Arthur was curled up

on Nim's belly, his left wing bandaged. Both of their chests were moving up and down, up and down. She couldn't tell which one of them the snoring was coming from.

'Nim?' she said again, this time much more quietly.

'She will be fine,' a familiar voice said softly. The sound felt like sunlight on her skin, warming her completely, from her toes to the wispy tips of her hair.

Peregrine turned, already knowing who she would see. 'Daedalus!'

Daedalus was getting up from an armchair next to her bed. He was wearing a crushed velvet waistcoat in an eye-popping shade of pink that was dotted in little golden suns. Something that was probably meant to be a smile, but looked more like a strangled wince, spread across his face. He must have got at least twice the poison that she had, and all the time that she and Rowan had been travelling, he had been spinning in those mist ropes . . .

The thought made her stomach gurgle.

Daedalus held up his hand, as if reading her thoughts, then collapsed back into the armchair. 'Nim had to puddle herself to get away from the BogBrethren.' His voice sounded strained. 'She'll be all right in a few days.'

'Puddle?' Peregrine looked again at the sleeping nyad. She looked so peaceful.

'Puddle – make herself liquid.' He sighed. 'Terribly dangerous for nyads to do, especially in cities. She's just come out of decontamination – to remove the pollutants.'

Nim was in here because she had fought Stan and Earl, to give Peregrine and Rowan time to get away. Peregrine's eyes widened. 'She helped me – us – in London, but also . . . in the Under Realm.'

Daedalus raised an eyebrow. 'She did, eh?'

Peregrine wiped her nose with her sleeve. 'You're sure she's going to be OK?'

'Oh yes.' The skin around Daedalus's eyes crinkled as he handed her a tissue. 'She's a tough old walrus.'

'And you?' Peregrine blew her nose.

'Me? Oh, I've always thought of myself less as a walrus, more as a gracefully ageing albatross . . .' He reached out his arms, flapped them slowly, then dropped them to his sides. 'Wingspans of up to three metres, you know!' His eyes glazed as he looked over Peregrine's head. 'Magnificent creatures.'

'No.' Peregrine rolled her eyes. 'I mean, are you OK? After . . .' She didn't want to say 'after Hekate stabbed you with her poisonous hairpin', though it was implied.

'Me? Oh, I'm fine, fine.' He reached out to squeeze Peregrine's hand. 'A touch embarrassed, to tell you the truth.' He settled back into the chair. 'I should have told you more about all this –' he gestured to the hospital room – 'sooner.'

Peregrine stared down at her hand. There was so *much* that Daedalus had kept from her, and she had always accepted it. A familiar anger began to bubble inside her. It's not as if she hadn't *wanted* to know. He hadn't told her *anything*, and then suddenly he had expected her to . . . what? Save the world? Save a world that she had only just discovered even *existed*? She looked up at him, her eyes flashing.

Daedalus met her gaze, dousing some of her anger. 'You'd have thought I would have learned by now.'

The heat ebbed from Peregrine's cheeks. 'What do you mean?'

Daedalus sighed. 'It means I am sorry, and thank you.' His eyes were watery. 'You really did save everything – *everyone*, you know.'

Peregrine realised that she had never actually seen Daedalus cry. He was always so annoyingly cheerful.

He squeezed her hand, then let go. Peregrine wriggled her fingers. They felt different somehow. She turned them over and saw the tiny frond-shaped marks where she had held the moss to the vines. She gasped.

'It is not enough, but perhaps this will act as something of an apology.' Daedalus patted his waistcoat pocket.

'An apology?' Tears pricked her eyes as she wound her fingers around each other. 'You were gone and I had to find my way to, to . . .'

Peregrine heard a familiar whirring sound. No . . . It couldn't be!

'GrumBug?' Peregrine pushed herself further up on the pillows and leaned towards Daedalus.

'In a way.' Daedalus wiped his eyes, then opened his hand. There, on his palm and buzzing excitedly, was a CosBug. It looked very much like GrumBug – deep sapphire-blue body, glassy wings and copper legs – but there were gold plates on the side that had been crushed by Hekate's boot, and three glittering sapphires had been added to its back.

'Nim's CosBug couldn't be fixed as it was, I'm afraid.' He paused to let Peregrine blink away some tears. 'But I took the liberty and added a few little tricks of my own invention.'

The CosBug chirped and bounced on Peregrine's outstretched

palm. She stared at GrumBug 2.0. 'Amazing,' she whispered. 'Hello.'

The CosBug bounded onto Peregrine's shoulder. Feeling its familiar weight, she sank back into the pillows, exhausted.

'You must have a lot of questions,' Daedalus said, blowing his nose into a fuchsia-coloured handkerchief.

Peregrine nodded. She had so many questions buzzing around her mind, even choosing *one* was making her brain hurt. An image of the pale mist-covered arm flashed across her mind. She needed to know. 'Discord?' She said the word quietly. 'What happened to . . . Discord?'

Daedalus sighed, and tucked the handkerchief back into his waistcoat pocket. 'With the astrological window now closed, Discord will be back in the Fourth Realm.' He steepled his fingers; his brow was furrowed and serious. He scanned Peregrine's face, watching her reaction. 'No doubt she is plotting her next escape attempt.'

Next escape? Peregrine's heart beat faster. 'And Hekate is with her in the Fourth Realm, right?' she asked. 'She got pulled through the portal too?'

'Ah, Hekate.' He tapped his fingers together. 'Hekate is . . . unaccounted for.' He sighed. 'You might indeed be right, and she is in the Fourth Realm, but we cannot be sure. I was wrong to underestimate her, very wrong.'

'She said that –' Peregrine took a deep breath, trying to calm her heart rate – 'that I must know what it felt like . . . to be underestimated.'

Daedalus looked at her then, his eyes clear and wide. 'Yes, yes, I can see that you must.' He nodded slowly. 'I fear I owe you many explanations, Peregrine, but I shall start with this one.' He leaned in. 'You see, Hekate was a pupil of mine, at the Academy, and then later she became my apprentice.'

Daedalus's other apprentice. That was what Hekate had said. Peregrine's brain fizzed.

'She was bright, gifted – like you in that regard – but I did not give her the attention, or the instruction, she deserved.' He shook his head. 'I was distracted, foolish, young.' He met Peregrine's gaze. 'Well, *younger*.'

Peregrine rolled her eyes. She felt a smile pull at her lips.

Daedalus sighed. 'I fear she may have found that instruction somewhere else.'

'Discord.' Peregrine gulped.

Daedalus nodded. 'Indeed.'

Peregrine hoped he would continue, but he did not. The silence extended, until Peregrine couldn't stand it any longer.

'And Stan and Earl?' she asked.

'Oh yes, the *real* villains of the piece!' Daedalus shifted in his chair. 'The harpies have got them. Stan was oddly excited by the prospect when I informed him, even asked me whether I thought they would sign his hat for him.' He shook his head in disbelief.

'*Your* hat,' Peregrine corrected.

'Ah.' Daedalus waved his hand. 'I told him he could keep it. I actually think it looked quite fetching on him.' He smiled.

Peregrine was about to loudly disagree when there was a quiet knock at the door.

'Come in, Rowan,' Daedalus called.

A bashful-looking Rowan tiptoed in. She was wearing a

clean jumpsuit and her face was flushed a vibrant green, as if she'd scrubbed it very hard.

Daedalus stood up from the chair with a groan. 'I'm going to check on the portal. I'll leave you two to chat.'

Rowan nodded, but she wasn't looking at Daedalus. Instead she was staring at a picture of Zeus that was hung on the hospital wall, underneath which was a plaque inscribed with the words *Zeus the Protector*. Rowan's bright eyes were narrowed and accusing.

Daedalus patted Peregrine's hand. 'I will be back in a few minutes.'

Peregrine caught his hand, and did not let go. 'I have one more question.' This was not true, she had many, but this one couldn't wait.

Daedalus raised an eyebrow. 'Yes?'

'Where were you going?' She squeezed his hand. 'That morning when you were kidnapped . . . did you know . . . did you know that Discord . . . ?'

'No, my dear, I did not.' Daedalus's eyes shone. 'There was no sign that anyone was using the window. I thought we were quite safe.' He blinked. 'I was . . . wrong.'

'So where were you –'

'I was going to Alexandria to see the portal. I knew their time was coming to an end.' He placed her hand back on the blanket, and placed his over his heart. 'I was going to . . . say goodbye.'

With that, he walked towards the door and closed it softly behind him. Peregrine stared after him.

'Er . . .' Rowan stood awkwardly at the edge of the bed.

She was holding a new jumpsuit in her arms, olive-green like hers. 'This is for you.' She placed it on the bed then took off her hat and began to turn it around in her hands.

'Thanks.' Peregrine sat up and pulled the jumpsuit towards her. She traced the embroidered apple over the pocket.

Spotting Peregrine's new CosBug, FlutterBug flapped its wings, hovered off Rowan's collar and whirred its way towards the bed. GrumBug 2.0 bounced off Peregrine's shoulder and the CosBugs met on the patterned duvet. FlutterBug lifted a front leg and prodded one of the new sapphires on GrumBug's back. GrumBug buzzed grumpily, and promptly pushed FlutterBug over.

Rowan laughed, then coughed to disguise it. 'Hi,' she said.

'Hi!' Peregrine grinned and waved weakly. 'What did Daedalus mean about checking the portal?' She gestured to Daedalus's armchair. 'Are they working again?'

Rowan slumped into the chair. 'My sister Hazel tells me that Portal Tunnel 9 is already fully operational for emergency transportation.' She shook her head in disbelief. 'That means that Bernadette has grown that section of the Network in less than *a day*!'

Pride wriggled its way through Peregrine's veins. 'Way to go, Bernie!' She beamed.

'That plant is unbelievable.' Rowan glanced shyly at Peregrine. 'Just like its caretaker.'

Peregrine grinned.

Rowan's face went bright emerald. 'I can't believe I didn't realise Bernadette was a portal. I mean, I'm a *dryad*, for Pan's sake! And a Librarian!' Rowan bit her lip. 'Apparently they only tell you that stuff in final year, once you've taken the Librarian's oath.' She sniffed. 'I guess they didn't tell me as I'm not a full agent yet.'

Peregrine stared at Rowan, who wouldn't meet her eye. Did Rowan think she was angry at her? 'Don't worry about it.' As she said the words, Peregrine realised she meant them. Rowan must have as many questions as she did – maybe even more. 'It sounds like they don't tell people a *lot* of things.'

It seemed as if Rowan was going to disagree, but instead, to Peregrine's surprise and – it looked like – to Rowan's too, she nodded. 'CSI aren't telling anyone about what happened in Alexandria,' Rowan said quietly. 'About any of it, really. The story is that the portal "self-destructed".'

'Self-destructed?' Peregrine winced as the image of the portal vines getting sucked back into the gateway raced through her mind. Black spots began to appear at the edges of her vision, and she gripped the blanket, willing herself to stay in the room.

Rowan nodded, her mouth twitching as if she wanted to say something. 'They're not telling *me* much, either. I mean, I did go against *direct* CSI orders. I didn't even memory-wipe you ... They could –' she inhaled deeply – 'they could expel me from the Academy.' She groaned and rested her forehead on her knees.

'They're not going to do that!' Peregrine's cheeks flamed. 'They owe you! And imagine what would have happened if you *hadn't* broken all those rules! Then I really *would* have been on my own.'

GrumBug 2.0 chirped loudly.

Peregrine grinned. '*Almost* on my own.'

Rowan sniffed into her knees. 'I guess I still have a lot to learn.'

Peregrine snorted. 'We all do. So –' she couldn't help but prod – 'what do you think about it?'

'About what?' Rowan was looking down at her hands, curling and uncurling her fingers.

'About Olympus, you know, *lying*.'

Rowan puffed up her cheeks, ready to give a practised answer, and then blew air out of her mouth as if she was deflating a balloon. 'I . . . don't know.' She sank back into her chair. 'It's all so complicated!' She pouted. Peregrine had never seen her pout before. 'I *hate* what Zeus did to the library.' Rowan shuddered. 'And what they did to cover it up, but maybe it's better that people don't know about –' she lowered her voice – '*Discord*.'

'I suppose it *was* a secret mission.' Peregrine shrugged.

'I suppose . . .' Rowan looked up, and they smiled at each other. It was a strange thing, sharing a secret this big. As Peregrine got changed, they caught each other up on their adventures, pausing in between tales to linger in their own thoughts.

'Now,' Peregrine said as she zipped up her jumpsuit, 'tell me what happened after you realised that *I* was totally right and you were totally –' she paused to click her fingers – 'wrong.'

Peregrine watched in satisfaction as Rowan's face went from a vibrant emerald to a pale cabbagey green. 'I was *not* totally wrong. I was –'

Peregrine smirked.

'A *little* wrong.' Rowan nodded solemnly. 'Just a little.'

There was a knock, then a gust of wind slapped the door open. Daedalus poked his head through. 'Rowan, I almost forgot. I have something for you.' He put his hand in his jacket pocket. 'Now, where did I put it?'

The breeze rustled Rowan's curls as she shrank back in her chair. 'Are you going to memory-wipe me? Because I promise I will never, *ever* tell anyone –'

Daedalus reached over and placed a golden apple pin in Rowan's palm. 'I was asked by Professor Demeter to give you this. I hear that you misplaced yours?'

Rowan nodded. Peregrine glanced from Rowan to Daedalus. How had Rowan lost her Academy pin?

'I understand that you might not want it –' Daedalus looked at the pin, then glanced at the picture of Zeus – 'now that you have a better understanding than most of its history.' He sighed. 'But you must remember, taking the badge doesn't mean you have to agree with everything it stands for. Olympus has let us down –'

Rowan started to speak, but Daedalus held up a hand.

'But they will need good people – now more than ever.' His voice hardened. 'This won't be Discord's last attempt to return, I'm sure.'

Two glowing red eyes burned in Peregrine's mind. 'But you said the astrological window was closed!' She inhaled. 'W-when is the next window?'

'In five hundred years.' Daedalus scratched his chin. 'Ish.'

'Oh!' Peregrine exhaled. 'Well, that's OK then.' She settled back against her pillow and folded her arms behind her head. Five hundred years might almost be long enough for her to forget those eyes. Almost.

'I wish I could tell you that this was all over, Peregrine.

But you have proved – you both have – that you are owed the truth.' His eyes flashed with pride.

Peregrine gulped. 'Truth?'

'The portals are just one route. A handy one, if I do say so myself.' Daedalus shrugged. 'But there are multitudes of paths that bridge the realms. *Multitudes*.'

'Multitudes?' Rowan stared down at the pin, as if, if she put it back on, she would be signing up for an awful lot more than Librarian duty.

Daedalus sat down next to Peregrine on the bed. 'I, for one, would feel safer knowing that there was somebody so brave, so wise and so *adventurous* on our team. Hmm?' He was looking at Rowan, but Peregrine felt that his words were for her too.

'Adventurous?' Rowan stared at him, then her CosPad buzzed, making her almost drop the pin.

Daedalus coughed. 'Well, it seems that our time here is up.' He looked at Rowan over the top of his glasses. 'We've got to get Peregrine to the portal.'

'What?' Peregrine pinched her brows together. 'So soon?' She didn't know how long she had been unconscious, but as far as she was concerned, she had only just got to the Cosmic Realm and she was in no rush to leave it.

'As much as I would like to show you the wonders of this realm, my dear, keeping your presence secret is a feat akin to hiding the sun behind the moon.' He smiled. 'It doesn't quite know how to dim its light enough, nor indeed should it try.' He winked. 'I can't ask our friends to shield us for too much longer.' He stood up and offered her his hand. 'It is time to go . . . home.'

44

PEREGRINE

'Pretty impressive, hmm?' Rowan elbowed Peregrine.

Peregrine couldn't speak. She just nodded, open-mouthed, as she gazed around the vast lamplit library.

They were the only ones there, and the only other sounds were the soft squeak of the trolleys wheeling themselves about the space and a chorus of gently flapping books as they reshuffled themselves on shelves, or arranged themselves on top of one another on one of the many, many desks. Then, a familiar hummingbird-hum filled the air.

'Portal transport ready!' Cal called from the desk, which was positioned in front of a many-panelled stained-glass window showing a flock of birds in front of a golden sun. He hopped down from his stool and trotted towards Peregrine. Peregrine tried not to stare. He was, if possible, even shorter, and even hairier, in real life.

'Pear-grinn!' He put his hand out. 'It was an honour to meet you.'

Peregrine shook his hand. 'You too, Cal.' She had the very strange sensation that she should be curtsying or something of that kind.

'Do you work for the Terran Travel Department now?' Rowan interrupted the moment. Her eyebrows were knitted together in confusion.

'Not *exactly*.' Peregrine noticed Cal's goat tail wagging excitedly. 'CSI are just borrowing the portal. We're not *strictly* supposed to have any Terrans here, you know.' Cal looked nervously towards the door, then hopped back on his stool. 'Best make this as quick as a flick of a centaur's tail, don't you think?' His voice went up a pitch. 'Before we get caught?'

'Talking of centaurs, where *is* Tyron?' Rowan looked around.

'He's already gone back to the Under Realm. Just temporarily,' Daedalus added when Rowan's face fell. 'To pack.'

'Pack?' Rowan asked.

'Yes.' Daedalus squeezed Peregrine's shoulder. 'I *might* have persuaded him to consider taking up his old position at the Academy.'

Rowan's face brightened. 'Really?'

'There's no point getting old if you don't get crafty.' He winked. 'There are tricks in this old sorcerer yet!'

'But what is he going to pack? He lives in a cave . . .' Rowan paused, then slapped her forehead. 'That blasted bat!'

Daedalus chuckled. Peregrine looked up at her godfather and scowled. She hadn't quite forgiven him for keeping so many secrets from her. That would take many, *many* trips to Comet and Gambles ice-cream parlour. With celestial sprinkles.

'One Terran to transport,' Cal said, practically bouncing on the spot in his efforts to speed up the process.

Peregrine nodded. Then stopped. 'Hang on. ONE?' She turned on Daedalus, her gaze fiery.

To his credit, Daedalus did look a little embarrassed. 'Olympus HQ seems to be down one Grand Architect – and, well, I've agreed to stay and, er, muck in for a while.'

The lava of Peregrine's anger was dangerously close to exploding.

Daedalus bent down so he was at her eye level. 'Hekate was *my* student. More than that, she was my apprentice. I'm responsible for so much of this . . .' He waved his hand around as if searching for a word.

'*Flooharght?*' Rowan offered, leaning in.

Daedalus clicked his fingers. 'Exactly! And Hekate was able to use my *own* CosTech to try to bring back . . .' He stood up and put his hands in his pockets. 'I need to be here to make sure that can't happen again.'

'So you're going to, what? Stay *here* for the next five hundred years? What about the . . . shop?' Peregrine yelled.

'Peregrine,' Rowan hissed. 'This is still a *library* –'

'I don't care!' Peregrine knew she was being selfish, that there were bigger things at stake, but she had tried so hard to find Daedalus and now it turned out, after all of that struggle, all of that pain, she was *still* going to lose him? The raw unfairness of it stung like a paper cut. Something twitched dangerously beneath her skin.

Daedalus traced a half-circle on the floor with his brogues. 'Everyone has a holiday now and then, Peregrine.'

'*You* don't!' she said, correctly. 'And also, can I remind you that I am *twelve*? I can't live by myself yet. That's not even legal!'

'Oh, don't worry about that.' Daedalus's eyes twinkled. 'You won't be by yourself.'

'What does *that* mean?'

He tapped the side of his nose.

Peregrine gritted her teeth. 'Are you *kidding* me?' Maybe *this* was the time to tell Daedalus that she had likely been suspended. 'If you leave me with Ms Kidman for more than one week, I *swear* I will get straight back through this portal!'

Daedalus pulled her in for a sideways hug. 'Goatcha.'

Cal huffed.

Stepping away from Daedalus, Peregrine edged towards the portal.

Rowan walked up beside her. 'I'm still a Librarian,' she said. 'Trainee,' she added quickly. 'But Professor Demeter is going to let me swear the oath!' She beamed. 'My shifts are Tuesdays and Thursdays. Maybe we could –'

'Hang out?' Peregrine asked.

'Hang . . . *out*?'

'Yeah. You know, have fun.'

'*Fun?*' Rowan looked genuinely confused.

Peregrine grinned and stepped towards the beautiful geometric gate. The familiar humming throbbed in her ears.

'*Fun?*' Rowan whispered to Cal, who shrugged, muttered something that might have been 'mortals', then pressed a button.

'*PORTAL GATE OPENING,*' a computer voice chirped.

There was a clinking, like shells rolling over each other on a beach, as the gate spiralled open. Peregrine gasped. Behind the gate was a vortex of iridescent green light. It was swirling like water draining through a plug, round and round and round.

It would have been a very grand moment indeed, had not a squeak of excitement erupted from the sides of the portal.

'Bernadette!' Peregrine reached out a hand. Tendrils of emerald light floated out to meet her palm and lick her fingers. It felt a bit like being greeted by an over-enthusiastic puppy. A very large puppy, who smelled like peppermint.

With one last glance over her shoulder, she saw that Rowan had taken off her hat and was waving. Daedalus was leaning against the desk, hands back in his pockets. Something shimmered on his waistcoat. It was the indigo feather he usually wore on his hat – a little battered but shimmering all the same. He hadn't let Stan keep *that* then.

Daedalus winked.

Taking a breath, Peregrine turned and stepped into the cool tickly green light. It enveloped her completely. Everything slowed down, even her breath, even her *blinking*; it was as if the whole world had been put on pause.

Then, just as suddenly, the world sped up.

Her stomach dropped, light rushed past her, and there she was, on the other side of the portal in Reading Room 3. It had been less than two days since she'd been there, but everything looked different.

'This is *real* magic,' Peregrine whispered. She even spotted a few golden apples shining from book spines. Had they been there before, and she just hadn't noticed them?

A smiling face was there to greet her. The face was chestnut-skinned, framed with dark curls and wearing a bowler hat.

'I'm Hazel. My sister has told me so much about you!' The woman shook her hand enthusiastically. 'Did you really go to the Under Realm? I've always wanted to –'

They were interrupted by a tapping. Peregrine froze. They were not alone.

Another woman stepped through the doorway of the Reading Room. She was wearing a wide-brimmed fedora hat, a tweed suit jacket and calf-high lace-up boots, one of which she was tapping loudly against the wooden floor. 'Peregrine Amelia Quinn! Where in *Hera's name* have you been?'

Peregrine blinked. '*Mum?*' A tidal wave of emotion crashed over her as her mum stepped towards her and Peregrine launched herself into her arms. She smelled just like she always did: of sand and old suitcases.

'You and I have got a lot of catching up to do, haven't we, pumpkin?' Her mum squeezed her tightly, lifting her off the ground.

'Yes.' Peregrine sniffed as she nodded into her mum's shoulder. Tears flowed freely down her cheeks, and she didn't even try to wipe them away. 'Yes, we do.'

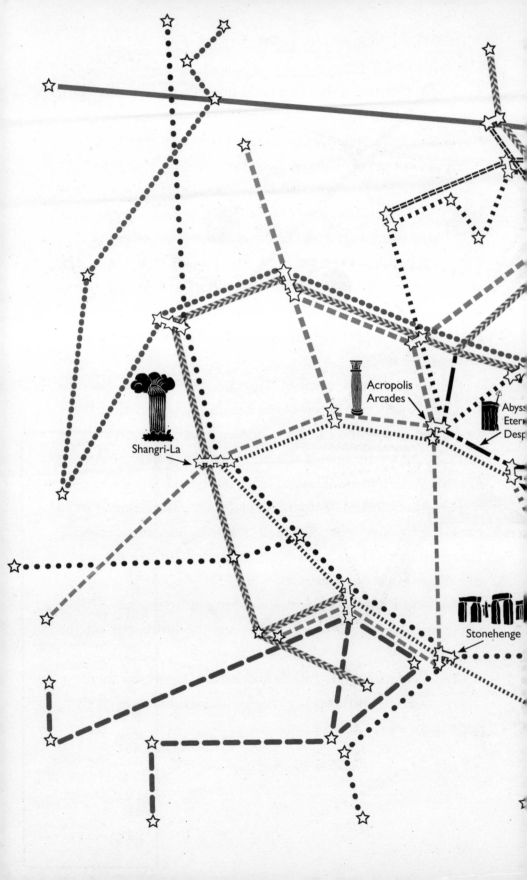

Shangri-La

Acropolis
Arcades

Abyss
Eter
Desp

Stonehenge

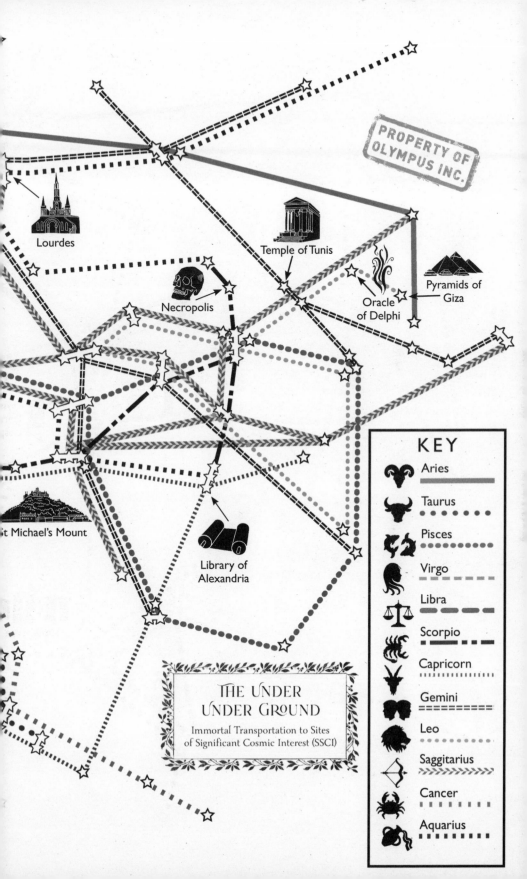

Lourdes

Temple of Tunis

Oracle
of Delphi

Pyramids of
Giza

Necropolis

St Michael's Mount

Library of
Alexandria

THE UNDER
UNDER GROUND

Immortal Transportation to Sites
of Significant Cosmic Interest (SSCI)

KEY

Aries

Taurus

Pisces

Virgo

Libra

Scorpio

Capricorn

Gemini

Leo

Saggitarius

Cancer

Aquarius

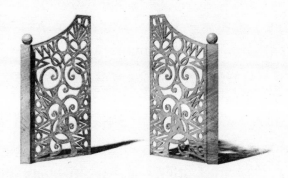

ACKNOWLEDGEMENTS

All books take a village (or, in this case, a Cosmopolis) and there are as many thanks to give as there are lights on in those windows. A few of those thanks are below.

To my fantastic agent, Jessica Hare, for her unswerving navigation of both Peregrine's journey and mine, I could not ask for a kinder, more generous guide. And to my editor, Ruth Bennett, who has used her unending skill to make this book's heart beat louder and fiercer, thank you. Most of the tears in this book are yours. To the wonderful team at Piccadilly - Dominica, Katie, Issie, Amber, Emma, Rob, Jess, Kate, Steph, Stacey, Talya, Jane and Charlotte – and everyone else who has contributed behind the scenes – I will be forever grateful for your belief in Peregrine and for your energy and enthusiasm in crafting her wings. To Two Dots for the fabulous cover, Brie Schmida for her stunning character pieces and Patrick

Knowles for the fantastically detailed maps – thank you.

To my teachers – Lucy Christopher, Jo Nadin and Steve Voake – thank you for being the people that I believed when you said this novel was good, and for the advice that made it that much better.

To my fellow writers, Rosie Brown, Olivia Collard, Helen Comerford, Natalie Harrison, Leigh-Ann Hewer, JM Joseph, Devyani Kothari, Carley Lee, Megan Small and Issie Smith. Knowing your eyes were on this made me want to write, and write to make you smile. And to Miranda Rose, for her wondrous feedback and for reminding me that I will always have a home in Oxford.

To my students, both academic and in the movement world, thank you for the inspiration, always.

And to my family – my brother, my mum, my dad and Moro – who make all of this possible.

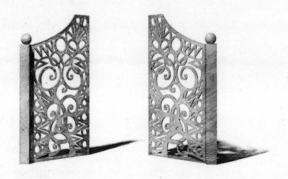

ABOUT THE AUTHOR

Ash Bond writes magical stories that have myth sprinkled through them like fairy dust. She is now studying for her PhD, focusing on the relationship between mythology and landscape, at the University of Bristol. Ash is also a yoga teacher and loves to move, insisting she gets her best ideas when swimming in rivers, stomping up mountains or doing cartwheels.

@ashbwrites
ashbond.co.uk

PEREGRINE QUINN

returns to the **Cosmic Realm**

in her next adventure . . .

COMING SOON!